Prologue

PRELUDE TO A KISS

Leeds, 1954

In the September evening light, Dan Markham paused at the corner of Byron Street, his key in the door of the Ford Anglia.

Over the road, on Regent Street, an ambulance stood outside Hart Ford, lights flashing in the sunlight, the back doors open wide, three black police cars beside it. He stood for a moment, watching the scene until one of the policemen glanced up, a familiar face staring at him.

Markham started the engine and drove away.

***

The next morning he'd only been in the office for five minutes when the door opened and Detective Sergeant Baker walked in, wheezing from the stairs and flopping into a chair. The man looked as if he'd been up all night, unshaven and worn, eyes like flint. He smelt of stale tobacco, a ring of grime around his shirt collar. A faded tea stain coloured the front of his mackintosh. He took off his hat, straightened the brim and placed it on his lap.

'I saw you down by Hart Ford yesterday evening. Do you know what happened there?'

'No.' A burglary, he'd thought, or someone injured. He hadn't heard the news on the Home Service or seen a newspaper.

'Someone killed Freddie Hart,' Baker told him. 'You know who that is, don't you?'

'Freddie Hart?' No, Markham thought. That wasn't possible. That just wasn't possible.

'Of course you do, since his wife hired you.' The sergeant stared at him. 'Want to tell me what you were doing there, lad?'

'I was working.' He could feel his heart thudding, palms slick.

Baker ran his hands down his face and sighed.

'Do I look like I came in on the milk train? I know you were bloody working. I want to know *what* you were doing, where you'd been and why you were parked there.'

Markham lit a cigarette. It gave him a few seconds to compose his thoughts. The truth was innocent enough.

'I'd followed one of Hart's employees home.'

'Who?' Baker asked.

'A girl called Annie Willis. She's the secretary, lives in Meanwood. I'd been on the bus. I was walking back to my car.'

'That's better.' The man's mouth smiled but his eyes showed nothing. 'Now, why were you after her?'

'I needed to find out who she was. Hart had taken her out after work on Saturday.'

'Oh aye? And what business is that of yours? Or were you just being a nosy parker?'

'Mrs Hart thought her husband was having a fling with someone. I'm an enquiry agent, that's what I do. You know that.'

'Divorce jobbie, was it?' Baker asked with contempt.

'She wanted me to find out what's going on.' The sergeant raised a thick eyebrow disbelievingly. 'After that it's her problem.'

'She also said you happened to be in the Harewood Arms in Follifoot on Sunday when she and Mr Hart arrived. Bit of a coincidence isn't it? Off your patch, lad. You've never struck me as the country pub type.'

'Hart had taken the secretary there the night before. I wanted to hear if anyone was talking about him.'

'Too bloody clever by half in the end, weren't you?' Baker sat forward and placed his palms on the desk. 'A little while after the business closed last night, someone came to see Mr. Hart and shot him.' He paused. 'Now, you're working for the wife, who thinks he's got a bit on the side. Maybe she just decided she was better off rid of him and paid you to do it.' His voice grew colder as he spoke. 'I know what you lot are like in this line of work. Bastards, all of you. I daresay you'd be willing to pull the trigger if the price was right.' Markham shook his head. He felt a bead of sweat run down his back. 'No one's straight in your game, lad, not if they want to make a bob. Everybody lies.'

'Look, I'm sorry about Freddie Hart,' Markham said. 'But it wasn't anything to do with me.'

'Have you ever seen someone who's been shot?'

'No.'

'Of course you haven't, you were too young for the war. I did.' He was silent for a moment. 'There are prettier sights in the world. I saw the bullet hole. Pound to a penny it was a .38 calibre. Close range.'

'There are still plenty of guns floating around from the war,' Markham said. 'Every officer had a sidearm.'

'Aye, and they were easy enough to buy and smuggle.' Baker ran a hand across his chin. 'You bring one back from National Service, did you?'

'No. I wasn't an officer.'

'Don't avoid the bloody question.'

'I don't have a gun.'

'But they taught you to shoot, didn't they?'

'Of course,' he answered. It was part of basic training. 'Me and most of the men in the country.'

'Be careful,' the detective warned. 'I've been up since yesterday morning and my temper's fraying.'

'I didn't kill Freddie Hart,' Markham repeated. 'Is that plain enough for you? I followed the girl on a bus to Meanwood.

She lives at 15 Bentley Grove. Then I bought cigarettes at the shop at the end of the street. The woman will remember me. I had to wait a quarter of an hour for the bus back.'

Baker nodded. 'Don't you worry, I'll be checking all that. And to see if that lass you were trailing had a jealous boyfriend of her own.' He placed the hat back on his head and pushed himself upright. 'I don't like what you do. It's a grubby trade. Enquiry agent.' He almost spat the words. 'Someone has to suffer for you to make money. I don't like that at all.'

Markham sat behind the desk after he'd gone, smoking a cigarette until it burned hot in his mouth. He ground it out in the ashtray and lit another, waiting until he was convinced that Baker wouldn't return. Finally he pulled the bottom drawer open. It was where he kept the Webley, the one he'd brought back from his time in Germany.

The drawer was empty.

Frantic, he scrambled around, feeling the panic rise as he ransacked the rest of the desk. It had been there on Saturday: he'd seen it.

He looked again. The filing cabinets, the cupboard in the corner.

No gun. Nothing else was missing.

Penny to a pound the bullet had been a .38, Baker said. The same ammunition as the Webley. And his fingerprints were on that revolver.

Someone was setting him up.

Someone had been in his office and taken the gun.

Why? Who?

He needed answers. He needed to talk to Joanna Hart.

Part One

BLUES IN THE NIGHT

CHAPTER ONE

She'd arrived the Friday before, in the middle of a balmy afternoon. Markham had the windows open in the office to draw in a little breeze. The third of September, a date everyone remembered, the day Britain went to war with Nazi Germany, fifteen years before. When he went out for his dinner he'd seen all the memories and loss on the faces.

She was waiting outside the office on Albion Place when he returned, dressed in a royal blue skirt, a white blouse and a hip-length jacket, the bag dangling from her hand. Her blonde hair set in short, neat waves.

'Can I help you?' Markham asked, bringing the keys from his pocket.

'I'm looking for Mr Markham.' It was a cultured voice. Expensively educated. Good breeding, his mother would have called it.

'I'm Dan Markham. What can I do for you?' He unlocked the door and she stood at the entrance, assessing the room with its worn lino floor and view of the old grey roof tiles before pursing her lips in disapproval. 'Please, sit down, Mrs …?'

'Jones,' she answered and he immediately knew what the job would be. Divorce. They always used the same names – Smith, Jones, Brown – as if they offered protection.

The woman perched on the chair and removed her gloves. About thirty, he guessed, with a porcelain complexion, her lips a deep, emphatic red. The clothes looked ordinary enough, but they hadn't come off the rack at Marshall's; some seamstress in a little shop had worked long and hard to make them. She had style. And money.

'Well, Mrs Jones …'

'Forgive me.' She lowered her eyes for a moment. 'I've never met an enquiry agent before.'

He gave a gentle, reassuring smile. 'Nothing like an American private detective from the films, I'm afraid.' His office was an unprepossessing room that had probably looked exactly the same before the war.

She hesitated. 'It's just that you're rather young.'

How long until they stopped saying that, he wondered?

'I've spent time in military intelligence and I've been doing this for four years now,' he told her with a smile. 'I'm a professional. And I'm good at what I do, Mrs Jones.'

This was the crux, the moment. Either she'd leave now or she'd tell him everything. She didn't move. After a moment she took a breath.

'I'm sure my husband's having an affair.' The women always blurted out the words. With men he had to work, to coax it out of them piece by piece, as if the admission cost them all their pride.

'Why do you think that?' He took out the pack of cigarettes and offered her one. She moved to take it, leaning forward into the match flame.

'He's out almost every night. I've smelt perfume on him. He doesn't seem to want to spend time with me any more.'

'Have you talked to him about it?'

'God no. Of course not.' She seemed horrified at the suggestion. 'How could I?'

'How long have you been married, Mrs Jones?'

'Five years.' She raised her head to look at him. 'Six in January.'

'And when did your husband's behaviour change?'

'About two months ago,' she answered after some thought. 'Just after that hot weekend we had during Wimbledon.'

The end of June. He made a note on the pad.

'Did anything unusual happen during that time?'

'Not that I can think of.' Now she'd begun, her gaze was squarely on his face.

'What does your husband do?'

'He owns an agency that sells motor cars.'

That explained the money. Cars were big business these days.

'And you'd like me to see if he's having an affair.'

'I'm certain he's having one, Mr Markham.' Her eyes blazed. 'I want to know who with.'

'I have to tell you, Mrs Jones, divorce is a messy business.'

'Oh, I don't want to divorce him.' Her voice turned cold. 'I want a hold over him.'

***

It took two more cigarettes to draw all the details from her. Her real name first – Joanna Hart. No children. A house out in Alwoodley. A golden life.

Reluctantly, like slowly drawing back a curtain, she'd revealed the rest of the picture. Freddie Hart was eleven years older than his wife, from a well-to-do family. His father had put up the money for a Ford dealership two years before. Now he was there all hours. Off first thing in the morning, then meetings and dinners until late. All business, that was what he told her. But the scent on his skin and the lipstick traces on his handkerchief told a different story.

'What do you think, Mr Markham?' Her voice was cool, no trace of emotion.

'I'll look into it, if that's what you want.'

She brought a five-pound note from her handbag and placed it on the desk.

'Is this enough to retain your services?'

'More than enough.' It was a full week's wages. 'How do you want my reports?'

'I come into town every Tuesday and Friday,' she said. 'I usually take luncheon at Betty's. You can meet me in the cafe there at noon.' She replaced the gloves on her hands. All the nervous gestures had disappeared and she moved with easy assurance. 'Good day, Mr Markham.'

He heard the click of her heels on the stairs, gave her ten seconds and followed.

She never looked back, swinging her hips as she moved down the street then turned up Briggate. He kept his distance, holding back as she stopped at the entrance to Thornton's Arcade.

She stayed for two minutes, checking her watch impatiently, until a man hurried up. They embraced and her face softened as he kissed her on the cheek and they walked away together.

★★★

He turned the car down Eastgate. At the roundabout, beneath the long grey face of Quarry Hill flats, he turned along Regent Street. The motor car dealers had gathered here, a cluster of them with their shiny new buildings of chrome and glass. Every one of them promised the future and the freedom of the road. They did a good trade; there were more vehicles on the road every month.

He didn't want a new car. He couldn't afford one; anyway, he knew a mechanic who kept his Anglia running sweeter than it had when it rolled off the production line. He passed Hart Ford, a place of yellow stone and large, gleaming windows that stood out brightly. The building spoke of solidity, of trust and modernity. The other half of the block was Victorian, decaying. The Reginald Building was carved over a boarded-up entrance. The past and the future, side by side.

Tomorrow he'd go and take a look. For now, though, he was content to go home. There was nothing more to keep him working today.

★★★

He ran a hot bath and soaked until the water began to cool. In the living room he selected *The Amazing Bud Powell* from the stack of records in the corner and put it on the gramophone, letting the strange sound of 'Un Poco Loco' fill the room, Powell's piano on its strange, mad journey.

Markham found eggs in a bowl on the shelf, along with half an onion, some cloves of garlic and a pair of mushrooms he'd bought at the market for a fancy Continental meal that never happened. It only took a few minutes to turn the ingredients into an omelette.

The LP finished and he swapped it for some Sarah Vaughan. Outside, beyond the window, the world was carrying on. Men were on their way home from work, wives were cooking tea. In here, though, caught in the music, he could close his eyes and try to imagine himself in a New York jazz club.

It was dark when he stirred in the chair. The record was still turning, the click of the needle in the groove sounding like a hushed birdsong. With a smile he remembered the way his father so often fell asleep after eating.

His parents had been dead for five years now. The summer of 1949. He'd only been back from National Service for two months when it happened, and still deciding what to do with his life. His parents went away on the holiday they'd booked to Scotland. He went down to the station to see them off and received a postcard from his mother three days later. The next he knew was the copper knocking on the door to say they'd died of injuries after a train crash in a place he'd never heard of – Ardler Junction. Somewhere and nowhere.

The house had been rented. After the funeral and the sad gathering of distant relatives, all that remained was to divide the possessions with his sister. The photographs, the furniture, the small keepsakes and the surprisingly large bank account.

His share had been enough to buy a second-hand car and still keep plenty in the bank. He found the flat and took a position as a clerk in an insurance company. The day he turned twenty-one, legally an adult, he handed in his notice at the job, took the lease on an office and set up in business as an enquiry agent.

He got by on divorces. God knew there was no shortage of them. People who'd married right after the peace and now regretted it. The wartime marriages that had sunk to nothing once the fighting stopped. They were his bread and butter. Those and the frauds that employers wanted discovered and kept away from the ears of the Inland Revenue. It was enough to pay his bills.

CHAPTER TWO

He was ready by nine the next morning, dressed in his best suit, brogues shined and the tie just so in a Windsor knot. Town would be busy; it was the same every Saturday. Consume, consume; it was beginning to feel like a national fever.

On Regent Street he pulled into Hart Ford, parking at the side of the building. Already there were couples, young and old alike, walking around the shiny new vehicles whilst earnest salesmen tried to convince them that Ford was the motor car that would improve their lives.

He strolled into the showroom, eyeing the models, the Prefect, Popular, Consul, Zephyr and the brand new Zodiac on gorgeous display. Idly, he wandered from one to another, opening doors to glance at the dashboards before moving on. Finally, on his second time around, a voice behind him said, 'That's a good car, you know. Top of the range. Better than a Wolseley, if you ask me. Terribly good value for money. Very smart with the two-tone paint and it'll go up to eighty when you put your foot down.'

He turned with a smile to face a man in his early forties, still trim, a dark David Niven moustache clipped close and the first hint of grey moving back from his temples. His nails were clean and manicured, with no nicotine stains on his fingers.

'How much is it?' Markham asked.

'Eight hundred and fifty-one.' He winked. 'But we've been known to let the spare pound go now and again.'

The voice held the ready charm and the confidence that only came with a lifetime of opportunity.

'Not cheap.'

'But worth it, old chap,' the man said. 'Unless you spring for a Jag, you won't find a better car on the road. I'm Freddie Hart. I own the place.'

He stood about five feet seven, his back straight, wearing tailored cavalry twill trousers and a blazer with the Royal Army Service Corps badge on the breast pocket.

'Dan Markham.'

'Do you drive now, Mr Markham?' he asked, as if he expected the answer to be 'no'.

'I have an Anglia.'

Hart nodded.

'Lovely little motor car. And one of ours, of course,' he added with another smile. 'Good taste on your part. But try this and it'll never seem the same again.'

'I'm honestly only looking. Curious.'

'Well, if you want to take it out and try it, just let me know. It's the only way to tell, isn't it? And if you're interested, I can give you a very fair price for yours.' He leaned closer. 'To tell you the truth, every Tom, Dick and Harry wants a motor car these days. It's hard to keep enough stock.'

'Good business to be in,' Markham said.

'Thriving. You take your time, old chap. If you want anything, just ask for me.' He held out his hand and they shook before Hart disappeared through a glass door, stopping in a secretary's office to lean over the desk.

Could it be that obvious, that clichéd: an affair with the secretary? The glass was frosted, but he could see that her hair was blonde. Hart's grin turned wolfish as he looked at her. If something was going on, at least it would be easy to discover.

DARK BRIGGATE BLUES

A DAN MARKHAM MYSTERY

CHRIS NICKSON

To Leeds Book Club, the little book club that could.
With gratitude.

Cover image © iStockphoto

First published 2015

The Mystery Press is an imprint of The History Press
The Mill, Brimscombe Port
Stroud, Gloucestershire, GL5 2QG
www.thehistorypress.co.uk

© Chris Nickson, 2015

The right of Chris Nickson to be identified as the Author
of this work has been asserted in accordance with the
Copyright, Designs and Patents Act 1988.

British Library Cataloguing in Publication Data.
A catalogue record for this book is available from the British Library.

ISBN 978 0 7509 6098 4

Typesetting and origination by The History Press
Printed in Great Britain

But it left one question. Who was the man Joanna Hart had met on Briggate yesterday?

★★★

He decided to go into the office for an hour, squeezing through the crowds that filled the pavements. The post lay on the floor, a bill and an onionskin airmail letter from Carla in Italy. He looked at the postmark. Sent six days earlier.

Ciao bella, cara … you see, it's easy to pick up the language! I'm having a ridiculous time. Spent a week in Venice that could easily have lasted a month or a year. I'm in Florence now and I can see why those rich young men used to relish the Grand Tour. Everywhere I turn it takes my breath away. My God, these Italians had a love of beauty that we English never seemed to discover for ourselves. While they dissect the soul, our Constables and Gainsboroughs paint these stolid scenes. Sometimes I think the only one worth a damn was Turner.

Anyway, the weather is beautiful (of course!) and I'm brown as a berry, although my bum's sore from Italian men pinching it! It really is true what they say. We should come here next year and you can look after me – what do you say? Everything's unbelievably cheap, we could live here on next to nothing. I leave for Rome tomorrow, all that history and grandeur they taught us about in school. Then home again. I bloody well hope you've missed me!

She'd signed it with three kisses, everything scrawled in her own disorganised fashion. Another eight days and she'd be back; he'd circled the date in his diary. Soon enough he'd see her smile and hold her again. He'd missed her.

Their meeting had been pure accident, a lunchtime in the record shop downstairs at Vallance's. He was looking through the LP sleeves, hoping they'd finally decided to stock some jazz, when he heard the woman next to him mutter, 'Oh bugger.'

He turned and noticed her, auburn hair, every inch as tall as him, in a bright, flame-patterned dress under a maroon coat. In a black-and-white world she was a splash of Technicolor.

'What's wrong?' he asked.

'I'm looking for something to inspire me. But this lot are all dead, aren't they?' She frowned. 'If they're not, they look it.'

'I know who you need,' he told her.

'Who?'

'Thelonious Monk.'

She burst out laughing, a hand covering the deep red of her mouth. 'You just made that up.'

He met her the next day and lent her the record. The following morning the telephone rang in his office.

'You sod,' she said, with no hello or how are you. 'He's brutal. He's bloody wonderful. Do you have any more?'

He asked her out, a meal at Jacomelli's, and they began seeing each other regularly. They enjoyed each other's company, and some nights they ended up in bed together.

She was an artist, making her living as an instructor at Leeds College of Art. The daughter of a Sheffield doctor, she'd been offered a scholarship and then stayed on to teach when she'd finished her diploma.

Carla had her studio at the college. He'd often find her there at lunchtimes or in the early evenings, bright clothes covered by an ancient smock, a scarf wound around her brilliant hair, sipping tea from a flask and working. She was good, everything striking and bold, even if he didn't understand any of her paintings.

They'd gone to London together once, a long dirty weekend in the capital. She had to go down, did he want to come with her? Of course he did. He hadn't been since he was a child, back before the war. She'd taken him around the National and the Tate, praising and criticising by turns. Then they spent an evening in Soho, eating real Italian food and eavesdropping on conversations in the pubs before heading off to Ronnie Scott's jazz club. They walked and watched the tarts in their windows before going back to the hotel.

The next morning, she announced she'd meet him at twelve.

'Where are you going?' he asked.

'Oh, I have a meeting at my gallery.'

'Your gallery?'

'Yes,' she told him. 'They sell my work. Didn't I tell you before? It's why I needed to come down here. Can you do the catch on this brassiere?'

★★★

He folded the letter, stuck it back in the envelope and slid it into his jacket pocket. Now she'd put thoughts of Italy into his mind. He decided to go up to Donmar's to eat. It wasn't Soho, and he was certain it wasn't anything like Naples or Milan, but it was all Leeds had to offer.

Carla had brought him here. She seemed to gravitate to places like this, to find them without effort. All he had to offer her was jazz.

★★★

By half past four he was parked on Byron Street, close enough to the corner of Regent Street to have a view across to Hart Ford. Time crawled by, the way it always did when he was waiting. At five he sat upright, a camera ready in his hands. The last of the customers vanished from the dealership and there was a short parade of salesmen and mechanics leaving to form queues at the bus stops. But no blonde woman.

Then she was there, in the passenger window of a shiny new Humber Hawk. He snapped a couple of pictures, enough to show her face, with Freddie Hart at the steering wheel. No Ford for him, Markham thought. As the car moved away, Markham started the Anglia and followed.

Beyond the city the traffic thinned to just a few cars and Markham had to keep his distance, hoping they wouldn't turn off the main road where he might lose them.

Finally, as they came to Pannal, the Hawk indicated a right-hand turn and he knew exactly where they were going. The Harewood Arms in Follifoot. A little country pub for the well-heeled set. He parked in sight of the entrance, in ample time to snap more shots of them going in, Hart's arm possessively around the woman's waist.

★★★

At ten he drove back into town. The crowds from the late shows and the Odeon and the Ritz filled the pavements, mixing with the drinkers leaving pubs before closing time. He parked and crossed the street, then pushed open a door and took the stairs down to the cellar and Studio 20. The only jazz club in Leeds. Open seven nights a week, as late as the musicians were willing to play.

It was early yet, just six people in the audience. A piano player he didn't recognise doodled on the keyboard, trying to herd an improvisation into a version of 'Lover Come Back To Me'. Everything would begin to come alive around midnight, when the musicians drifted in from their paying gigs, ready to have some fun.

Bob Barclay, the owner, sat behind his partition, tapping his hand in time on the wood, nodding at Markham as he saw him. The club had no alcohol licence, so it was tea, coffee or orange squash, and uncomfortable chairs. Somewhere only for the jazz faithful. And when the sound took flight, it was worthwhile. But not tonight. The air was flat, without any sense of expectation. He turned on his heel and went back to the car.

Out past Sheepscar he turned on to a side street. This had probably been a respectable area once, he thought. Now it had been left to run down and fade away. He walked up the path to a detached Edwardian villa, every window carefully blacked out as if the war had never ended.

Inside, Markham paid his half-crown to Marvin, the large West Indian man on the door, and entered. Apart from one back room the house was empty, sounds rattling up the stairway. A thick old dining table with heavy, lovingly turned legs served as a bar. Other small tables and chairs were scattered around. Music played scratchily from a gramophone in the corner, some American rhythm and blues to liven up the atmosphere.

'Whisky, Mr Markham?' Thomas the barman held up a bottle with no label and a dark amber liquid.

'Is it?'

'Fresh from the glens,' the man answered with a grin. 'Just distilled it yesterday.'

He could believe it. No one came to the International Club for the quality of the drink. Just for the fact that it served alcohol outside licensing hours. It wasn't even a real club; there was no membership, simply an entry charge, and any trouble dealt with efficiently and viciously by Marvin and his knife.

He lifted the glass, took a tiny sip and nodded.

'The real thing,' he said with surprise.

'Only to special customers,' Thomas laughed. 'But don't tell everyone.'

The place had been around since just after the war. Plenty of backhanders went to the coppers to stop them closing it. He'd spotted enough of them in here, knocking back the booze until the small hours. But the International catered to everyone, from councillors and businessmen wanting the seamy side to those who craved one extra drink then another, eking out the last of their wages.

The man he hoped to find was huddled on a chair by the darkened window, hands turning and turning an empty glass on the table. Markham sat next to him.

'Keeping busy, Brian?'

The man glanced up and shrugged. He was in his mid-thirties, sandy hair already fading away from his forehead. His eyes were glazed, the worse for wear after a long evening of drinking. But every night was the same for Brian Harding, one more chance to obliterate the world and his inheritance. He was lucky: he'd been doing it since he was demobbed, his liver hadn't packed up yet and he still had money left.

'Do you know someone called Freddie Hart?'

'Course.' He gave a small chuckle. 'Freddie. He was always a bit of a bastard.' There was no hint of slurring, every word clearly enunciated. Whatever horrors the drink smothered, it didn't affect his speech.

'What about his wife?'

'Joanna?' Harding snorted dismissively. 'Everyone had Jo. Well, everyone but Freddie. I think that's why he married her, to show he could go one better than the rest of us.' He turned the glass upside down and stared pointedly. Markham passed over his own whisky. 'Why are you interested in that pair, Dan?'

'Just a passing curiosity,' he said. 'So what made Freddie Hart a bastard?'

'His father wangled him a billet in the Service Corps and he was quite happy to sit on his arse while the rest of us were out there fighting.' He knew that Harding had been amongst the first troops into the Bergen-Belsen concentration camp, and since then he'd spent his time trying to erase the sights from his head. 'Feathered the nest a little, that's what I heard. And then his father set him up with that Ford place. A licence to print money.'

'Wealthy family?'

'Buckets of the stuff. Grandfather made his money with something or other, bought up a chunk of the North Riding and settled back to become lord of the manor. All very feudal. That's the way Freddie was brought up. My brother was at school with him. Said he was a shit even then. A sneak.'

'What about Joanna?'

'Harrogate,' Harding said simply, as if that explained every-thing. Markham waited. 'Joanna Wilson – that was her maiden name. Mad for everything in trousers when she was younger. A real looker back then, too.' He turned. 'Have you seen her?'

'Yes.'

'She's still quite the thing. But her family's skint. They're squeaking by these days, from what I hear. Sold off everything they can.'

'So she has nothing of her own?'

'Only the notches on the bedpost.' Harding smiled and showed a row of brown, rotted teeth. 'Nothing that'll buy you a cup of tea and a sandwich.' He downed the drink in a gulp.

'Look after yourself, Brian.' Markham stood.

'I always do, Dan. A few glasses is just what the doctor ordered.'

CHAPTER THREE

On Sunday lunchtime he was back at the Harewood Arms. The car park was filled with Morgans and MGs, their tops down to enjoy the September sun. He left the Anglia around the corner and out of sight. There wasn't a single face he knew in the pub. That was good: it meant he could listen. With luck he'd overhear something about Freddie Hart.

He leant against the bar, surveying the crowd and cocking an ear to the conversation. Horses, wives, motor cars. His thoughts had drifted away when a hand clapped him on the shoulder and he turned with a start.

'Hello, old chap. I didn't expect to see you here.' Hart stood there, a guileless smile on his face, his wife at his side.

'Oh you know, it's a lovely day,' Markham said with a shrug. 'I just fancied a run out.' It sounded a likely lie.

'Any more thoughts about that car?' Hart asked.

He shook his head. 'A bit rich for me, I think.'

'Ah well.' He shrugged. 'You won't have met my wife.' He put his arm around her and squeezed her shoulder. 'This is Joanna. Darling, this is Mr—'

'Markham. Dan Markham.'

'He was looking at a Zodiac yesterday.'

'Very pleased to meet you,' she said, shaking his hand as if she'd never seen him before and was barely interested now.

'We're meeting a crowd,' Hart said and gestured to a group in the corner. 'Why don't you join us? They're great fun.'

'Thanks, but no.' He held up the half-empty pint glass. 'I'm going as soon as I've finished this.'

Hart shrugged, ordering a pint of bitter and a gin and tonic from the barman. Joanna kept her face bland.

'What do you do, Mr Markham?' she said.

'I'm an enquiry agent.'

'Really?' Her eyes widened. 'That must be exciting.'

'It has its moments.' He drained the rest of the shandy. 'It's been a pleasure to meet you.'

Outside, he lit a cigarette and strolled back to the car. She'd been cool. Not a hint of surprise or anger. A good enough actress to be in pictures. And Hart … he was daring. Taking his girlfriend to the pub on Saturday evening, his wife on Sunday. Maybe the man liked danger.

★★★

By Monday the sun had gone. It was chilly enough to take the overcoat from the wardrobe. He set off early and parked in town, but didn't go straight to the office. Instead he cut through the splendour of Country Arcade, then into the market on the other side of Vicar Lane. Up the stairs, looking down at all the stalls and the market clock, he entered the small cafe that catered to the workers.

It smelt of grease and stale smoke, condensation running down the windows, the air heavy with steam. He ordered a cup of tea and sat down next to a middle-aged man engrossed in the *Daily Express*, a cigarette dangling from his lips.

'Who do you fancy at Sandown?' the man asked without looking up.

'I haven't a clue.' Markham took a ten-shilling note from his pocket. 'Whatever you fancy, have a bet on it.'

The money disappeared into a fist.

'What do you need?' Harsh light glistened on Ted Collins' bald head. He adjusted his glasses and sat back. Collins was a civilian chief clerk for the police, working out of Millgarth station just down the road. For a fee he was happy to provide confidential information. Pay enough and damning records or evidence could disappear without trace. It was a good little earner, enough to feed the man's losing habit on the horses and provide well for his wife and three children.

'Frederick Hart. He owns Hart Ford. Wife Joanna, née Wilson.'

Collins said nothing, picking at a tooth with his thumbnail.

'How much do you need to know?'

'Any criminal records, rumours.'

The man considered the request.

'Ten bob more,' he said, and Markham passed it over. 'Kardomah, half past twelve.' He turned back to the newspaper.

★★★

The Kardomah stood on Briggate, a fixture that seemed rooted since the beginning of time. Soot had turned the red bricks almost black, rubbing off on clothes as people brushed passed. The ground floor was overwhelmed with the heady smells of tea and fresh coffee. Up the stairs was the tea room. Markham took a table by the window and glanced out at the traffic.

'Don't often see you in here for you dinner, Mr Markham.'

He looked up to see Joyce, the waitress, poised with a pencil and pad in her hands. Their paths regularly crossed on the way to work. She looked smart in the black and white uniform, a cheery smile on her lips.

'I'm meeting someone.'

'Do you want to wait, luv?'

'No, it's fine,' he told her. 'I'll just have a cup of coffee and a ham sandwich.'

'I've seen that ham.' She pursed her lips. 'I'd not bother if I were you.'

'Cheese?'

'Can't go wrong with that,' she agreed. 'I'll pop them out to you in a minute.'

'Thanks, Joyce.'

Half past came and went and Collins didn't appear. He ate the sandwich and sipped at the coffee, smoking the last cigarette in the packet. The man finally arrived at quarter to, bustling through the room, his mac flapping as he moved. He settled on the chair with a sigh.

'Had something urgent come up,' he said. There was no apology; Collins wasn't the kind of man who ever said sorry. 'Tea,' he ordered as Joyce hovered. 'Nothing to eat.' As she left he passed a piece of paper across the table. 'That's what I found.'

Markham studied the note. Hart had been arrested once for drunk and disorderly in '46. Joanna's past was more interesting. She'd accumulated six fines for her own drunk and disorderlies. The last was six years ago, probably just before her marriage. It looked as if a wedding ring had curbed her excesses.

'She has a juvenile record, too,' Collins said. 'That's sealed. It'll cost you more.'

Markham shook his head. It would only be more wild behaviour, a confirmation of what he already knew.

Collins slurped his tea and tossed a sixpence on the table.

'Too much to do. You know where to find me.'

Markham paid the bill and walked back to the office. The information was nothing useful. Hart's arrest had probably come when he was celebrating being demobbed. There was nothing unusual there. One of thousands, probably.

★★★

He parked on Byron Street a little before five. When the blonde appeared, marching purposefully down the street, he followed on foot then took the same bus out to Meanwood.

He was behind her when she alighted, crossing over the road and vanishing down Bentley Grove. Markham was just in time to see a door open and close. He waited five minutes then walked quickly down the block, noting the house number from the corner of his eye.

It was a working-class street, neat terraces with net curtains and clean windows. There was a shop on the corner, the type of place where they'd have chapter and verse on every person in the neighbourhood. Inside, there was a bare board floor and all the basics, jars and tins, displayed on wooden shelves. A handwritten note saying 'no credit given' was pinned to the wall. Behind the counter a woman in a nylon overall stared at him.

'Ten Craven As, please,' he asked, taking a ten-shilling note from his wallet.

She waited a moment before she handed them over.

'Don't get much passing trade.'

'I had to deliver a message,' he lied. 'But there was no one at home.'

'Which one?' Her ears pricked at the possibility of gossip.

'Fifteen.'

'Aye, well.' She shook her head. 'You'll never find Arthur Willis home before seven. Allus stops for a drink on the way back from work. And that Annie, she's out till all hours. Her fancy man drops her off on the corner in his big car and she thinks no one will notice.' She snorted. 'Little madam.'

'I'll just go back later,' he said.

'I'd do that if I were you, luv,' she advised as she gave him a handful of copper and silver.

The bus into town took a long time to arrive. He strolled along Regent Street, back to his car. Then he saw the ambulance and police outside Hart Ford, and Detective Sergeant Baker glancing up and catching sight of him.

And everything changed.

CHAPTER FOUR

The houses in Alwoodley were expensive, but they were as much alike as any terrace street. Every one had its carefully-tended front garden hidden behind a privet hedge, and borders of rose bushes and bright perennials beginning to wilt with the approach of autumn. He stopped outside number three, listening to the Anglia's engine tick as it cooled. An empty Wolseley Six was parked down the street.

Markham walked down the drive, soles scuffing along the gravel, knocked on the door, waited and knocked once more. Finally he heard the sound of feet clicking sharply over the floor and the handle turned to show a middle-aged woman wearing a light brown overcoat, with a scarf over her hairdo and a handbag clutched in her fingers.

'Yes?' she asked.

'I'm looking for Mrs Hart.'

'She's not here, luv.' The woman had a thirty-a-day voice and lines so deep they seemed to cut her face into sections. Her gaze turned suspicious. 'Who are you, anyway?'

He considered lying. But there was nothing wrong with the truth.

'She employed me for a job. I just heard about her husband.'

'Murdered in cold blood.' She shook her head. 'He was a lovely man, too. He was at home a few times when I come to clean. Always had a good word. I hope they hang the bugger as did it.'

'I'm sure they will,' he assured her. As long as it wasn't him. 'Where's Mrs Hart?'

'Her father come for her not half an hour since. Coppers had her half the night asking their questions, then the telephone's been ringing all morning. The only thing she could do was sit there and cry. I made her phone her parents. She needs her family around her, people who'll look after her. Poor lass was shaking like a leaf when I arrived. She's torn to pieces by it.' She glanced up at him. 'Who wouldn't be, eh?'

'True,' he agreed. 'Thank you.' He began to turn away.

'Do you want me to tell her who called, luv?'

'Mr Markham.'

'Don't you worry, I'll let her know. Markham.' She repeated the name with a satisfied nod.

He sat in the car, hands gripping the steering wheel. Not even the middle of the morning yet and he felt as if he'd lived through an entire day. He started the engine and set off back into town.

The telephone rang before he had a chance to sit down, the bell ringing loud and urgent.

He answered with the number and heard the clunk of coins dropping in a telephone box.

'Mr Markham?' a man's voice said.

'That's right.'

'I understand that you're missing something.' The hairs on the back of his neck prickled and he drew in a breath without thinking. The Webley stolen from his desk. 'Well, Mr Markham? Do you know what I mean?'

'I do,' he answered quietly. 'Who are you?'

'Tell me,' said the caller, ignoring the question, 'would you like the return of the … item? Or perhaps I should see it ends up in official hands?'

He didn't know the voice. Not local. From the South. Long vowels.

'What do you want?'

'Many things, Mr Markham.' The man sounded amused, in control and taking his time. 'But for the moment I'll settle for your attention.'

'You have it,' he said.

'Do you know the Adelphi?'

'Yes.' It was a grubby old Victorian pub at the top of Hunslet Lane, just over the river.

'Be in there at, oh, let's say one o'clock. I'll tell you more then.'

'How will I know you?'

The voice turned to a chuckle.

'You won't need to, Mr Markham. After all, I know you.'

CHAPTER FIVE

The line went dead. Markham replaced the receiver and looked at the clock. A little after noon. Soon enough he'd know exactly who was so keen to set him up. Someone had known he was back in the office. Why? he wondered. What the hell was going on?

***

In the service, as part of his military intelligence training, they'd taught him how to shadow someone and how to throw off a tail. Everything hammered into him in drill after drill. He'd never been as good as some of the others. His friend Ged Jones seemed able to disappear in a crowd. But Markham could get by. He walked out purposefully, taking a quick note of the faces on the street as he crossed Briggate, slipped through County Arcade and Cross Arcade, then along Fish Street, ending up staring at the reflections in a window on Kirkgate to see who was behind him.

The man was an amateur. By the time he came out into Kirkgate he was almost running, staring around nervously until he spotted Markham. Older, NHS specs, his overcoat buttoned up and belted with a scarf at the neck and a hat was pulled down on a ruddy, jowly face. It was no one he recognised, no one he could remember ever seeing. But the face was imprinted on his memory now.

He set off again, ambling back to Briggate and stopping often, then down to the bridge over the river Aire. The buildings were old, decayed and black from a hundred or more years of dirt that had built up layer on layer.

The Adelphi probably hadn't changed since the turn of the century. An old gas lamp still hung over the front door. Inside, the pub was dark wood, dull brass and bevelled etched glass, all neglected and in need of a thorough cleaning. At the bar he ordered an orange squash.

A table and two chairs sat in the middle of the snug. This room was different; freshly scrubbed, the hearth black-leaded, tiles gleaming and windows shining.

'Have a seat, Mr Markham,' the man by the window said. The voice on the telephone. He checked his wristwatch. 'You're right on time.' He smiled. 'Punctuality is a good sign.'

'Of what?'

'An organised man.' He was probably in his late forties but well-kept, broadly built, neat dark hair shot through with grey. His nose had been broken in the past and there were small scars across his knuckles. But he didn't have the look of a bruiser. His eyes shone with intelligence. The dark suit was costly, a subdued pinstripe, cut smartly enough to hide the start of a belly. The tie was real silk. He sat and gestured at the chair opposite. 'We have things to talk about.'

'One thing, at least.'

'In my experience one thing always leads to another. It's the way of the world.' And he had the air of someone who'd spent a fair bit of time in the heart of the world.

'I like to know who I'm talking to.'

'I'm David Carter.' He brought out a pack of Dunhills and a slim gold lighter. 'Does that name mean anything to you?' he asked as he blew smoke towards the ceiling.

'No.'

'Good.' He sipped from a glass of whisky, savouring the taste before swallowing it. 'Never wise to be too public. If people see a name cropping up a few times they tend to become inquisitive.'

'So what do you want with me?'

The man cocked his head. 'Your co-operation.'

'You should have just asked, Mr Carter.' The words were calm enough, but he was shaking inside. Whoever this man was, he knew exactly what he was doing. 'You obviously know where my office is.'

Carter reached into the side pocket of his suit and threw a packet of Lucky Strikes onto the table.

'I'm told you liked those during your National Service in Hamburg. That American colleague of yours used buy them for you from the PX. Have them. My compliments.'

All he could do was sit and stare. Oscar, the American Pfc he'd worked with in Germany, had been able to buy the cigarettes on base for next to nothing. That and the jazz records. Carter possessed a long reach. All the way to the War Office. And far beyond. It was a powerful little gesture. Impressive. And chilling.

'What do you want in Leeds?'

'Oh, I've been buying some businesses here in the last few months. You won't have heard.' He gave a quick, tight smile. 'And those who work for me are good at staying out of sight. Except for one of the chaps following you today. But you didn't notice the other, did you?' He stared at the burning tip of his cigarette for a moment. 'Tell me, Mr Markham, what do you know about crime in Leeds? This is your home, after all.'

'I don't really deal with criminals,' he answered slowly. 'If you think I do, you've got the wrong man.'

'Indulge me. What do you *know*?'

He shrugged. 'There are tarts. Shebeens. I imagine there's illegal gambling and some protection rackets. I don't really know.'

'Penny ante stuff,' Carter said dismissively. 'And if someone's caught they end up in prison.' He paused. 'In some cases, on the gallows.'

Markham unwrapped the cellophane from the Lucky Strikes, broke open the packet and lit one. The taste brought quick memories of Germany.

'What do you want?' he said.

'I'm more interested in guineas than change. Let's say a man signs over half a profitable business to someone. A little while later he sells the rest of it to his new partner at a knockdown price. All above board and completely legitimate. Do that with a number of places and there's good money to be made.'

'Hart Ford?' he guessed.

'Poor Freddie.' Carter shook his head sadly. 'But I had to make an example of him. We had a few discussions but he wouldn't sell me an interest in the business. The fellow was adamant. Still, he didn't suffer. All it took was a single shot. But it means that the next person I talk to will be more amenable. And in case you're wondering, I didn't pull the trigger. There's nothing to connect me to the crime.'

'So why use my gun?' He realised he was barely breathing. He was a minnow swimming next to a shark.

'I never claimed anyone did, Mr Markham,' Carter corrected him. 'If you think back, I never said that at all. Your gun disappeared, shall we say, and a man was shot. I'll leave you to guess whether those two events are connected.' He frowned. 'But a wrong guess could be fatal, of course.'

'So what do you want from me besides co-operation?'

'You did well during your National Service, I understand. They wanted you to stay on in military intelligence. Someone like that can be an asset to my business. You have a mind, Mr Markham. That's what I was told. I can use a good mind. The only thing I did was put you in a position where you can't refuse.'

'What if I go to the police and tell them all this?' he asked.

'Then a certain weapon appears. As simple as that. Do you really want to gamble that your weapon wasn't connected to a crime?' He raised an eyebrow.

For a long time the only sounds were the clatter of glasses and the low murmur of voices from the bar.

He sighed. 'Like you said, I'm in no position to refuse.'

'I'm glad you see it my way, Mr Markham. Martyrs are such tedious people. I'll be in touch very soon. I have a use in mind for you.'

★★★

His first thought was to run. To leave Leeds and never come back. But the gun would appear and the police would find him. Or he could do what Carter wanted, whatever use for him the man might find.

No. It was as simple as that. No one was going to use him. He was going to fight back. And he was going to beat the bastard, whatever it took.

★★★

For the most part Markham steered clear of pubs. He rarely drank, he'd never seen the joy in them. But by eight he was standing in the public bar of the General Elliott, squashed between men wanting their orders filled, voices loud next to his ear. The place was full, a thick fug of smoke hanging beneath the stained ceiling.

Michael Doughty was sitting alone on the other side of the room, huddled into a booth where the red velvet had worn away from the seats. He was a man who heard all and said nothing unless someone paid him. Words seemed to find their way to him, names, places and dates, every one of them lodged in his head.

He was barely noticeable, so ordinary that eyes passed over him, but that was how he liked to be. Doughty always wore a cap, and with an old shirt, a jacket that was frayed at cuffs and heavy boots, he looked exactly like a working man who'd just finished his shift, bags sitting heavy under tired eyes. The only giveaway was his clean, soft hands. A flat pint of mild sat on the table in front of him. Markham put another beside it and Doughty looked up.

'Slumming it?' he asked with a smile.

'I was looking for you.'

'Come to cross my palm with silver?' He always seemed amused by life, the working man who dressed the part but made a living from secrets and tales. A hidden man. 'I hear you're in trouble.'

'Don't believe everything people tell you.'

'Oh, I don't, Mr Markham. I'm too long in the game for that. But this is from a very good source.'

'I'm here, aren't I? It can't be too bad.'

'We'll still make it cash, if you don't mind. What do you need?'

'David Carter.'

Doughty sucked on his dentures.

'If he's giving you problems, then you'd do right to be worried.'

'How much?'

'A quid,' the man said after consideration. 'That'll get you everything I know.'

Markham opened his wallet and took out a pound note. In a second it had vanished into Doughty's pocket.

'Well?'

'I don't know where he's from, so there's no point in asking. Posh, though, you can tell that. Started out here about nine months ago. You remember Nat Early? He ran that club down on Wellington Street.'

'The Kit Kat?'

'That's the one. All of a sudden he had a partner named Carter. Out of the blue. Three months later he sold up altogether. Not long after that Carter had a finger in a couple of drinking clubs in Armley and Hunslet. Soon after that it was his whole hand. You get the picture?' He waited for a nod. 'They were all doing well. There was no reason for Nat or the others to sell up. And since then there have been a few more. Another club. Some businesses here and there.'

'He's putting together an empire?'

'On the quiet. Unless you were looking you wouldn't even know he was around. But he's becoming an important man, there's no doubt about that. A dangerous one, too.'

'What's he done?'

'Him?' Doughty lit a Woodbine, coughed, and plucked a strand of tobacco from his tongue. 'He's not the sort to do anything himself. He has people to do all it for him. You know the type. They come around for a quiet chat and the threat's usually enough.'

He'd run into men like that over the years, men who thought with their fists and their feet. All you had to do was wind them up, give them their orders and let them go. The war had produced thousands of them who'd never made it all the way back to Civvy Street.

'A man to avoid?'

'If he's after you, it's probably too late. The way I hear it, he knows plenty of important people down in London. People in the ministries.'

'What do the police think?'

Doughty shrugged. 'Maybe they have a weather eye on him. Perhaps some of them are taking a few quid from him. No one's made any complaints against him yet. Happen they have more important things on their minds. And Scotland Yard …' He shook his head sadly.

'Who works for Carter around here?'

Doughty counted out the names on his fingers.

'Big Chalky White, you know, the one from Burmantofts, John Dodge, Rob Anderson. Familiar?'

'Anderson. I've met him a couple of times.' He was a man who stuck in the mind, easily six feet three, with a scar that ran the length of his cheek and a pair of dead eyes.

'If he comes for you, Mr Markham, the best thing you can do is run.' He downed the pint in a single, long gulp. 'And that's your lot. I've given you value for money.'

'Where does Carter live?'

'He keeps a room at the Metropole. Doesn't stint himself. But he doesn't need to, does he?' Doughty put the cigarettes and matches in pocket and stood. 'Good luck. If you're dealing with him, you'll need it.'

After he'd gone, Markham sat for a minute. He felt in his pocket for cigarettes and brought out the packet of Lucky Strikes. American cigarettes were almost impossible to find in England. But Carter had them.

At least he now had an idea who he was up against. He couldn't go to the police, not if they were certainly receiving backhanders from the man. Baker wouldn't believe him, and if the gun appeared he'd be happy to see Markham banged up. He was on his own. He finished the smoke, crushed the butt in an ashtray and left.

CHAPTER SIX

The telephone rang, the bell a stark sound that filled the office. For a moment he considered ignoring it. If Carter wanted to reel him in, let him do it later rather than sooner. But the sound persisted; finally he picked up the heavy Bakelite receiver.

'Mr Markham, this is Mrs Hart. Joanna Hart.' Her voice was subdued and tentative.

'Mrs Hart. I heard about your husband. I'm very sorry for your loss.'

'Thank you.' She hesitated. 'My father's taking care of all the details. I just can't face it.' She sounded completely different to the scheming woman who'd come into his office the Friday before. All the brightness had been dulled and the words made her seem younger and fragile. 'The housekeeper told me you'd been by. I just wanted to ask you to destroy whatever you'd found. It doesn't matter any more, does it?'

'I don't suppose it does.' There'd been next to nothing, anyway. 'I'll return the rest of your retainer.'

'There's no need,' she answered quickly. 'You can keep it. It's only fair.'

'OK,' he agreed. 'But tell me something, Mrs Hart.'

'What?'

'What made you pick me?'

'You?' The question seemed to surprise her. 'There aren't many enquiry agents in Leeds. And a friend of mine mentioned your name.'

'Who was that?' He doubted they knew anyone in common.

'Celia Dawson. I've known her since we were at school. Why do you want to know?'

'I was just curious.'

'Her husband, Will, works with someone who'd heard of you.'

'I see,' he replied thoughtfully. 'There's just one other thing. When you left my office the other day you met a man. Who was he?'

'Goodbye, Mr Markham,' she told him curtly and the line went dead.

Will Dawson. He knew he'd never heard the name before. But he'd find out who the man was. First, though, he needed to make some telephone calls.

★★★

Markham was back in Chapel Allerton by four, parking by the flat. Inside, he put some Monk on the gramophone. The music was as disjointed as his thoughts, raw and awkward and impossible to ignore. He began cooking a stew, adding sprigs of herbs and a little red wine before leaving it to cook on the gas ring.

He felt like a man at the bottom of a deep pit, wondering if he'd be able to climb up out. As long as Carter had the Webley, he had power over him.

Carter thought he'd won. He needed to let the man believe that.

And then he needed to use all those skills the British Army had taught him. They were the ones who selected him for military intelligence. They'd shown him all the techniques and sent him over to Hamburg for the better part of two years. He was there while the Berlin crisis played out and everyone waited for the tanks that never rolled.

He'd seen a city of rubble where the men and women came out every day to clear stone and metal. A country of spies. He'd worked with the Americans, vetting Germans for their Nazi pasts. He'd picked up Russian misinformation from safe drops and passed on plenty of his own. A game. And once his time was up he'd happily walked away from it all. Some, like Ged Jones, had stayed on made a career, but it wasn't for him. Now he needed to remember it all.

The Monk record finished and he replaced it with Charlie Parker. It was exciting, exhausting music. He played like a desperate man, the sax breathlessly chasing up and down the scales, seeming to leave the rest of the band behind. And it was fruitless. Whatever was in his mind, fuelling the frantic rush, he'd never manage to catch it. He'd never be satisfied. It was the sound of a man finely balanced on the edge, always in danger of toppling over into the abyss. There was nothing that could follow a disc like that, nothing that could keep his mind jangling.

★★★

He'd never been in the Eldon. It sat across from the university, but it wasn't the kind of place likely to draw students. The paint had worn away to grey wood and the plasterwork was crumbling. It was dying on its feet, just like the rest of the area. A warren of cobblestoned streets lay a short way beyond it, decrepit back-to-back houses cascading down the hillside, still standing, still lived-in.

He pushed open the door to the public bar. Glum men consumed their lunchtime pints as they glanced at newspapers. A pair long past retirement age were playing dominos, too focused on their game to even glance up as he walked in.

He ordered an orange squash and asked the barman for Billy Harper.

'Who wants to know?' he asked suspiciously.

'Do I look like a copper?'

The man glanced over at a corner, waiting until he received a nod. 'There.'

Harper folded his *Express* and studied Markham as he crossed the old, bare boards and sat down.

'I don't know you.' He was a small man, built like a jockey, dark hair Brylcreemed down flat. In his middle forties, Markham guessed, years of nicotine stains colouring his fingers. A Park Drive burned down in the ashtray and he picked another from the packet, lighting it from the nub.

'Dan Markham.' He extended his hand. Harper didn't take it, sitting back. He had a sour face with thin, miserly features and hard eyes.

'What do you want?'

'I might have some work for you.'

'Oh aye?' He took a slow draw on the cigarette and gazed at the tip. 'We've never met but you know my line of work? Right bloody know-it-all, aren't you?'

'It depends if Harry Dalton was telling me the truth.'

Dalton knew people, and the ones he knew lived on the edge of the law or beyond it. That was his real business. Markham had rung him the day before at the second-hand shop the man kept on Hunslet Lane. He'd described the job and Dalton had answered without a moment's hesitation,

'You want Billy Harper. He doesn't look like much but he's the best. Never been pinched. He won't bugger you around.'

'Where do I find him?'

'In the Eldon. Regular as clockwork every lunchtime. That's going to cost you a pound, Mr Markham.'

Harry's assistant would come calling at the end of the week, just like a tally man, marking off payment in a little notebook.

'Wait here,' Harper said, standing and digging change from his pocket. In two minutes he returned, jingling coins as he sat.

'Enquiry agent, eh?' he said.

'That's right.'

'What do you want nicked?'

'I want you go to through someone's hotel room.'

The man rubbed his chin. 'Which hotel?'

'Metropole.'

Harper ran his tongue over his teeth.

'What would I be looking for?'

'A gun, if it's there. And whatever papers you can find.'

'I don't like shooters. Didn't even like 'em in the war.'

'I just need you to find it and bring it to me.'

'What papers do you want?' he asked. 'I won't have hours to go through everything.'

'Anything you find.'

'Whose room?'

'A man called David Carter.' He wondered if Harper would know the name, but he gave no indication.

Harper rubbed a stubbly chin. 'How soon?'

'When can you do it?'

'I haven't said I will yet.' He finished the cigarette and lit another, leaning back on the chair and considering. 'How much?'

'Tenner?'

Harper gave a croaking laugh.

'For the Metropole? Don't be so bloody stupid. Twenty, and that's if there's no problems. And I keep anything else I take.'

Twenty pounds: plenty of money. But Harry had insisted the man was the best. Finally Markham nodded his agreement.

'How long will it take you?'

'Come back here in two days. And not a word to anyone, right?' He tapped the side of his nose. 'I hear you've been talking to people in the meantime and you can go whistle.'

'Don't worry about me.' He stood.

'Are you forgetting something, Mr Markham?'

'What's that?'

'My money,' he replied. 'I'm not doing owt unless I'm paid in advance.'

He had to dig through his wallet and his pockets to come close. Nineteen pounds, eighteen shillings and elevenpence, and Harper staring at him as he counted it all out, the contempt of the professional for the inept amateur.

'You can owe me the shilling,' he said finally with a dismissive shake of his head.

'What happens if you're caught?'

Harper snorted. 'Didn't Harry tell you anything? I don't get caught. Never have been and I'm not going to let it happen now.' There was pride in his voice, the sound of a craftsman who enjoyed his work. 'You understand?'

'Yes.'

'Good lad. You come back the day after tomorrow.'

★★★

He'd thought long and hard. It was a gamble. There was no guarantee that the Webley would be in Carter's hotel room. But if it was on him, he'd keep it close and safe where no one else might accidentally find it. If Billy Harper was as good as his reputation, it would be worth twenty pounds or more to have the weapon back.

And papers. Every scrap of information was useful. It was power.

★★★

He hadn't expected to see her again, but Joanna Hart was standing meekly by the office door, waiting for him to invite her inside. She wore black well, a tailored suit, the skirt just below her knees and a white blouse with a cameo of black jet at the throat, her perfume faint and subtle. Her eyes widened as she approached, a mix of fear and beseeching.

She sat on the edge of the chair, with the small hiss of nylon as she crossed her legs. He offered her a cigarette and she bit her lip, looking for all the world like a helpless young girl. Her eyes were red from tears she'd cried and even expensive make-up couldn't hide the paleness of her face. He let the silence build around them, in no hurry to begin.

'I'm sorry,' she said. 'I was short with you on the telephone.'

'I daresay you have other things on your mind. My condolences again.'

She gave a brief, polite smile.

'I had a letter in the post this morning.' She reached into her handbag and held out an envelope. He didn't take it and she placed it on the desk.

'I thought you were staying with your parents in Harrogate.'

'I am,' she said. 'It came there.'

'What can I do for you, Mrs Hart?'

'The person who wrote that wants to discuss buying Freddie's motor car dealership.'

'There's nothing wrong with that,' he told her. 'Do you want to run it yourself?'

'No, not really,' she admitted. 'I know this chap talked to Freddie when he was still alive about a partnership. The amount he offered then was an insult. Freddie just laughed him off.'

'Did he mention a figure in his letter?'

She shook her head.

'Just that he'd be interested in the place if the price was right. You can read it.'

'I don't need to,' he said. 'It was sent by David Carter, wasn't it?'

Her eyes widened. 'Yes. How did …?'

'Call it a good guess.'

'He wants to meet to discuss figures.'

'I'm not sure what you want from me.' Markham asked. 'I'm no expert on business.'

'Freddie said this Carter had been putting pressure on him.'

'Pressure?'

'Ringing him all the time, turning up at the showroom.'

'Then you should tell the police about him, Mrs Hart.' He weighed his words. 'That could make him a suspect in your husband's murder.'

She hesitated and drew something else from her bag, letting it flutter down on top of the letter. It was a photograph of a man, the one he saw her meet after she'd hired him to find out about her husband's infidelity.

'That's the other reason I've come to you, Mr Markham.'

'Who is he?'

'Jamie Parker. His brother was an old army friend of Freddie's. I met him at a cocktail party about six months ago.'

'Did your husband know you were having an affair?'

'No.' She paused. 'I don't think so.'

'Then why are you telling me about him?'

The woman took a deep breath.

'Freddie had started talking about divorce. We … we hadn't been happy for a while, I suppose. I thought if I had ammunition, I could stop him.'

'Tell me, did you love your husband?'

'I …' she began, then stopped. It was enough of an answer.

'Do you love …' he tapped the picture, 'Mr Parker?'

'No,' she replied. 'But he's mad about me.'

'You think he killed Mr Hart?'

'I don't know.' She looked up at him. 'He was a commando in the war. He killed people back then, he told me that.'

'You should tell the police about him. And about Carter,' he repeated. It would set Detective Sergeant Baker sniffing elsewhere.

She gave a small nod.

'I still don't understand why you're here.'

'I want you to be with me when I meet David Carter.'

'Why me?' It didn't make sense.

'Because I don't trust him.'

'You could take Mr Parker.'

'No,' she replied with firmness. 'I don't want him knowing about Jamie.'

He was willing to bet that the man already knew everything about him.

She stared at him. 'Freddie made out that business was booming.' He nodded. It was what the man had told him, too. 'It wasn't quite the truth. He was spending far more than he was taking in. He's left me bills but no money. I'm stoney. I need a good price for the business.'

'I see.'

'It's the truth, Mr Markham. You know it all now. I hope you'll come with me. I paid you five pounds before.'

'And I offered to return it,' he reminded her.

'Do this and we'll call it even then,' she offered.

He thought quickly; maybe he could use her as a lever to bring Carter down.

'When and where?'

'I have to telephone him and arrange things.'

'Do that and let me know. But don't tell him I'll be with you.'

'All right,' she agreed quickly.

'Sometimes a surprise can be a good thing.'

★★★

There was little he could do except wait. Carter would ring when he was ready, expecting Markham to be at his beck and call. Joanna Hart would be in touch when the meeting had been arranged. He wasn't seeing Billy Harper until Saturday.

Waiting. He'd always hated it. His life had been full of it. All through the war he waited, ready to be done with school, to join up and do his part. Then it was over and his National Service began. Once he was at home again there was all the time spent in queues until rationing ended. Hurry up and wait.

At least by now he knew how to do it.

★★★

The door to the flat was open. Someone had sprung the lock. He entered cautiously, ready for anything except the man sitting in his armchair.

'Decent little place,' Carter said. He nodded at the records in the corner. 'Queer taste in music, though.'

'Making yourself at home?' Markham asked. There were three cigarette ends in the ashtray. Carter had been here a while.

'You need a telephone here.'

'I have one at the office.'

'I told you I'd have something I wanted you to do.'

'You know my number.'

'I'm a man who likes the personal touch, Mr Markham.'

'What do you want?'

'I'm looking at buying a certain business.'

'Hart Ford, perhaps?'

Carter's smile was cold.

'Very good. Give yourself a gold star. It belongs to his widow now. You know her, I believe?'

'She hired me for a job.'

'Then perhaps she'll listen when you advise her to sell the business to me. I'll pay a fair price.'

'Fair?'

'What I consider fair.'

'I see.'

'I don't care how you do it, as long as she accepts my offer and signs of her own free will. I don't want any comebacks later.' He rose and buttoned his jacket. 'One last thing. I expect quick results. And I don't take no for an answer.' He put a hand on the doorknob. 'You need a better lock if you want to keep people out.'

He'd been hungry when he climbed the stairs. Now he couldn't eat a thing. He filled the kettle and made a pot of tea, standing at the window to gaze down at the Harrogate Road. The shops had closed for the day, only a few people still walking along the pavements. Buses passed, crowded with people on their way home from work. A delivery van rattled by on its way back to the depot.

Of course Carter already knew about his connection with Joanna Hart. The man was thorough. The only thing he didn't seem to know was that the woman had visited again and wanted him on her side. But he couldn't tell her that Carter expected him to work on her, to persuade her to sell. She'd never trust him. Both sides against the middle, he thought. And he was dead centre.

Markham searched through his records for something to take away the oppressive silence. Basie. Something by the Count would always lift the mood, a roar through 'One O' Clock Jump,' full of life and verve. But by the time the needle clicked in the end groove he'd hardly heard the tune.

He was trapped in the middle of a bloody mess. Carter wanted him as a pawn, something to be moved around and sacrificed. Joanna Hart wanted him as her protector. And he … he didn't want to end up in court for murder.

CHAPTER SEVEN

'I told Carter I'd meet him at seven on Saturday,' Joanna Hart said. Her voice sounded different on the line. Brittle, more metallic.

'Where?'

'The Chained Bull. There's a decent room where we can talk privately.'

He'd driven past the place, but he'd never been inside. It had that pre-war look, full of a future that was starting to show its age all too quickly.

'I'll be there,' he promised.

'Thank you,' she said, as if he'd taken a weight off her mind. 'I need a good price for the business.'

'We'll hear what he has to say, then.'

'Tomorrow evening, then?' she asked. It could have been a social engagement.

★★★

He was restless. The hands of the clock barely seemed to move. He tried to read and threw the book aside after a few minutes. Finally he walked up and down Briggate, staring in shop windows without remembering a single item. By three he'd given up, climbing into the Anglia and driving home.

Women were finishing their shopping, arms weighed down by bags. A few pushed prams, stopping outside the butcher, the baker and the post office. He stood in the flat, looking down at the road and smoking Friday away.

★★★

He parked on Woodhouse Lane and walked into the Eldon at exactly noon on Saturday. The public bar was quiet, just a few people at the wooden tables, men with nowhere better to go or nowhere they'd rather be.

Harper was there, as good as his word. In the same chair, wearing the same clothes, he looked as if he hadn't moved in the last two days.

'All done?' Markham asked as he sat. He could feel his heart pounding and the breathless feeling in his chest.

'In there.' He nudged a shopping bag with his leg.

'The gun?'

'Daft bugger had it in a drawer with his underpants.'

Markham gave a long sigh of relief. He was free.

'What else did you find?'

'Papers, just like you wanted.' Harper paused. 'I'll tell you something, though.'

'What's that?'

'Whoever your friend is, he's not too careful. He had a hundred nicker just sitting there. That's a bloody fortune.' A smile crossed his grim face. 'He used to have it, anyway.'

'No one saw you? You didn't leave any prints?'

Harper shook his head scornfully. 'I'm a professional, sonny. I was doing this before you were born. You got what you wanted.'

'Thank you.' He stood and picked up the bag, feeling the weight of the Webley inside.

'I'd get rid of that shooter if I were you,' Harper told him quietly. 'They're nowt but trouble.'

★★★

There were no pedestrians crossing Crown Point Bridge, only the occasional vehicle heading in or out of Leeds. He pulled the gun from the bag and sniffed the barrel. It had been fired. He held it for a moment, then let the weapon drop into the water. No one noticed. There was a small splash, the ripples spread for a few seconds and then it was over. Gone. He closed his eyes and breathed deeply.

In the flat he looked through the papers Harper had taken. Carbon copies of letters and documents, all of them relating to the businesses Carter owned in the city. Ten, by his count. Two night clubs, a pair of drinking clubs, four shops and two garages dotted around Leeds. By the figures they were all good earners, enough to fill Carter's bank account. But beyond profit, he couldn't see any pattern between them. And now he wanted a Ford motor agency.

By three he felt drained. He'd spent the last few days living on his nerves. Now the threat had gone, and he was running down.

It had turned six by the time he woke. Markham washed his face before changing into his best suit, the dark grey worsted that cost seven pounds and worth every penny. If clothes really did make the man, these changed him into someone of substance.

There was still one thing to do before he left. He bundled the papers into an old arch folder and took them down to the cellar, a set of pokey, brick-lined rooms behind an anonymous door. No one came down here. Probably none of the other tenants even knew it existed. Everything would stay safe and hidden.

It was little more than a mile to Moortown. The shops on the parade were all closed for the night. The only place with any life was the Chained Bull. He ordered a shandy, lit a cigarette and leant against the bar. He'd arrived early; there was no sign of Joanna Hart or Carter yet.

She came five minutes later, hair up in a chignon to show off her long neck and a simple square-neck black dress that flared out from the waist. It was sombre, elegant and effective. It suited her perfectly. Several men watched her cross the floor.

'Thank you for coming,' she said, putting her hand on his arm.

'I told you I would. Get you a drink?'

'G and T, please.'

She led him to a quiet corner at the back, set apart from the main bars and furnished with a low table and comfortable club chairs.

'What do you want me to do?' he asked.

'I hope you being here will be enough,' she told him with a smile.

'Carter can be persuasive,' he warned.

'That's why you're with me. I know exactly how much I need. I can't settle for a penny less.'

Time to change the subject, he thought.

'Have the police said more about your husband's murder?' The story was still on the front page of the *Post*, but it had moved below the fold. And Baker hadn't been back to see him.

'No,' she answered slowly. 'Not that they've said to me. That fat detective came to ask me more questions. I've told him everything I know.'

'About Carter and your friend?'

'Yes. Even Jamie.'

He nodded and brought up the topic that had been worrying at him for a few days. 'That's him. Tell me, Mrs Hart. You said the husband of a friend recommended me?'

'That's right. Celia's husband, Will.'

'It's odd. I've never heard of him. What does he do?'

'He manages the Kit Kat Club on Wellington Street. Why?'

'It doesn't matter. I was just curious.'

The Kit Kat. The very first business that Carter had bought at a knock-down price in Leeds.

There was no time for more. David Carter bustled in, as if the thought had been his cue, a glass of Scotch in his hand. He wore a sports jacket and cavalry twill trousers, a cravat at his neck, looking every inch the businessman dressed down for the weekend.

'Mrs Hart,' he said extending an arm. 'Thank you for seeing me. I know this must be a trying time for you.' She shook his hand and gestured him to the empty chair. As he sat he glared at Markham, a look that was eager to kill.

She nodded her head graciously.

He sat forward, elbows on his knees, looking at her.

'As I explained in my letter, I'd talked to your husband about buying his business. I'm very sorry about your loss, but I want you to know that I'm still eager to purchase Hart Ford.'

'Freddie told me about your offer, Mr Carter. And the answer he gave you.'

'We'd barely begun negotiations.' He gave a smile that showed white, even teeth and looked at Markham. 'Is this gentleman your representative?'

She shook her head.

'Just a friend I asked along.'

'I'm sure he'll tell you that running a business isn't easy. I know your husband had built the Ford agency into something worthwhile, but do you really want all the day-to-day responsibility to make it even better?'

She took a long, thoughtful drink of the gin.

'What I want is a fair price for the business.'

'Of course,' Carter said politely, dipping his head as he drank.

'That means I need a great deal more than you offered Freddie.'

'Mrs Hart—' he began, but she cut him off.

'That's not negotiable,' she said firmly, her voice rising so that people turned to watch. 'And I'll tell you something I don't appreciate, Mr Carter. I don't like someone pursuing me this way before Freddie's even been buried. The only reason I agreed to meet you was to see what a ghoul looked like. I'm sure you feel that preying on widows is a perfectly legitimate tactic, but I'm afraid I don't. If you want to make a realistic offer after the funeral, I'll listen. Now, if you'll excuse me.'

She stood quickly and gathered up her handbag. The men rose with her, and Markham followed her from the room. He glanced back, seeing Carter's face set with fury.

He found her leaning against the Humber, holding a cigarette. Her hand was shaking slightly. He struck a match and watched her pull smoke down to her lungs.

'I hadn't expected that,' he told her.

'Oh, I did, Mr Markham.' Her eyes were strangely bright, her lipstick bloody in the evening light. 'What an odious man.'

'He doesn't give up easily.'

'I don't imagine he does. But maybe it'll make him think and come back with a higher offer. I've given him some food for thought. He's not the only one who can play a game. Next time he'll be serious.' She dropped the cigarette and ground it out under her shoe. 'Thank you for coming, Mr Markham. I appreciate the moral support.'

Then she was gone, her car moving away, just the vague scent of her perfume lingering for a few seconds.

In the Anglia he looked at his watch. Barely half past seven: the encounter had only lasted a few minutes. His stomach rumbled and realised he'd barely eaten all day. At the flat he fried up bacon and eggs and sat at the table. Carla's letter from Italy still lay there. Tomorrow she'd be back, arriving on the five-fifteen from London. And he'd be waiting on the platform, glad to have her home.

Carter would come calling again soon. He was sure of that. Not only his anger at being rebuffed by Joanna Hart. All too soon he'd realise the gun and the papers were missing. The man would want his revenge.

★★★

A little after ten he drove into town. There was hardly any Saturday night traffic on the roads, no more than a few buses and cars and the flashing tangerine lights of the Belisha beacons.

He parked on New Briggate, close to the Wrens Hotel, and walked the few yards back to Studio 20.

The music began just as he walked down the stairs, piano, bass, drums and a young tenor player he'd never seen before. He barely looked old enough to shave and dressed awkwardly in something that could have been his father's demob suit. But he could play, twisting a world of ache and pain through the melody of 'Someone To Watch Over Me' with a heartbreak that went beyond his years. Markham waited in the doorway until the tune ended in a slow flurry of notes that rose like smoke.

It was a small crowd so far, no more than a dozen, but they applauded wildly. Everyone knew they'd just heard something special. The young man blushed, and Markham eased into the back room where Bob Barclay, the club's owner, sat watching everything through a hatch in the wall where he dispensed the tea, coffee and squash.

'Who is he?'

'Good, isn't he?' Barclay said as the piano took a long introduction to 'Stormy Monday Blues', the sax player replicating the tone of Billy Eckstine's smooth voice over the chords. 'Just showed up with his instrument this evening. Lives in Huddersfield, would you credit it?' He nodded his head in time with the beat.

'He's going places,' Markham said. 'What's his name?'

'Michael Goodman. He's off to London tomorrow to audition for Dankworth's band.'

'He'll get the gig.'

'Be a crime if he didn't.' He beamed as Goodman caught a solo, a series of short, anguished phrases that built in intensity. 'I tell you what, Dan, we're seeing the birth of a new star here.'

'I think you're right.'

He stayed for the rest of the set. It was pure joy to hear. The lad played his heart out, tearing through 'Donna', some Ellington and more Gershwin before closing with a take on 'Somewhere Over The Rainbow' that trembled with hope.

When the lad took the reed from his instrument, Markham left. There was nothing else he could hear tonight that could come close to that. He felt warm, happy in the glow of the music, replaying it in his mind as he walked to the car, just the sounds of the night around him.

They came out of the shadows. Two men, both big. One strayed into the light of a street lamp, showing a boxer's face with a broken nose and a long scar down his cheek. Rob Anderson. Carter's man.

The other held up a knife.

'You're coming with us,' Anderson said. He had a voice that sounded as if it had been dragged over gravel. Markham weighed his chances. 'Don't,' the man advised, making his hand into a large first. 'Right?'

He was pushed into the back of a Vauxhall Velox parked a few yards along the street. The man with the knife sat next to him, the tip of the blade pushed hard against his stomach. Anderson started the engine and pulled away.

'You'd best hope we don't need any sudden stops else you'll be pulling that out your belly.' It was all he said as he cut through the centre of town, over Leeds bridge and left onto Dock Street, going slow over the cobbles as they passed the old wharf and turned into a small road that ended in the brick wall of a factory.

The street was lined with small workshops and garages. The door to one opened and Carter came out.

'Bring him in here.'

The knife point pricked the back of his neck, just enough pressure for him to feel the sharpness without breaking the skin. The room was bare brick walls, an old table and two wooden chairs in the middle of the floor. A single bulb cast a harsh light into all the corners.

'Sit down,' Carter ordered as he paced around slowly.

Markham sat. He was in for a beating, he knew that. A lesson. He'd expected it. He could take it. But Carter wouldn't dare kill him. Another murder in Leeds would bring too much unwanted attention. He'd started to reach for his cigarettes when a fist landed on the side of his skull, hard enough to send him sprawling on to the concrete.

He shook his head, trying to clear it as he slowly pulled himself to his feet, leaning heavily on the table. This next blow caught him in the gut and sent him back to the ground, gasping for air.

This time he stayed down, waiting until he could breathe again before he stood. His stomach burned and he could taste the bile in his throat. A heavy throb beat in his head as he moved. Someone had righted the chair and he sat once more.

Carter took the other seat.

'You think you're a clever little fucker, don't you?'

'Do I?' His voice surprised him. It seemed to come from miles away, something faint and half heard.

'Think getting the gun lets you off the hook, do you?'

He didn't reply. Anything he said would mean another blow.

Carter shook his head. 'You just think it does, sonny boy. Stupid. Don't you worry, I'll find out who he was.'

Markham kept his silence, blinking and trying to keep his gaze from slipping out of focus.

Carter paced again and said, 'Do you know what's painful?'

'What?' The word was a croak.

'Broken fingers. It's a funny thing, they never heal quite properly. It's a shame you don't play an instrument. You'd really notice it then.' He nodded. Anderson darted forward, holding Markham's arm in a tight grip, left hand forced flat on the table, palm-down. He tried to struggle, to pull back, then the knife was at his throat, the blade cold against his skin. 'People don't cross me, Mr Markham. You're going to learn that. You can scream all you like, there's no one around to hear.'

Carter leaned over and picked up a hammer.

'This is going to hurt,' he said with no emotion. 'But maybe it'll make you remember. I told you to persuade the Hart woman to sell. I give you a job to do, you do it.'

Swiftly, he brought the hammer down once, twice.

Markham screamed. It was done, all over before he could even move. He was still yelling as they grabbed his collar. Carter stood in front of him and brought up two fingers like a gun barrel against his forehead. Very quietly, staring into Markham's eyes, he said, '*Bang.*'

They threw him out into the street. The door closed and he was lost in the dark, yelling over and over until his throat felt raw. The pain was intense, the ruined fingers burning and sending flames shooting up his arm. He bent forward and vomited, so weak he thought he might fall.

He managed to steady himself against the wall, cradling the hand, not even daring to look at it. Finally he felt strong enough to try one pace, then another, gritting his teeth and sweating, more stumbling than walking. He stopped, gathering strength before making himself move further. It seemed to take hours until he was back on Dock Street. Every step jolted and hurt. He bit his lip, gathering it all in.

Markham stopped on the bridge, resting his forearm on the parapet. He forced his hand to open. Where his ring and little fingers had been was just blood and tissue, and the sharp, ugly white of bone. They were broken. Useless. He vomited again, leaning over to empty his stomach into the river until there was only the taste of acid left in his mouth.

The pain was worse than anything he'd ever known. He drew in a deep breath and began to move again, urging one foot in front of the other along Briggate. Step by step, each one a little victory. First to Duncan Street, then rest, leaning against the wall, almost in tears. On to Kirkgate. Another break to gather his strength. Eventually he crossed the Headrow. He was soaked, face drenched in sweat, legs as heavy as lead. With his good hand he fumbled for the car keys and sat in the Anglia, head down on the wheel.

He stayed like that, waiting for the nausea to pass as his skin dried under his clothes. Finally he turned the key and put the car into gear, gasping as his fingers touched the lever. It was only a few hundred yards to the Public Dispensary at the top of North Street.

Casualty was a quiet place of green tiles and old cream walls. The nurse took one look at his hand and led him straight through to a cubicle. The doctor bustled in a minute later, no older than himself, pulling on the white coat as he entered and covering a yawn.

'Christ Almighty, what happened?' he asked in shock.

'Someone decided they didn't like me,' Markham managed. He tried to smile but his mouth stayed set.

'Let's get some anaesthetic in that hand so I can look at it properly.' He rubbed his chin. 'It'll just be a local, no need to knock you out.'

The nurse appeared with a tray. He watched the needle go in and a few minutes later it was numb. The doctor worked for an hour, stitching skin and splinting. He stopped to sigh and clean his glasses, then continued, finishing with a bandage to hold the two fingers tightly together.

'That's the best I can do,' he apologised. 'With luck you'll have full usage in time but they'll never look too good, I'm afraid.' He paused. 'What's that on your head?' Gently he felt around the knot, the residue of the blow he'd received on the other side of the river. Markham winced under the touch. 'I'd like to get that X-rayed, just to make sure there's no concussion,' the doctor said.

'I'll be fine,' he answered. All he wanted was to go home, to settle into bed and sleep long into Sunday.

The doctor shrugged.

'It's your funeral. I can't make you. I'll write you a prescription for some painkillers and give you enough to last until the chemist opens on Monday. If you experience any dizziness, I want you back here immediately. That could be a concussion.'

He vanished and returned with a piece of paper and a small bottle of pills.

'Take two of these once you're home. Another two every four hours tomorrow.'

'Thank you.'

'Go and see your GP, too.'

'I will.'

'I mean it, Mr Markham.' The doctor stared at the hand. 'That's a nasty injury; it's going to need a lot more care to heal well.'

★★★

He could barely feel anything as he moved to change gear. The eastern sky was starting to brighten. Ten minutes later he climbed the stairs to the flat, weary, angry and needing sleep. He swallowed a couple of the pills with a glass of water, stripped off and sank under the covers.

Part Two

SOMEONE TO WATCH OVER ME

CHAPTER EIGHT

Markham woke with the sun on his face, turned over and blinked at the clock. Ten past two. As he tried to rise he yelled out in pain as his broken fingers pressed against the mattress. He swallowed two more of the tablets with a cup of tea, switched on the immersion heater and studied himself in the mirror.

The lump on his head was tender. But at least his vision was clear and the wound only ached when he touched it. A few days and it would be gone. He gazed at the fingers, useless and bound. They were a different matter. Carter had done his work well. The scars would remind him for the rest of his life.

He bathed, shaved and dressed. At quarter to five he started the car, the sense of anticipation rising in his stomach. Another half hour and Carla would be home. He could already picture her, skin brown from the sun, climbing down lazily from the train, happy to be back. And to see him again.

He parked and walked into the station. It was a cauldron of noise, voices, engines and the stink of coal and smoke all gathered under the glass ceiling, dimming the light. A whistle sounded, followed by the familiar slow chug of a train pulling away.

Markham stood by the entrance to the platform and lit a Craven A. The pills had reduced the agony to a low ache that pulsed through his body. He watched the hands move on the clock, finishing the cigarette and lighting another.

At quarter past the train pulled in, exactly on time, letting out an exhausted sigh of steam as it came to a standstill. His right hand tensed against the barrier. The doors of the compartments opened and people alighted. Not many passengers, even for a Sunday.

Carla was the last, climbing down and pulling a heavy suitcase after her, then reaching back for second and a third and hauling them down with both hands. A porter appeared, expertly sliding everything onto a trolley and following her as she strode down the platform. Markham waved; she spotted him and her face lit up. She moved faster, almost throwing her ticket at the clerk. Then she was in his arms and grinning at him.

'I missed you, you bastard,' Carla said, before giving him a long kiss. She stood back, taking his hands, and the smile turned to horror. 'My God, Dan, what happened?'

'I've been in the wars,' he answered.

She stroked the bandaged fingers lightly, then the side of his head. He pulled back a little from her touch.

'Right,' she told him. 'Come on, let's go home.'

He tipped the porter a shilling for arranging the cases in the boot, started the motor and pulled away.

'Where?' he asked.

She leaned her head back against the seat and let out a sigh.

'Can we go to yours? It feels like I've been gone forever. I just want to spend some time with you before I go back to my flat.'

He smiled.

He carried one case in his good hand while Carla grunted and cursed the others up the stairs. Spread out, they filled most of the room. He put Monk on the gramophone to welcome her home and she tapped her feet in time with the music as she sorted through the things she'd brought back with her. Her dress lapped around her in shades of red, orange and black, perfect for her colouring and her figure. After a few minutes of digging, clothes, papers and packages strewn all across the floor, she announced, 'Aha!' and held up two large bags. 'For you. Souvenirs.'

He looked at her warily.

'What are they? Sticks of rock with Italy all the way through?'

'Philistine.' Carla stuck out her tongue. 'Here.'

He opened the first, bringing out a bottle of red wine, the bottom half covered in woven straw. Chianti Classico, he read from a label with the image of a black rooster.

'That's the real thing,' she told him. 'Not the muck we get over here. Delicious, too. I thought we could have it when we eat.'

'I don't have anything in.'

She gave a wide grin.

'I've taken care of that, too. Look in the other bag.'

He did, and saw dried pasta in a packet. Not spaghetti, but wide noodles and a glass jar holding a dark red liquid, yards of Sellotape wound tightly around the lid to stop it spilling.

'What is it?'

'Sauce. I persuaded the cook where I ate on Friday to put some in there for me.' She grinned, kissed her fingertips and opened her hand, a woman who could charm a bird out of a tree. 'Perfecto. And all you have to do is heat it. Wait a mo.' She knelt and rummaged around some more before holding up one more bag. 'Here. To finish it off.'

'My hands are full,' he said.

She drew out a packet of coffee, opening it so the heavy aroma filled the room, then dug down for a small steel pot.

'For making espresso,' she explained. 'After we've eaten.'

Markham laughed.

'Is there anything you haven't thought of?'

'Not a thing.' Her eyes shone.

'I have plans for after the food.'

Carla ran a tongue teasingly over her mouth.

'You'd bloody well better have after I've been gone so long. Just think of the meal as, what did that Kinsey chap call it? Foreplay.' She came and kissed him, only their lips touching. She was warm and beautiful, wicked and bright, the skin on her bare arms warm and soft. There was no one in the world he'd rather be with right now.

'Was it worth all the money and time?' He knew she'd saved for two years to afford the month in Italy.

There was a whole world in her sigh.

'Every penny. Oh Dan, it was wonderful. We have to go, you'd love it. The art was bloody marvellous. I think I could have stayed in Florence for a year and still not seen it all. I was sketching like a mad thing. I feel like I'm going to burst with all these ideas. I'd seen pictures of these things in books but until you're there …' She shook her head. 'Go on, start cooking, I'll tell you whilst we eat.'

The food was as delicious as she'd promised, the sauce light, not sweet, clinging to the pasta, the flavours blending on his tongue.

'This is glorious,' he told her. 'Thank you.'

'Wind it round your fork,' she said and demonstrated for him, hand moving deftly as she twisted the fettuccine. 'Like that.'

It took him a couple of attempts to master it with his right hand, Carla laughing at his clumsiness.

The wine matched the food, a hint of sweetness and an aftertaste that stayed on the tongue. He found an old candle in a drawer and set it in a saucer, turning off the electric light to create the atmosphere. As they ate she chattered about Italy, the memories piling one on top of the other: the scenery, the people, the ridiculously cheap prices. Finally, when they were done and they'd managed to understand how the espresso maker worked, she looked at him.

'So what happened?' She stroked the knot on the side of his skull again with her soft fingertips and held up his left hand. 'Someone's done you over.'

He hadn't planned on telling her any of it. But after the wine, having her home and close again, he let it all spill out, from Joanna Hart's first visit to last night's beating. She was silent for a long time, smoking her Italian cigarettes, elbows resting on the table, the empty cup and wineglass in front on her.

'It's a mess, isn't it?'

'Yes,' he agreed with a sigh. 'And it's going to get worse.'

'What are you going to do, Dan?'

'Beat the bastard.'

She was quiet for a long time.

'This Carter sounds nasty.'

'He is.' He held up the fingers as proof. 'He has connections, too. He knew what brand of American cigarettes I smoked in Germany.'

'Christ. Look after yourself, Dan.' She stared into his eyes. 'Please.'

'I will,' he promised and smiled. 'Now, weren't we talking about something for after the meal?'

★★★

He woke in the early light, hearing her soft breathing beside him. Their lovemaking had been rowdy, a need in them both, powerful and loud. She'd straddled him, taking the lead, speeding up then slowing down, making it last until he was bucking under her into a final explosion. He reached out, fingers running lightly down her spine, feeling the small bump of each vertebra as she stirred for a moment.

'What time is it?' she mumbled.

He turned to glance at the clock.

'Six.'

'God. Wake me in an hour, will you?'

★★★

She'd never been a morning person. She lingered over tea and toast, telling him more about Italy, little highlights that popped into her head. The statue of Donatello's Magadalene Penitent in Florence, so raw that it looked as if it could have been sculpted yesterday, the crowds around the Forum in Rome, the light in Naples.

'What about your luggage?' he asked as she applied her lipstick.

She turned to him, eyes wide and hopeful. 'Would you really mind if I left it all here until tonight? I need to see the head of department in an hour about all the students starting next week.'

He surveyed the mess. There were clothes all over the floor, dresses, slacks, underclothes, paths snaking between them. It would take more than an hour for her to re-pack, longer still to transport everything to her flat in Headingley.

'Of course. You want a lift into town?'

'You're a godsend.'

Markham parked and they parted with a kiss. He took time to watch her walk away towards the Art College on Vernon Street, hips swinging, heels clattering against the pavement.

★★★

He sat in the office, staring at the calendar on the wall without seeing it. His fingers hurt; he'd filled the prescription and taken two more of the pills. All the tiny things he'd always taken for granted became a trial – knotting his tie, tying his shoes, even buttoning his fly.

Carter, he thought. Bloody Carter.

Some memory flickered in his head, words he'd heard his American colleague in Hamburg say one day: the best defence is a good offence. Markham hadn't understood then. Was he talking about the Russians? But now it made sense. What he needed was a good offence.

He'd brought Carter's papers from home. Now he spread them out and began to read properly, jotting notes on a stenographer's pad.

He worked until noon then packed everything away in a folder. He heard footsteps on the stairs, and Detective Sergeant Baker walked in without knocking, sitting hard on the client's chair and fanning himself with his hat.

'Off somewhere, Markham?'

'I was just going to eat. Want to join me?'

'Your belly can wait,' Baker decided. 'What's happened to your hand?'

'I had an accident. Broke two fingers.'

The man looked doubtful. 'Messing about where you shouldn't?'

'Just a normal accident.' Markham shrugged and settled in the chair. Joanna Hart's lover must have come to nothing as a lead. 'What can I do for you, Mr Baker?'

'I still like you for the Hart killing. You fit.'

'I told you before. I wasn't there and I didn't do it.'

'What if I said I had a witness who says you were there around the time it happened?'

'Then he's mistaken or a liar. I'm sure you followed up on what I told you.'

Baker nodded. 'The shopkeeper in Meanwood says someone came in and bought Craven As,' he acknowledged. 'But she can't describe him. Just that he was young.' He stared. 'Could be anyone.'

'Not anyone. Me.'

'And my witness could be telling the truth about seeing you at Hart Ford after it closed.'

'Who is he?'

Baker's smile was as grim as death.

'You think I'm going to say and give you a chance to nobble him? I wasn't born yesterday, lad. All I need now is the weapon and they can start preparing the hangman's noose.'

'Then you'll be looking for a long time.'

For a fat man Baker moved quickly. He was up from the chair, leaning across the desk and pulling Markham by the tie until their faces were an inch apart. He could smell the rank sourness of the policeman's breath.

'Don't play the clever bugger with me. Someone's dead, lad. It's not a fucking game. I can get a search warrant for this office and that flat of yours like that.'

'Look all you like. You won't find a gun because there isn't one. Help yourself. I tell you what, I'll even give you the run of the place whilst I'm out.'

The detective let go of the tie and stood up.

'You're a cocky little bastard, Markham.'

'I've got nothing to hide.' He picked up the folder and riffled through it. 'See? No gun hidden inside. I'm taking this with me.' Then he opened the top drawer, produced a key and placed it on the desk. 'I'd appreciate it if you'd lock up when you leave and pop this through the letterbox. If you want me I'll be at Lyons.'

On Albion Place he lit a cigarette and glanced back at the building. He could leave Baker there. The man might loathe enquiry agents, but he was honest. He wasn't a copper who planted evidence or lied for a conviction.

And the gun was safely in the river. But who was the witness who claimed to have seen him at Hart Ford? Carter's doing, it had to be. Trying to tighten the screws just a little more. But as soon as Baker dug deeper he'd see it was all lies.

He ordered a cheese sandwich and a cup of tea, reading through more of the papers. He couldn't find anything illegal, but it told him the extent of Carter's empire. Clubs, shops, businesses. If he carried on at this rate, in a couple more years he'd be someone with real power in Leeds; too big to dislodge.

Markham had just put the papers away when something metallic dropped on his empty plate. The office key. He looked up to see Baker standing there.

'Your office is clean.'

'I told you it was.'

'You could have ditched the shooter.'

'I could, but I didn't.' A lie, he thought, but it was also true. He hadn't used the gun to murder anyone.

'Or it could be in your flat.'

'Come and take a look, Sergeant.'

'All right,' Baker agreed. 'I want to see how someone like you lives.'

***

The man was thorough. He went through all the drawers and cupboards, checked the mattress for rips, felt every pillow. On top of the high cistern in the toilet, the back of the dressing table. Baker looked distastefully at Carla's clothes thrown all across the floor and the records stacked against the wall.

'You think you've been clever, don't you, Markham?'

'I've been honest with you.' He'd even made a cup of tea for them both as the policeman searched.

'I still think you're behind this.'

'And I know I'm not. So do you, really. If I were you I'd take a closer look at this witness you have.'

'You would, would you?' Baker's tone oozed sarcasm. 'I suppose you'd teach your granny to suck eggs, too. I don't need lessons from a kid on how to do my job, Markham.'

He paused at the door. 'You should teach your slut to pick up her clothes. This place is a bloody tip.'

***

Carla arrived in the late afternoon, looking worn and despondent.

'I'd forgotten how dirty this bloody city is. I've only been back a day and I feel grubby already.'

'It's Leeds,' was all he could say.

By seven they'd moved the luggage back to her flat in Headingley. It was a garden flat — a cellar in everything but name — with front windows that looked out to the lawn and a bathtub that backed up whenever it rained heavily. She opened the windows to air it and he kissed her goodbye.

At home he put Sarah Vaughan on the gramophone as he worked through more of Carter's papers. He had the information. Now, how could he use it?

Midnight came and he still didn't have an answer. All around him the city had gone to sleep.

***

The morning brought a chilling rain that was too heavy for the windscreen wipers. He dashed the few yards from car to office and was still soaked. Inside, he smoked and stared out of the window, watching runnels of water glide down the glass.

He picked up the telephone on the first ring.

'It's Joanna Hart.'

'What can I do for you, Mrs Hart? Have you heard from Carter?'

'He rang me yesterday,' she said. She sounded drawn. 'I tried you but you were out.'

'Has he made another offer?'

She told him the figure. To Markham it seemed a fortune, but she treated it as an insult.

'He wants to meet again to discuss it.'

'What did you say?'

'I'm trying to arrange Freddie's funeral.'

'Then don't let him bully you.'

'He was very insistent.'

Markham stared at his bandaged fingers. 'Yes,' he said. 'Men like that can be.'

'What should I do?' she asked

'Let him stew. He might raise his price.'

'OK,' she agreed after a while.

He'd no sooner set the receiver down than it rang again.

'Have you heard about Billy Harper?' Harry Dalton asked. He was the man who'd put Markham in touch with the burglar.

'Billy Harper? No.'

'He did a job for you last week, didn't he?'

'Yes.' And he'd done it well, recovering the gun and taking the papers from Carter's hotel room. 'But I haven't seen him since Saturday.'

'Someone gave him a hell of a beating last night. He's in the Infirmary. Broke his jaw and messed up his hands. He'll survive but he's in a bad way.'

'I'm sorry.'

'Don't know if he'll ever work again. Do you know who did it, Dan? The last thing he did was for you.'

'I'll try to find out.'

'You do that. Billy has plenty of friends who'll be looking for revenge.'

He lit another cigarette and stared out at the rain again. It was beginning to seem like war.

The post plopped onto the mat. Just bills. Never anything worthwhile.

CHAPTER NINE

Markham walked into the hush of the bank. People talked in whispers, as if they were in church. The woodwork and brass all gleamed. He waited in the queue, mackintosh dripping rain on the parquet floor.

The cashier took his cheque and walked away. Two minutes later she returned.

'I'm sorry, sir, but we can't honour this.'

'What?' He was loud enough for people to turn. 'It's only twenty pounds. There's plenty in my account.'

She glanced down, embarrassed.

'Would you like to see the manager, sir?'

★★★

He had to wait half an hour. Finally the manager invited him into the office. Mr Atkinson, the nameplate on the desk read. A spare, ascetic man, almost bald, eyes hidden behind heavy glasses. He opened a file and looked at the papers inside.

'I believe you're an enquiry agent, Mr Markham.' Atkinson said finally. He pronounced the words as if they were something distasteful.

'That's right.'

'Aren't you a little young for that?'

'What does that have to do with anything?' he asked angrily. 'I want to know why there isn't enough in my account to cash a cheque.'

Atkinson held up his hand.

'I merely mentioned it because my experience has shown that the young tend to be rather irresponsible with money.'

'My account's in the black.'

Atkinson tapped the folder

'No, it isn't, Mrs Markham. You have three pounds and ten shillings in it.'

He started to rise.

'What?' That wasn't possible.

Atkinson held up a piece of paper.

'In black and white, Mr Markham.' He held up a piece of paper. 'You took out four hundred pounds on Friday morning.'

'Don't be so bloody ridiculous.' He could feel the anger rising as he gripped the chair arms. Atkinson stared at him. 'Where did it happen?'

'In London.' He read. 'On Charing Cross Road.'

'I was here on Friday. In Leeds.'

But even as he spoke, he knew. Carter.

'It's right here, Mr Markham.' Atkinson gave an indulgent smile, as if explaining to a backward child.

'Then someone's made a mistake. Christ.' He banged his good hand on the desk hard enough to make the bank manager look towards the door.

'Please, Mr Markham. There's no need for that.'

He leaned forward.

'There's every bloody need for it. I want you to get on to your head office and have them check again. I wasn't in London and I didn't take out four hundred pounds. Do you understand that?'

'I can ask them to look into it,' Atkinson said quietly. 'But you understand that at the present time I can't honour your cheque.'

Markham slammed the door behind him, footsteps sharp over the wood floor. Outside, in the steady rain of Park Row he checked his money. Carter had shown him he was powerless. All it took to destroy him was a telephone call.

***

He sat in the basement cafeteria at Marks and Spencer on Briggate. Mothers chatted in groups around large tables; others balanced trays and shepherded young children. The noise was as deafening as a factory canteen. But that was what he needed: something to block out his thoughts.

He finished the sandwich and pushed the plate away, lighting a cigarette as he stirred the tea. The woman at the cash register had glanced at him sympathetically as he counted out his coppers for the meal.

'Don't look so down in the mouth,' she said. 'It might never happen.'

But it already had.

Hands in pockets, he made his way back to the office. The rain was still falling, sluicing the rubbish off the pavements and leaving the slabs a dark, shiny grey.

Who was Carter? What had brought him to Leeds? He smoked a cigarette down to the filter, stubbed it out and lit another. There was someone he could call who might be able to give him a few answers.

Markham took out his address book and flipped through to 'J'. There were two London telephone numbers for the name, one home, another for work. He picked up the receiver and called the operator, waiting until he heard her say she was connecting him.

'Hello.' No name, no business.

'I'm looking for Ged Jones. This is Dan Markham.'

'Danny boy.' He could sense Jones' smile, the slight Welsh lilt in the words. They'd done their National Service together, the pair of them stationed in Hamburg. But Jones had been the one with the brilliant mind, the one who'd stayed on and been recruited by MI5. A useful friend to have. 'It's been a long time, boy. How are you?'

'I'm in a bit of a fix,' he answered honestly.

'That doesn't sound too good. Are you still in the detective business?'

'I am. What about you? Still working for Her Majesty?'

'I'd be a section head by now if I had the right accent and school tie,' Jones answered cynically.

'I'm hoping for some help. A favour …'

'Always on the cadge,' he laughed. 'I remember what you were like over there, looking for cigarettes.'

'Which I gave to the Germans in exchange for information. How many Nazis did they help to bring in?'

'Fair enough,' Jones agreed with a chuckle. 'So you're after something. What do you need?'

'David Carter. Does it ring any bells?'

'Not even a tiny one. Should it?'

'That's what I want to find out.'

'He been causing you problems, Danny?'

Markham looked at the broken fingers.

'You might say that. He knows things, Ged. He gave me a pack of Lucky Strikes because he knew Oscar used to get them from the PX in Germany.'

'I see.' Jones' voice was suddenly serious and professional.

'And he's also managed to clean out my bank account.'

'Jesus, boy. Sounds like you've managed to make a powerful enemy.'

'I'm saving the best for last. He's killed someone and he's trying to set me up for it.'

He heard the intake of breath.

'What about the coppers? Aren't they doing anything?'

'He's under their radar. Or there are backhanders. I need to know who he is.'

It only took a moment for Jones to consider the request.

'Give me an hour or so and I'll ring you back. But,' he cautioned, 'you won't have heard anything from me. All right?'

'All right.'

'Stand by your telephone.'

Markham replaced the receiver, feeling more confident. Ged would dig out the truth. Then he'd have some ammunition.

He'd been pacing the room slowly for five minutes when the phone rang again. He answered with the number; it was far too soon for Ged to be calling back.

'How do you fancy taking me out tonight?' Carla asked. 'These students are bloody awful. I'm going to scream if I don't have something to look forward to.'

'What did you have in mind?'

'Dinner somewhere and the pictures?' she asked hopefully.

'What's on?'

He heard the rustle as she glanced through the newspaper.

'There's *On the Waterfront* at the Ritz. It's supposed to be good. Marlon Brando.'

'OK. Why don't you come to the office when you finish? We'll go on from there.'

'You're an angel.' She made a kissing sound. 'Really, you are. 'I'll see you later.'

At least he'd enjoy the evening.

He sat and smoked and paced, glancing at the clock only to watch the minutes moving too slowly. Finally, three hours later, the telephone rang again. Even though he'd expected it, been waiting for it, the sound still startled him.

'Danny boy, you sound nervous.' Ged chuckled.

'I am. I've got a couple of broken fingers to keep me on edge.'

'Courtesy of your friend?'

'Yes.'

'From what I've learnt that doesn't surprise me. Turns out there's quite a bit on him.'

'What have you found out?' Markham asked.

'How long do you have?'

'As long as you like. You're paying for the telephone call.'

'Good to know you're still a Yorkshireman, anyway.' He laughed. 'Anyway, let me tell you about this chap. Do you remember those men in suits who used to wander around the office in Hamburg? Always closed the doors before they talked with each other?'

'Of course.' They'd always speculated about them, the ones who never smiled or laughed.

'Carter was one of them, but in Berlin.' He paused. 'It's interesting, though.'

'What is?'

'I was looking for his war record and it's not available. I'd need a higher clearance to see it. What does that tell you, besides the fact that I need a promotion?'

'Enough.' It meant Carter's work had been top secret and even nine years after the war it was still kept hush-hush.

'He knew people,' Jones said. 'At that level he must have done. I did manage to find out that he was in Berlin a couple of days after it fell. That means he was one of the first spies in there. He was one of the big boys. I'm reading between the lines here, Danny. I had to put all this together from bits and pieces. That's why it took me a while. His is one of those files that doesn't say too much, so you know there's plenty hidden.'

'I appreciate it, Ged.'

'It's fun,' Jones laughed. 'For once I'm actually making use of all that bloody training they gave me. Anyway, Carter stayed in Berlin until the airlift was over. So he must have gone up against the Russians, but you remember what that was like. Everyone thought it was going to be war against the Reds.'

He remembered it all too well. Tension every single day. They had to pore over every communication, to keep a close check on so many people who might have been Communist agents.

'Funny thing, though,' Jones continued. 'Less than a week after it was over he was back in London and out of the service in a rush. Make of that what you will.'

'What do you think?'

Ged was slow to reply.

'Reading between the lines again, which is fancy talk for guessing, something happened in Berlin. More than a few people died under mysterious circumstances there.'

'What are you saying? He killed someone? A Russian high up?'

'Let's put it this way: from what I've read about Carter, it wouldn't have been the first time.'

'I see.'

'He's a nasty piece of work, boy. I daresay he had a racket or two on the side. Everyone did, a chance to make a bob or two. The best thing you can do is steer clear of him.'

'It's a bit late for that.'

'Then you'd better keep your wits about you.'

'I've learnt that,' he said ruefully and looked at his bandaged fingers again. 'What about his background? Do you know anything about that? And any connections to Leeds?'

'Not unless he has a maiden aunt there.' Markham heard the sharp sound of a match and Jones exhaling. 'Grew up in Sussex. Minor public school, read Arabic at Cambridge in the Thirties. You know they sent me there on one of those Russian courses? My mam was so proud, her little boy going to a place like that.'

'Hard to imagine you in a cap and gown.'

'Oh Christ, boy, there was none of that. I was just glad to be out of uniform.'

'Thank you. You've been a bloody marvel.'

'I've just been providing value to a taxpayer,' he said with a laugh. 'And don't you worry, no one will know I was ever looking. I just wish I had more to tell you.'

'You've given me a start. That's something.'

'Then you can buy me a pint the next time you're down here.'

'At least.'

Jones' voice turned serious.

'I meant what I said, boy. Watch your back around Carter. He's a ruthless bastard. And it's a long time since you had your training.'

'I know.' Just as he also knew exactly what Carter could do. 'I wonder if the people in Whitehall know what he's up to here?'

'More to the point, would they really care?' Ged asked.

'What do you mean?'

'Down here we look outwards, mostly at a certain country that should remain nameless but is coloured bright red. We've been very attentive since the man with the bushy moustache died. No one cares what's going on in England, as long as we're not giving away all the secrets. If Carter still has the ears of the high and mighty, he could be getting away with murder.'

'He is,' Markham said.

'Then watch yourself.'

'So I'm on my own?'

'Unless you can convince the flatfoots.'

'They don't care for my profession.'

'Then I don't know what to tell you, Danny. I wish I did.'

'Thanks, anyway, Ged. I appreciate it.'

'Don't you worry, boy. Anything else I can do, just give me a ring. It's good to keep the old skills sharp.'

So he was up against a man who was experienced, professional and deadly. At least he knew now.

He doodled on the notepad for a few minutes, trying to marshal his thoughts. After the beating Harper had received, no one in Leeds would help him. Markham rested his elbows on the desk and stared at the wall. The best defence is a good offence. He had to take the fight to Carter.

★★★

Carla was standing outside the office when he returned from the market carrying a string bag with its brown paper parcels. Her mouth curved into a smile.

'You'll make someone a lovely wife one day, Dan.'

'The perils of bachelor life.'

She arched her brows. 'If that's a hint I'm going to pretend you never said it.'

He shook his head and she laughed.

'Where do you want to go to eat?' Markham asked. 'Delmor?'

'Not in this weather.' She pouted. 'I want Italy to be all sunshine in my mind, not this bloody awful Leeds rain. Jacomelli's?'

'We could.'

'Someone told me about a Chinese place on Bishopgate. Do you fancy it?'

'Chinese?' He'd never tasted it before, never even thought about what they'd eat. 'Why not? I'd better warn you, I don't have much cash. The bank's been buggering with my account.'

'I'm flush,' she told him. 'Don't worry about it.'

'Let me put these in the car and we can find it.'

★★★

The restaurant was a hundred yards from the railway station, with red paper lanterns over the tables and heavy, embossed Oriental wallpaper. Rain ran down the windows. They were the only customers in the place and the waiter hovered around them as they sat. Markham studied the menu.

'What should we order?' he asked. 'I haven't a clue.'

'I'm going for the fried rice. Anne said the sweet and sour pork was good.'

'When's the film?'

'Not until half seven. Don't worry, we have plenty of time.'

The food was better than he expected. Strange, but not so alien after all. Quite tasty once he grew used to it.

'What do you think?' Carla asked.

'Not bad,' he answered after a few mouthfuls. 'How's yours?'

'Rather good. Different.'

They settled into eating and talking. She told him more about Italy, all the dilapidated beauty of Rome and the waterways and churches in Venice. He was happy to listen, simply to hear her again, so vibrant and alive. They strolled arm-in-arm along Boar Lane, past all the business closed for the night, like any young couple out for the evening. The rain had turned to drizzle, puddles all over the pavement. The air smelt fresh and clean.

With its plush seats, the Ritz always seemed like luxury to him. He folded his raincoat and lit a cigarette. The cinema was packed, barely room for another couple anywhere. People were rapt, caught in the action and tension. And it was good, he had to admit. He didn't often bother with the pictures, but this was worthwhile. Brando seemed to seethe and burn in his role. He really could be a contender.

'Would you really mind if I went off and worked?' Carla asked as they stood outside, the rest of the audience flowing around them.

'Now?' he asked in surprise. 'At this time of night?'

She nodded. 'I just feel inspired. That last scene, where Brando walked into the docks. It ...' Her eyes were shining. 'I'm sorry. Would you mind terribly?'

'It's OK,' he answered. He'd hoped for another night with her, but by now he knew Carla. When she wanted to do something, she needed to do it *now*. And being away in Italy she'd had no chance to paint. They'd have other nights together. Plenty of them, he hoped. 'I'll walk you up there.'

'I'll be fine.' She smiled at him and squeezed his arm gently. 'But thank you, Sir Galahad. At least the men here don't pinch your bum as they pass you.'

They kissed, and he watched her walk away through the Grand Arcade. Hands in pockets, he ambled back to his car, senses alert for anyone behind him, but no one was there.

The Tuesday night streets were empty. Only the pubs had life about them, and when he glanced through the windows they looked quiet. He considered turning back and going to Studio 20, but for once the idea of music didn't appeal.

No car tailed the Anglia along North Street and out of the city centre. But why would Carter need to? Where else would he be headed at this time of night but home?

Ten o'clock. Still too early for bed. Markham looked through his records. Ella Fitzgerald, he decided. He'd let the warmth of her voice wrap around him and carry him off into the night.

It had been a long day. The bank was bad enough, but that would be corrected in a day or two. The real worry came with everything Ged had told him.

★★★

Tuesday's rain became Wednesday's sun. A clear day, according to the forecast on the Home Service, with temperatures into the sixties. He put on a plain, pale grey suit that a tailor had made up for him in Germany. He'd found the shop in a side street, one of three buildings still standing, the old man waiting in the doorway with a tape measure around his neck and an army of pins in his lapels, patient and hopeful of any custom.

People were smiling as they walked through the city centre. The telephone was ringing as he unlocked the door.

'It's Joanna Hart.' She spoke her name quickly. 'I've been trying to reach you for the last ten minutes.'

'What can I do for you, Mrs Hart?' He glanced at his wristwatch. It was still only twenty to nine.

'He rang again last night.'

'Carter? What did he want?'

'The same thing.' She sighed. 'He told me he could make a slightly better offer, but I have to make a decision quickly. He understood my situation, but he wants to act and he has the money.'

'I see. What did you tell him?'

'That I wasn't going to make any decisions before my husband was buried. The police haven't even released his body yet.'

'You did well.'

'He said he was happy to make provisional arrangements for the sale. His solicitor could draw up the papers and we could sign them after the funeral. He'd put down a deposit right away. Cash.'

'That sounds unusual.' Carter must be desperate for the business, he thought. Why?

'He was polite enough, quite charming, I suppose. But he was pressing me all the time. Every time I said no to something he had another suggestion.'

'I told you he would,' Markham said.

'He wants to meet me again. Without you there.'

'I'm sure he does.'

'I told him I'd make up my mind today. He's going to ring back later.'

'Don't do it. Keep him waiting.'

'I need the money. I told you that.'

Would Carter know? Probably. The man was thorough and he had a long reach.

'I've given you my advice, Mrs Hart.'

'Yes,' she agreed. 'I just wanted you to know.'

***

Markham stood on Wellington Street, close enough to the station to be able to smell and hear the trains. He was surrounded by Victorian grandeur, tall and solid, all of it ruined by generations of the soot of factory chimneys.

He was watching a building that was faced with terracotta tiles. Half a century before it would have been the height of fashion. Now, like an aged aunt, it seemed to have faded into the background. A gaudy sign, colourful against the grubby old street, was attached to railings in front of a basement. The Kit Kat Club, it read, with an arrow pointing down a set of steps.

He glanced at his watch. Half past two. Someone would be there to take care of deliveries and the things that could only be managed during normal working hours. Finally he crossed the road and hammered on the door.

The man who pulled back the locks stood in his shirtsleeves. He'd been working, his face flushed, but he still looked smooth and sleek. A trace of annoyance flickered in his eyes for a moment.

'Can I help you?' It was the voice of a man who already had too many things to do.

'I'm looking for the manager.'

The man sized him up carefully.

'I'm Mr Dawson. But if you're a musician or a singer, we go through an agency.'

'My name's Dan Markham.'

'Ah, I see.' He hesitated for a moment, then said, 'Come in.'

He was an inch or two shorter than Markham and probably close to thirty-five. His body was still trim, but the face was just beginning to turn pasty and stale. He led the way through the club, tables waiting to be set for the evening, the bandstand empty, and through a door to a corridor of old brick and linoleum. The office stood at the end. Dawson sat behind a desk stacked with papers and invoices and gestured to an armchair on the other side of the small room.

'You're the one Jo hired,' Dawson said. 'It's terrible what happened to Freddie. He was a good chap. Have the police found his killer yet?'

'I don't know. They don't confide in me,' he answered.

'Oh. I just thought ...' Dawson said.

'We're not close friends.' He paused for a heartbeat. 'Do you know Mrs Hart well?'

'Not that well. But she's been pals with my wife forever.'

'You recommended me to her.'

'She was looking for an enquiry agent. I asked around and someone mentioned you. I passed on the name.' He shrugged. 'That's all.'

'Do you remember who told you about me?'

Dawson shook his head.

'I don't. It was just one of those things that came up in conversation, you know?' He'd only been seated for a minute. Now he stood again. 'I'm sorry, but I'm rather busy. I'm expecting a delivery and the bloody help hasn't shown up for work.'

'Of course.' Markham rose.

'Stop in at the club one evening. Good dancing, a very lively crowd.'

'Who knows,' Markham answered, 'maybe I will.'

Outside, the sky was a clear, brilliant blue. Maybe they'd have an Indian summer after all. People sweated as they walked, raincoats folded over their arms. In the Kardomah the windows were open wide. He stirred his coffee and lit a cigarette.

He knew full well who'd given Dawson his name. But why him? He was just a man scraping a living. His work was perfectly legal. He'd never put the strong arm on anyone, he wouldn't even know how. And now Carter had tried to frame him for murder, tried to bankrupt him by clearing out his bank account and broken two of his fingers. He held up his left hand to look at the mangled digits.

Why?

★★★

Detective Sergeant Baker was waiting out on the street, leaning his bulk against a lamppost and smoking his pipe.

'Waiting for me?'

'I knew you'd be out sooner or later. And the chat I want is better in private.'

'Oh?' Markham raised an eyebrow.

'Let's take a little stroll down to Millgarth. I know you're not daft enough to run so I'll spare you the cuffs.'

'I thought we'd settled everything.'

'Nothing's settled until there's a conviction. Everything legal and the judge putting on the black cap.'

CHAPTER TEN

They headed down George Street towards the police station, side by side, for all the world like two colleagues out for a walk.

The building had stood in the same spot for the best part of a century, bits and pieces tacked on over the years, but still looking more like an old school than a nick. Inside, the desk sergeant stood behind the counter, watching him as he passed. Baker took hold of Markham's elbow and led him through a door then up an old set of steps.

'In there,' he said.

The interview room was small. The barred window looked down on the area behind the station and over to the outdoor market, no more than thirty yards and a lifetime away.

'Sit down,' Baker ordered.

Markham sat on the plain wooden chair and lit a cigarette. The room smelt of hopelessness and fear, as if they'd seeped into the plaster.

The detective lowered himself onto the other seat and placed his elbows on the table.

'Freddie Hart,' he began.

Markham sighed. 'We've been over this. I told you where I was.'

'This time it's official.' He gestured around the walls. 'I told you before that I had someone who saw you at Hart's after the place closed.'

'I wasn't there.'

Baker gave a slow smile.

'You said you'd gone into a shop in Meanwood. But the lass there couldn't definitely identify you.'

'She knew someone had been there buying Craven As.'

'Yes.'

'And the bus conductor might remember me. Coming back into town it was running late.' His head came up quickly as he recalled something.

Baker continued to smile.

'We've got a gun. It's being tested.'

Markham kept his face impassive.

'Any prints?'

'A few,' Baker allowed. 'Happen yours are among them.'

'No,' he replied with certainly. His gun was safe at the bottom of the river. 'Whoever told you I was at Hart's that day was lying.'

'We'll see. I want to fingerprint you to check.'

Markham held out his good right hand.

'Whenever you like.'

'You're a clever little bastard.' All the warmth had gone from Baker's voice. 'Let's see how smart you are when you feel the noose around your neck for murder.'

'If that happens it'll be because you've rigged the evidence. You and I both know that.' Baker started to rise as Markham stubbed his cigarette out in the ashtray. 'And you're not that kind of copper. Bring in the ink and the paper. Then you can see I've been telling the truth.'

By the time the constable had been and gone, another hour had passed. Markham tried to clean off the ink but the dark stains remained. Baker had vanished but a bobby stood silently inside the room.

Finally the detective returned with a face like fury.

'You can go,' he said quietly.

'Is it the murder weapon?'

'No,' Baker answered dully.

'And no prints of mine on there.'

'No.' The man said again as he sat down heavily. 'What do you know about Billy Harper?'

'He's a burglar.'

'He probably won't be again. He took a very bad thumping the other night.'

'I'm sorry to hear that,' Markham said. 'Or are you trying to pin that on me, too?'

'Just wondering if you knew him. Maybe he'd worked for you.'

'Can't he say who did it?'

'His jaw's wired shut and his fingers were broken so badly he probably won't be able to use them properly ever again.' Baker glanced at Markham's hand. 'What did you say happened to yours?'

'An accident.'

'Not someone breaking your fingers? Very painful, I hear.'

'An accident,' he repeated.

'Have it your own way,' Baker sighed. 'But if I find you taking the law into your own hands, I'll be on you like a ton of bricks. You're right, Markham, I don't like you. If it was up to me I wouldn't let you operate in Leeds.'

'What I do is legal.'

'Doesn't make it any better. But you know more about this Hart murder than you're saying. I know it in my water. I want whoever pulled that trigger. You hold back on me and I'll see your life here's not worth living. I saw that body. It was done in cold blood. I'm after a killer. I'm not playing fucking games, lad.'

'There's a fellow called David Carter. He wanted to buy Hart Ford.'

Baker gave him a withering look.

'Do you think I'm daft or something? Clean as a whistle. I've looked into him. A solid alibi with two councillors.' Of course. Who'd doubt a councillor? 'And before you say a bloody word, I looked at Hart's wife, too. If you know something, better tell me, son.'

'I've told you what I know.' He glanced at the sergeant. 'Tell me, Mr. Baker, why do you hate me so much?'

'You?' Baker looked at him with contempt. 'It's your profession. I've told you that. Taking advantage of people's misery.' He shook his head. 'It's not honest.'

'I do my best for every client,' Markham told him. 'It's not my fault I wasn't old enough for the war, you know.'

'Go on, get out of here,' the sergeant said wearily. 'But if you hear anything, come and tell me.'

★★★

Outside, the air was warm and heavy against his skin. But after Millgarth it felt fresh and clean. He breathed deeply as he walked back to the office, thoughts jangling like electricity in his head. He stopped on Albion Place, turned and went to his car. It was time to ask a favour from someone who wielded power.

In the Anglia he joined the procession of traffic leaving the city. Out along the Otley Road and finally into the country, beyond the Chevin and to the quiet gentility of Ilkley. He parked on a side street of tall Edwardian terraces, walked through a tidy garden, heavy with roses, and let the knocker fall on a glossy black door.

The man who answered peered at him, cloudy blue eyes behind gold-rimmed spectacles. What hair remained was white and thin, carefully combed down across his scalp. A few grey bristles showed on his chin where he'd missed them with the razor. He wore a threadbare cardigan over a checked shirt and tie. Slippers peeked out from under a pair of baggy corduroy trousers.

'Daniel Markham?' he asked in a hoarse voice.

'Hello, Mr Smith,' he answered with a smile.

It was still the easiest case he'd ever had. The man had shuffled into his office one Friday afternoon, heavily wrapped up in an overcoat, scarf and flat cap. He'd introduced himself as Mr Smith; he believed his wife was having an affair. There was nothing unusual about that, except he had to be close to seventy and she was half his age.

It only took Markham four days to gather the evidence. Mrs Smith came into Leeds every day to spend time with a butcher in Bramley. Straight from the bus stop to the shop. It wasn't glamorous deception; it wasn't anything much at all. He took the pictures and presented them quietly to his client.

Mr Smith really was Smith. Ted Smith. He had a small fortune; he'd designed and patented something for aeroplanes then built it in his small factory. The RAF had bought the device during the war, then the commercial airlines had been clamouring once the fighting was over. When he told his wife he wanted a divorce she'd threatened to take him for everything he was worth. Then he produced the photographs. She went off to Bramley without a penny.

'I'm grateful, lad,' he said as he wrote out a cheque with a very generous fifty pound bonus. 'If there's ever owt you need, you come and see me. I appreciate someone who does a good, fast job.'

Now was the time to see if he'd meant it.

'Come in,' Smith said. 'I'll put the kettle on.'

They settled at the kitchen table. Smith moved aside a pile of papers covered with sketches for some component and put down a plate of biscuits. He might have looked frail but Ted Smith was a powerful man. His name opened every door in the Civic Hall; he knew everyone important in Leeds and plenty down in London. He poured the tea, nibbled on a digestive and said, 'It must be summat important.' He nodded at Markham's left hand. 'Anything to do with those?'

'Yes.'

'What do you need?'

Markham didn't hesitate.

'Access to people on the council.'

Smith looked thoughtful. He pulled a pipe from the pocket of his cardigan and lit it, puffing until he was satisfied that it was drawing properly.

'Councillors or them as really run things?'

'Is there a difference?'

'A big one, lad.' He smiled. 'Councillors come and go. But they're not the ones who get things done. It's mostly the folk as run different departments as have the power. Tell me something.'

'What?'

'Do you know who your councillor is?'

'No,' Markham admitted.

Smith pointed with the pipe stem.

'See, that's what I mean. Most people couldn't even tell you who was Lord Mayor.'

'I can't.'

'Need to keep your finger on the pulse. What happens here is as important as what those buggers in Whitehall are doing. So who do you need to talk to?'

'Someone in licensing and someone in planning,' Markham said. 'People with influence.'

Smith nodded.

'I know just who you need.' He puffed on the pipe for a few more seconds. 'How powerful is the person you're up against?'

Markham laughed. Ted Smith had always been a perceptive man.

'Very. He killed someone but I can't prove it.'

'That murder in the newspapers?'

'Yes.'

'Talked to the police?'

'They say he's clean.'

'Aye, well, most coppers share a single brain cell. Let me ring a few people. You'll hear in the morning. That do you?'

'Thank you.'

Smith waved away the gratitude.

'It's nowt. From the look of you, you're still going to need plenty of luck.'

'Very likely.'

'If there's anything else I can do to help, make sure you let me know.'

'I will.'

'I mean it, Daniel. You saved me a lot of money and grief. I've not forgotten that.' He stood. 'Wait here a minute.'

He disappeared and Markham looked around the room while he was alone. A small refrigerator stood in the corner, next to the larder, and there was a new gas cooker. All mod cons, but Ted Smith was a man who welcomed progress: it had been his business, and from the drawings on the table he hadn't retired yet.

Smith returned with a sealed envelope.

'Take that. You might find it useful.'

Markham looked at him quizzically but slipped it into his inside pocket.

'Thank you, Mr Smith. I mean it.'

'Just do me one favour, lad. When it's over, come out and tell me about it. I don't get to live much these days.'

'I promise.'

★★★

The telephone bell shrilled at exactly five minutes past nine.

'Mr Markham?'

'Yes,' he answered.

'I'm John Hay. I'm the clerk to the licensing committee. Mr Smith asked me to give you a ring.'

Markham smiled. Ted Smith's name conjured up people eager to help.

'There's something I'd like to talk to you about. It's delicate.'

'We'd better meet, then,' Hay said cautiously. 'About noon at Whitelocks? It's far enough from the Civic Hall for us not to be disturbed.'

Or seen together, Markham thought. 'That would be fine. How will I know you?'

'My teeth,' the man replied with a small, self-conscious laugh. 'Honestly, you'll know.'

'Then I'll see you there.'

★★★

Ten minutes later the phone rang again.

'I'm looking for Daniel Markham.' It was a woman's voice, calm and assured.

'That's me.'

'Oh good. I've been talking to Ted Smith. He asked me to ring you. I'm Carol Kingston.'

'With the planning committee?'

'I'm a secretary there.' She paused for a moment. 'I'm the one who handles all the applications and complaints.'

Smith had promised him the ones who really ran things.

'There are a few things I'd like to talk to you about.'

'I imagined that from what Ted said,' she said with amusement. 'Look, why don't we meet later? How about one o'clock outside the entrance to Marshall and Snelgrove?'

That would give him plenty of time to talk to Hay.

'Perfect,' he agreed.

He took out the envelope Smith had given him. He'd slit it open the night before, astonished to see ten twenty-pound notes inside. Nothing had been said, but he knew what it was – money to grease palms, to make the system work. Money talked; this amount of money only needed to whisper. And right now, with no cash in the bank, it was a godsend.

★★★

104

As soon as he walked into Whitelock's he understood what Hay meant about the teeth. They protruded enough to make him look like a horse. He was standing by himself at the end of the polished bar, a half pint of beer in front of him. The pub was busy, high murmurs of conversation and laughter filling the air. A few men in suits stood around, but most of the customers wore donkey jackets and caps.

'Mr Hay,' he said. 'I'm Dan Markham.'

The man smiled briefly and nodded as a table was vacated.

'Let's sit there.'

Once they were settled, Hay was all business. His gaze moved around nervously for a moment, then he said, 'What can I do for you?'

'I'd like some questions asked about a couple of licences.'

'I see.' He turned the glass and took a swift drink. 'Which ones?'

'The Kit Kat Club on Wellington Street. And the Bass Note up on Merrion Street.' The two clubs that Carter owned.

'What do you want?'

'Ideally? Their licences revoked for a few days.'

'It's possible.' Hay nodded, and the action made him look even more equine. He gazed at nothing, thinking. 'Suspending the licences would be difficult. A couple of raids and regular checks would be easier.'

Markham took two of the twenty-pound notes from his pocket, folded them and slid them across the table.

'Would that help?'

'It would make a difference,' he agreed. 'Might I ask why?'

'I think it's best for both of us if I don't say anything.'

Hay nodded again.

'Tell me, do you think it's possible that the club is serving under-age customers?' the man asked slowly and deliberately, giving a wink.

'I think it's very likely,' Markham answered, understanding.

'We're duty bound to act whenever there are reports of violations like that. You can leave this with me.' The notes vanished into a trouser pocket and Hay stood. 'I think you'll find there'll be action very soon.'

Then he was gone, head down as he moved quickly through the crowd and out into Turk's Head Court. Markham looked at his watch. It had been quick; he had three quarters of an hour to kill before meeting Mrs Kingston.

He arrived right on time. She was already there, standing and swinging her handbag in front of her, a bemused face like a young Ann Sheridan, with carefully shaped eyebrows and a red bow mouth. She was dressed in a stylish skirt and short jacket, her dark hair carefully set.

'You must be Carol Kingston.'

'I am,' she said. 'I'm glad you're punctual.' She began to move away to the department store, the doorman quickly opening the door for her. Inside, she walked around confidently, as if she was a regular customer. 'Now, Ted said I should help you.'

'Do you know him well?'

'Oh, we go back years. He's a poppet. He said you're an enquiry agent. Is that exciting?' She nodded at his bandaged fingers. 'It sounds rather dangerous.'

'It has its moments.'

She stopped to glance through a rack of blouses, pulling one or two out to study them.

'So what can I do for you, Mr Markham?'

'How closely can the committee look at planning applications that were granted a while ago?'

She pursed her lips.

'It's certainly not usual. But the committee looks at what I give them. And they usually do what I recommend.' She stood in front of a mirror and held up one of the blouses in front of herself before giving an approving nod. 'What do you have in mind?'

'I have a list of properties. Most of them are businesses.'

'Let me see.'

He passed it over, along with two more of the twenty-pound notes. She glanced at the names and addresses before putting the paper in her handbag.

'I'm sure we can send out a letter and an inspector. There might be all manner of violations there that need to be investigated. The businesses might need to be closed whilst they come up to scratch.' She arched a brow. 'Would that suit?'

'Perfectly.'

'Good.' She smiled. 'Now if you'll excuse me, Mr Markham, I'm going to try this on.'

CHAPTER ELEVEN

He parked on Chapeltown Road and darted across to Cantor's for fish and chips. The smell filled the Anglia as he drove home.

He saw her legs first, a pair of cigarette ends by her feet, then the calves that disappeared into a dress of brilliant reds and yellows.

'I was beginning to think I'd have to go to the pub to wait for you,' Carla said. Her eyes narrowed. 'You've got fish and chips, haven't you? There'd better be enough for two.'

At the table he divided up the food and set out the salt and a bottle of vinegar.

'How are the new students?' he asked.

'As green as you'd imagine. One or two look like they might have some talent. Most of them just seem to be passing the time.' She shrugged. 'Anyway, how's your quest?'

Quest? He hadn't thought of it that way, but maybe it was a good word. And quests sometimes did succeed.

'It's starting to move,' he said cautiously. 'I think it is, anyway.'

'You'd better look after yourself.' She put a hand over his. 'I don't want anything else happening to you.'

'I will.' But once Carter realised what was happening, that it was concerted and organised, he'd know who was behind it. What Markham needed was to find a way to increase the pressure, to keep Carter too busy for revenge.

'You're miles away, Dan.'

'Sorry.'

'Do you have a plan?'

'Mostly I'm making it up as I go along.'

'That's the best way,' Carla told him firmly. 'Be spontaneous.'

'I think I'll need to be.'

'Good. Now, I don't suppose you have anything like a drink around, do you? I'm parched.'

★★★

A bored doorman stood outside the Kit Kat Club. He was a big and brawny, wearing a tailcoat with epaulettes and a top hat. But the man's scowl and pug face made a mockery of any welcome. Reluctantly, he held the door open, no greeting, and let the handle go as soon as Markham was through.

He'd dropped Carla off in Headingley and decided to see what the club looked like when it was alive. For a Thursday night, business was slow. Couples were dotted around the room, fewer than half the tables filled. The dance band plodded rather than swung, playing the charts with a lack of enthusiasm. The singer hit the right notes, but that was the best anyone could say.

It was depressing, he thought. He sat at a table and lit a cigarette, ordering an orange squash when the waitress appeared.

He'd been there fifteen minutes when Dawson bustled through the front entrance, tightening his tie and adjusting his jacket. He stopped, glancing around, his gaze lingering here and there. After a few seconds he made his way over to Markham, a smile on his face.

'I'm glad you decided to visit,' he said as he sat. The waitress appeared with a glass of Scotch. 'Something for you?'

Markham held up the orange squash.

'I'm fine.'

'It'll pick up later. It's still early.'

'I'm sure.'

'And it's packed on the weekends,' Dawson insisted. 'Everyone wants to have fun and we provide it.'

'Good little earner, is it?'

'It does well enough.'

'You're not the owner, are you?'

Dawson lifted his chin.

'I never said I was. I'm the manager.'

'And Mr Carter owns the club?'

'That's right.'

'You know he's a dangerous man to work for?'

'Is he?' The man took a drink. 'I've found him very fair.'

Markham held up his hand to show the broken fingers.

'There's the proof.'

Dawson glanced at the hand then turned away sharply.

'I find that hard to believe.'

'You shouldn't. He did it himself. With a hammer. And he enjoyed it.'

'Mr Carter is a businessman.'

'You know what they say: business can be cutthroat.'

'I'm sorry, I don't buy that.'

'I'm not selling it, Mr Dawson.' He shrugged. 'It's a fact.'

'If you don't like the owner, what brought you back here?'

'I'm curious. And you invited me, remember? How's your girlfriend?'

'What?' The question took him by surprise.

'That's who you slipped out to see, isn't it?' Dawson didn't respond. 'You'd better clean the lipstick off your cheek before you go home.'

The man pawed at his face.

'What do you want?'

'How much do you know about David Carter?'

'All I know is that he hired me to manage this place.'

'How did that happen?' The band started a half-hearted version of 'String Of Pearls', taking all the glide out of the melody.

A few couples moved to the dance floor, shuffling around to wartime memories.

'I was knocking about, looking for something. I'd done a few things for my father and some of his friends, but nothing really struck my fancy.'

'That must have been difficult. You're a married man. Do you have a family?'

Dawson shrugged. 'Celia's parents give her an allowance. It let us get by.'

'Who introduced you to Carter?'

'An old school chum. He knew I lived up here. He gave me a ring after David bought the club and everything fell into place.'

'Do you know what other business Carter owns?'

'He told me there's another club, the Bass Note, a shop or two and a garage. I've never paid that much attention.'

'How often do you see him?'

'He stops in once or twice a week,' Dawson replied. 'And every Tuesday afternoon I meet him to go over the figures. So far he's been pleased enough.'

Markham took a sip of the orange squash. It had been diluted too much.

'Who does he entertain here?'

'Businessmen. He's brought in a councillor or two sometimes.'

'Has he asked you to supply girls?'

'You mean tarts?'

'That's exactly what I mean,' Markham said.

'He sort of hinted at it once. I told him I didn't know any and he didn't mention it again.' He finished the Scotch and looked around for the waitress.

'I'm going to give you some advice, Mr Dawson.'

'Advice?' The man stared. 'What do you mean?'

'Start looking and find yourself another job. There must be plenty around, the government's always telling us we have full employment.'

'Why should I?' Even in the dim light he could see the flush rising on the man's cheeks.

'Because Carter won't be around too much longer. His little empire is going to fall apart. If I were you I'd want to avoid being a casualty.'

Dawson gave a small laugh.

'Who's going to tear it down? You?'

'Yes, Mr Dawson, me,' Markham answered seriously.

'You know what David will say when I tell him, don't you?'

'He can say whatever he likes.' He stood. 'I'll wish you good-night and good luck.'

***

The wind rattled against the flat and the weather forecast on the radio spoke of a gale. So much for any hope of that Indian summer, Markham thought. The tree branches were flailing, people on the pavement wrapped in their overcoats as umbrellas turned inside out. A bus passed, the windows of the upper deck opaque with condensation, as he waited to pull out into traffic in the Anglia.

By noon it had passed, only a few heavy gusts left as a reminder. Litter had been blown into awkward piles against walls. A few slates had come off the roofs and shattered on the pavement. The cafeteria at Marks and Spencer was crowded with workers and housewives, each with their tales of the morning. He sat with his sandwich and listened, drinking tea and smoking a cigarette before returning to the office.

She came about three, still dressed in black, a pencil skirt and angora twinset under a thick coat and a small hat with a veil. A widow, but she wore her weeds with style.

'Sit down, Mrs Hart,' he said as he showed her in. He'd expected another telephone call, not a visit.

'I had to come into town and take care of some things,' she explained as she lit a cigarette.

'Did Carter ring again?'

She nodded. 'This morning.'

'What did you tell him?'

'The same as before, that he'll have to wait. That the police haven't even released Freddie's body yet.'

Her grief sounded convincing. He wondered how real it could be when they'd both spent their time in bed with other people.

'How did he react?'

'He's very smooth,' she said, and there was a hint of admiration in her voice. 'He builds up the pressure so one hardly notices. He's not someone who likes to wait, is he?'

'No,' Markham agreed. 'He isn't.' He decided to change the subject a little. 'Have the police told you when you can have your husband's body?'

'Monday. The undertaker is collecting it.' She paused for a moment of reflection. 'The funeral's on Wednesday in Richmond. That's where he grew up.'

'And what then?'

'If Carter offers a fair price, I'll sell to him.' She stubbed out the cigarette. 'After all, I need to live.'

'He won't. He likes to deal on his own terms.'

'Then he won't get his hands on Hart Ford, Mr Markham. It's a simple as that.' She smirked. 'I have another offer, anyway.'

'What? You didn't mention that.'

'It's not really an offer,' she corrected herself. 'Just someone who might be interested.'

'Who?'

'Will Dawson.'

He breathed evenly.

'Do you know who he works for?'

'Himself. He owns the club.'

'No, Mrs Hart. He's the manager of the Kit Kat. Carter owns it.

'What?' She was full of outrage and disappointment. 'He never told me that.'

'It's true.'

'Damn him.' Joanna Hart set her mouth firmly then loyalty won out over anger. 'But Will's family has money. So does Celia's. He could afford it.'

'Maybe he can. But Carter will be behind any offer he makes. I'd bet on that.'

'I know Will,' she protested. 'He's an honourable man.'

Markham sighed. He wasn't sure that honour had any place in the world these days.

'I'm sure he is.' He'd allow her that. 'I don't understand you. I've just told you that Dawson's working for the man who wants your business and you shrug it off. I don't know what you want from me.'

'Support, advice. And to stand up to Carter.' She eyed him. 'You seem to be doing a good job of that.' She opened her black handbag, took out a purse and produced a ten-pound note. 'Will that keep your services for a little while?'

'Yes,' he told her. He had hardly any money in the world but didn't reach for the note.

'Daddy lent me a little.'

'I see.'

'You're a strange man yourself.'

'Am I? I feel like a confused one right now.'

'Aren't we all?' She stood by the door.

'Perhaps we are.' He paused. 'Next Thursday.'

'Thursday?' She turned her head.

'You said the funeral's on Wednesday. Carter will ring you on Thursday.' He nodded at the money on the table. 'You can guarantee it.'

***

He knew exactly where he'd find Carla – in her studio at the Art College. It was where she spent every spare minute. He strode through the corridors, feeling so old next to the earnest students. The room was on the top floor, nothing inspiring about it, just another room behind a door, but inside it was her kingdom. She was standing back, absorbed in studying the painting on the easel, and didn't even hear him enter.

The figure was a woman. He felt certain of that, although he couldn't say why. The long hair, probably, and the slim fingers of the praying hands. But everything else had been stripped away. The flesh of the face was almost down to the bone, the eyes sightless, the clothes just rags covered in mud.

'God, that's good,' he said.

She turned with a smile.

'Thank Donatello, then,' she told him.

'Who?'

'Italian sculptor. Renaissance. This is inspired by a statue of Mary Magdalen that he did.'

'It's …' he began.

'For God's sake don't say beautiful, Dan.' She delved under her smock for cigarettes and matches. 'Please. I don't want any beauty in there. I want pain, suffering, redemption.'

'You've got that.' He was impressed. It was completely different to anything else she'd done. In spite of what she said, there was beauty in the honesty of anguish.

She kept her eyes on the painting.

'Not yet. Who knows, maybe I'll manage it.' She shrugged off the mood. 'What do you want to do this evening?'

'I don't know. A meal? The pictures?'

She pouted.

'There's nothing on I want to see. Some friends of mine are having a party later. We could always go there.'

'We could.' He'd met some of her friends. They had little in common.

'Or we could go out to eat then back to your flat and shag our brains out.'

'That sounds a much better idea,' he replied with a grin.

'Give me ten minutes to change and do my face.'

★★★

They went to Donmar. He had enough left to afford it. She'd brightened at the suggestion, but once the meal arrived her enthusiasm dimmed.

'What's wrong? I thought you liked it here.'

'I do.' She pushed the pasta around with a fork. 'It's just after Italy, the real thing, it's just not the same.'

'It's still good. You always enjoyed it before.'

'I know,' she apologised. 'It … it just doesn't taste Italian to me now.'

'We can leave if you want.'

'No. You eat. I'll just have the wine and a coffee.'

'Are you sure?'

She nodded but he knew all the magic of the evening had already evaporated. Nothing would seem right, the mood had shattered. They could go through the motions but neither of them would be happy.

He ate in silence until his plate was clean while she sipped her wine and smoked. The waiter brought their small cups of dark, hot coffee.

'Would you rather just go home?' he asked.

'Would you think I was really terrible if I said yes?' she asked glumly. 'I'm sorry, Dan. I hadn't thought this would make me feel like this.' She shook her head and gave a weak laugh. 'It's all rather silly, isn't it?'

'It's fine,' he told her.

'I can just take the bus …'

He shook his head.

'I'll take you home.' He lifted a hand for the waiter. 'Can I get the bill, please?'

★★★

He drove. During the few minutes to Headingley they barely exchanged a word. Carla fretted with her handbag and stared out of the window. When he parked she turned to him.

'I'm sorry,' she repeated. 'I really am. It's such a stupid little thing. I know that.'

'It doesn't matter.'

She gave him a peck on the cheek.

'I didn't mean to ruin everything.'

Studio 20 was almost empty, the musicians still setting up, piano, drums, bass, trumpet and saxophone. A few people sat around, everyone in his own little world. Did he want to wait and hear jamming that would probably be uninspired? No, he decided, and turned on his heel.

'Dan.' Bob Barclay's voice called him back.

'What is it?'

'Do you remember that young tenor player from last weekend?' Of course he did. The boy felt the music in his fingers and his soul. A rarity for British jazz. Rare enough even in America. 'He sent me a letter. He got the job with Dankworth.'

'I'm glad.'

'There's talk of Big Bill Broonzy touring over here again. Sonny Terry and Brownie McGhee, too.'

He'd heard them on record. Blues on acoustic guitars and harmonica. Good stuff but it didn't touch his heart like jazz.

'Let me know if they're coming to Leeds.'

'Not staying?'

'Not tonight.'

★★★

At home he looked through his records. Not so many of them, really. Finally he selected some Coleman Hawkins, ballads that moved languorously, suiting his mood. By the time the needle clicked in the final groove he'd smoked his way through three cigarettes, not thinking of anything in particular, just letting the sense of regret and loss weigh down on his mind.

★★★

The grey morning suited him. It was Saturday. He didn't need to go to the office. Instead he took the list of properties that Carter owned and spent the day driving from one to another, walking each neighbourhood. They had nothing in common, other than the fact they'd becomes his for next to nothing. But it wasn't wasted time; now he could place them all if he needed.

★★★

Markham put a shilling in the gas meter and heated up a tin of tomato soup. A concert played quietly on the Home Service, Rachmaninov's 'First Piano Concerto'. A book, an evening of the radio and an early night. But he hadn't even finished ten pages before there was a timid knock on the door. He opened it, wondering who'd want to visit, and saw Carla standing there, biting her lip and looking bashful.

'I'm sorry about last night,' she said. 'I must have seemed like a shit.'

'I didn't know what to think.' He'd wondered if her final words the night before had meant it was all over.

'Can I come in?' she asked and held up a bottle of the Chianti she'd brought back from Italy. 'Peace offering.'

'What would you have done if I'd been out?' he asked later. They were sitting on the floor, only the light through the window illuminating the room.

'Camped out on your doorstep until you came home,' she answered. He couldn't make out her eyes. 'I mean it, I would. And if you'd brought some floozy with you I'd have told her to get lost.' She sighed. 'I don't know. I was fine until we went into the restaurant. I know they want to make it seem like Italy, but as soon as I walked in it just seemed so, I don't know, false. It made me wish I was back there and I started feeling sad. I took it out on you, I'm afraid.'

'But you're here now.'

'I had a little cry last night.' She gave a wan little smile. 'Well, a lot of a cry, actually. And this morning I told myself not to be so stupid. I like it here, really. If I moved to Italy I'd have to learn the lingo. It's cheap there but it's not as if I have pots of money to support myself.'

'And you have me,' he ventured.

'If you still want a silly cow.'

'I do.'

Carla put down her glass.

'So yesterday we were talking about shagging. Do you still fancy it?'

★★★

He woke feeling chilly and realised she'd pulled the sheet and blankets around herself, cocooned and blissful as she slept on. Typical, Markham thought. He washed and dressed, watching her face, then slipped out to buy the Sunday papers.

They were sitting by the window, drinking tea and reading the weekly scandal and titillation when Carla stretched and said, 'I should go. I want to do more on that painting.'

'You don't have to.'

She leant across and kissed him.

'I do,' she insisted. 'I don't suppose you'd like to give me a lift to the college?'

★★★

He left her on Woodhouse Lane, striding away purposefully. So close to the city centre that he might as well go to the office and see if there'd been any interesting post the day before. The streets were empty, the shops were shut; even the pubs in the middle of town didn't open on the Sabbath.

Bills – rent, rates, another form from the Inland Revenue – nothing he wanted to think about today. He tossed them on the desk and left, feeling happy. They'd had a good night, a very good night that made him smile.

He turned the corner on to Briggate and paused for a moment. He knew the man leaning against his car, drawing on a cigarette and then studying the glowing tip. Detective Sergeant Ronnie Graham. Someone had pointed him out once. A hard man with hungry pockets and fists that saw more use than his brain.

Graham was in his early thirties, as bulky and muscled as a boxer, hair so short it seemed to barely colour his scalp. But the dark mackintosh and big, booted feet gave him away as a copper.

'Can I help you, Sergeant?'

The policeman stared at him as if he wanted to memorise every feature of Markham's face, the look slowly turning to contempt.

'I think it's you who needs help, lad, not me.'

'Why's that?'

'A little bird told me what happened to those fingers of yours.'

'You must know some very talkative birds,' Markham said.

'It also told me what you were supposed to do. Seems like you haven't been doing it.'

'So it sent down a crooked copper?'

Graham made one hand into a meaty fist.

'You'd better be careful.'

Markham had been enjoying Sunday. He felt at peace with the world after time with Carla. He didn't want this. And he didn't have to prolong it. He unlocked the car door.

'Was there anything else?'

'I don't waste the time of day on people like you for no reason. Two things. A reminder to do what you're told.'

'Anything else?'

'What do you know about a raid on the Kit Kat Club last night? Seems it was ordered by the licensing committee.'

'Maybe someone tipped them off.' He started the engine. 'Good day, Sergeant.'

'We'll be meeting again.'

He glanced in the mirror as he drove away. Graham was standing, hands on hips, looking at the vehicle.

Carter was bound to have a copper or two on his payroll. It was inevitable that he and Graham should find each other. The policeman lived with his hand out. He beat confessions from people. He planted items on searches.

Still, he'd learned something. The licensing committee had already taken action. Twenty quid of Ted Smith's money well spent. And over the next week it would become more interesting when the inspectors from the planning department visited Carter's other businesses and found faults.

CHAPTER TWELVE

'I hear you saw Sergeant Graham yesterday.'

Baker stood by the table in the Kardomah, his face flushed after hauling his bulk up the stairs.

'For a minute or two.' Markham waved at a seat. The letter from the bank had arrived that morning. No apologies, just excuses. A mix-up in accounting. But he had money again. He was flush.

'Don't mind if I do.' The man put his hat on the crisp white cloth and mopped his face with a handkerchief. Joyce the waitress appeared, her steps silent on the thick carpet.

'Cup of tea, luv,' Baker said, 'and a slice of cake.'

'We've a nice sponge today,' she told him.

'Aye, that'll be grand. Just put it all on this young man's bill.'

'It'll be a pleasure,' Markham said wryly.

'What did you do to annoy Graham? He's not often about on a Sunday.'

'He seemed to think I'd done something that I hadn't.'

Baker eyed him sharply.

'There seems to be a lot of that about lately. I think you might have shot someone but you haven't. Now Graham thinks you've done summat else and you've not. You're innocent as a newborn bloody lamb, aren't you?'

'Not my fault people make mistakes.' He finished the last of his soup and roll.

'Maybe not. But there's something going on. Why don't you tell me what and get it off your chest. You'll feel better. If Graham's involved it must have a stink to it.'

'No love lost between you two?'

'He's a disgrace to the bloody force.' Baker's voice was serious and flinty. 'And if you ever claim I said that, I'll deny it and break two more of your fingers. Got that?'

'Perfectly.'

'Good lad.' He stopped talking as Joyce returned, then gave his attention to the food.

Markham stirred his coffee and lit a cigarette, letting the smoke drift up towards the ceiling.

'Why are you so interested in Graham?' he asked.

'I told you why,' Baker answered finally as he slurped the tea. 'A little fix here and there when you know in your bones that someone's guilty but you can't prove it. That's fair enough, that's justice is all. But what he does is wrong and it makes us all look bad. If you have something going with him, I'll see you go down, too.'

'Yesterday was the first time I'd met him.'

Baker gave a small nod.

'Then make sure it's the last. If he wants something from you, walk away. Consider that a warning.'

'I don't want anything to do with him.'

'Then he wants something from you.' The policeman sat back and lit his pipe. 'What is it?'

For a moment Markham considered telling him about David Carter. But he didn't know how far the man's influence reached. Not to Baker, that was certain. But those higher up, where everything could become lost? He was safer keeping it all to himself.

'I didn't give him the chance to tell me.'

'I don't believe you,' Baker said flatly. 'I don't like you, but you're not a bloody fool. Don't get mixed up with him.'

'I'm not going to.'

'And when you're ready, come and tell me what's going on.' He paused for the length of a heartbeat. 'If you don't, I'm going to take you in again and question you properly. You know things you're not telling me.'

'I promise.'

Baker nodded again and rose, gathering his mac around his body and placing the hat on his head before lumbering away.

'Is that everything?' Joyce's voice took him away from his thoughts.

'Yes, thank you.'

'I don't know who that man is but he's a messy eater.' She looked down at the crumbs on the tablecloth.

'He tries,' Markham told her. 'How much do I owe you?'

★★★

The fingers. He'd barely thought about them for a couple of days until Baker mentioned them. The pain had turned to a faint ache at the back of his mind, always there but easy to ignore. He gazed down at his hand and saw how dirty the dressing had become. It needed changing and he knew the damage should be inspected to see how it was healing. First, though, he'd finish his tax return.

He could pay an accountant. But in his first year he'd made so little that it had been impossible. Now he'd acquired the habit of doing it himself. He could be creative and he hadn't been caught. So far.

He was adding a column of figures to claim as expenses when there was a knock on the door and he saw a shadow through the glass.

'Come in.'

The man was probably forty, but he could have passed for fifty, face weighed down by the heavy bags under his eyes. A fifty-shilling suit, shiny at the elbows, the tie knotted at his throat, a moustache bristling above his upper lip.

'Are you Mr Markham?' he asked.

'I am. Have a seat.'

The man looked around the room as if he wasn't sure what to expect.

'You're an enquiry agent?'

Markham smiled.

'That's right.' He kept a small advert in the *Yorkshire Evening Post* classifieds. It didn't cost much and it brought in trade. The man had it in his hand. 'How can I help you, Mr …?'

'Jenkins. Roger Jenkins.'

'Mr Jenkins. What can I do for you?'

It was divorce, he was sure of it. The man had that diffident manner, putting off the words as long as possible, eyes darting everywhere.

'It's my wife,' Jenkins answered finally. 'I think she's seeing someone.'

'What makes you think that?' he asked, pen poised over a notepad.

'She's … I don't know.' Jenkins pursed his lips. 'She's just different. Colder at home.'

'What's your wife's name?'

'Laura.'

'Do you have any children?'

'No. I'm afraid we were never blessed that way.'

It took another quarter of an hour to draw it all out. Laura Jenkins rarely went out in the evening, but the man suspected she might be seeing someone during the day. He had no idea who it might be. He seemed baffled by it all. Their friends were all good, upright, hard-working people. He wanted Markham to keep an eye on her, to see if she was having an affair.

'And if she is?' It was the question he always asked. Divorce was a messy business, one that ruined lives. Co-respondents would be cited, it would be dirty and ugly and it would all be out in public in the courtroom.

'I'll make my decision then,' Jenkins said calmly. 'We've been married fourteen years. Right before I went off to fight. You don't throw that away like tea leaves.'

'No,' Markham agreed.

He had the address, in the Carr Manors. Comfortable semi-detached houses from the 'thirties. Jenkins might not look much but he had some money. Or far too many bills.

'How much do you charge?'

'A five-pound retainer. The fee's dependent on what I need to do. And expenses, of course.'

The man pulled the wallet from his suit jacket and took out a note, rubbing it carefully to be sure there was only one. Markham began to write out a receipt but Jenkins refused.

'What if Laura found it?' he asked with a horrified look. 'How would I explain that?'

'What's your line of work?' Markham asked.

'I'm a manufacturer's agent.' Jenkins reached back into the wallet for a business card. 'Knitwear,' he explained. 'I sell it to wholesalers around here and up in the Northeast. I'm gone one week in four – Newcastle, Sunderland, around there.'

'And you think Laura's unfaithful when you're away?'

'Yes.' There was quiet defeat in the word.

'And you've no idea at all who she might be seeing?'

'None,' Jenkins answered after a small hesitation.

'Are you sure?'

'I …' He shook his head. 'No, not really.'

'Does she have a job?'

'Of course not. She's a housewife.' He said it with a kind of pride, that he earned enough to support his family.

'Do you have a photograph of her?'

'No.' He seemed surprised by the idea. 'Why?'

'So I can recognise her.' He said it with a gentle smile.

'She's the only woman who lives there. You'll be able to follow her. That's what you do, isn't it?'

'Yes. Does she drive?'

'No. I can take her wherever she needs and she walks to the shops. When can you start?'

'Tomorrow?'

The man nodded.

'That would be good. The sooner, the better.'

'Leave it with me, Mr Jenkins. How do you want me to contact you with my reports?'

'I'll be in touch with you.'

'Of course.' It was often the way. They didn't want someone ringing at work or to receive anything at home. 'Give me a few days and I'll see what I can find.'

★★★

He drove by the Jenkins' house, a semi with a bay window and a small front lawn tucked behind a privet hedge. There was a place towards the end of the road where he could park and watch. Tomorrow.

On the way home he stopped by the doctor's surgery, spending half an hour in the waiting room before the physician could see him.

'You look like you've been in the wars,' he said as he snipped off the bandages and put on fresh ones.

'A little.'

'Yes.' The man pronounced the word slowly. 'It's nasty but it's healing, Mr Markham, but you need to be patient.' He pushed his lips together. 'I'll be honest with you, though. I'm not sure how well those fingers will work after this.'

'I understand.' Another reason to make Carter pay.

★★★

The next morning he was parked on Carr Manor Parade, slumped down in the seat of the Anglia, eyes on the Jenkins' house. He'd made a sandwich, wrapped in greaseproof paper on the passenger seat, and a thermos flask of tea.

The man had left promptly at half past eight, driving off in a Ford Popular. Laura Jenkins emerged a little after nine. There was nothing glamorous about her. Flat-heeled shoes on thin legs, a dark woollen coat, scarf over her hair and a shopping bag in her hand. As ordinary as she could be.

He could have walked down to the parade behind her. But at this time of day a man on his own would have stood out. Mornings were when the women went out to the grocer, the greengrocer, the baker, while the men were at their work. A chance to gossip and see someone else, to decide what to make for tea.

This was the stuff of his life, tracking all this, making quick notes on a pad. All too often suspicions turned out to be nothing more than groundless fears. Inside, he felt sure that Laura Jenkins was a faithful wife. Ground down and unhappy with the routine perhaps, but not about to do anything about it. He parked by the parade and saw her arrive, moving quickly from shop to shop before starting the short trek home.

He was there, down the street again, to see her arrive and unlock the door. By afternoon nothing more had happened. She hadn't gone out again. The coal man delivered his load along the road, hoisting the hundredweight sacks easily on his shoulder. Later it was the soft drink man with his bottles of lemonade. Neither of them stopped at the Jenkins' house.

At four he turned the key in the ignition and drove away. Nothing. He'd return tomorrow and do it all again. But he doubted that he'd discover anything.

★★★

As soon as he walked into the office he knew something was wrong. The chair was pulled away from the desk; he always pushed it in before he left. The blotter sat left of centre; he kept it squarely in the middle. Someone had been here. He breathed slowly and looked around, taking in everything.

He'd decided to come back and finish his damned tax return. It wouldn't take more than an hour at most, then the evening was his own. But now his heart was beating faster and his mouth felt dry. Carter. He searched quickly through the desk drawers and the filing cabinet. Nothing was missing. What did the man want? The papers that had been stolen with the gun? No. If they'd been so important he'd have had someone in the office before. And they weren't even here.

If nothing had been taken, then something must have been left.

A chill prickle of sweat rolled down his back as he hunted. At first he was methodical, exactly the way they'd taught him in military intelligence, under and behind desk drawers, checking the lino for a loose corner where something could be hidden. Not a thing. All the files in the cabinet were exactly as they should have been. No papers or packets added.

As the minutes passed he became more frantic, looking anywhere and everywhere. Think, he told himself. Bloody think. Finally he dragged out the filing cabinet, grunting with effort. There was only wall behind it. On his knees he reached under the bottom drawer. Then he felt it. Slowly, cautiously, he tried to grip with his fingertips, pulling it out into the open.

A bulky brown envelope he knew he'd never seen before. Carefully, he broke the seal with his thumbnail as he shouldered the cabinet back into place.

Money.

He counted quickly, then again, scarcely able to believe his eyes. Five hundred pounds in white five-pound notes. A fortune. Almost two years' salary. He flicked through the notes once more.

He smoked a cigarette, the money spread out across the desk. It was here for a reason and it wasn't generosity. Markham licked the glue and sealed the envelope again, then hurried down the stairs to the floor below. Miss Jacobs' secretarial agency did work for many small businesses; he used her whenever he needed a letter typing. He was barely in time; she was just locking up, the girls who worked for her leaving in a rapid shower of heels on the steps.

'Mr Markham,' she said. 'If you need a letter it'll have to wait until tomorrow.' She was always immaculately turned out, grey hair set in neat waves around a bony, disapproving face. She wore an engagement ring, the memento of a fiancé who never returned from Ypres all those years before. A photograph of him in uniform, trapped in time, sat on her desk.

'It's nothing like that,' he told her, trying to put some charm into his smile. 'I was hoping you could keep this for me until tomorrow morning.'

'I suppose I could,' she agreed with a prim sniff. After so many years she was used to strange requests from men.

'I'd be very grateful.'

She put it securely in her handbag, wished him goodnight and left. He returned to his office, lit another cigarette and ran a hand through his hair, trying to make sense of what he'd just found.

***

He heard the footsteps clambering up to the third floor and sat behind the desk, straightening his tie as he waited. The door flew open and Detective Sergeant Graham marched in, a pair of uniformed constables behind him.

'Here you go, lads,' Graham said, eyes already hungrily scanning the room. 'Meet an enquiry agent. Likes to think he's one of those private detectives from the films.' One of the coppers smirked. The other, younger, a glimmer of intelligence in his eyes, looked embarrassed. 'A little bird told me you have some dodgy money here.'

'That little bird again? He's busy, isn't he?' Markham took the wallet from his pocket and produced the money Jenkins had given him, flattening it out on the desk. 'This looks fine to me.'

'Not that,' Graham said. A flush of anger rose on his cheeks. 'Don't get clever with me, lad.'

'That's all the money I have here.'

'Aye, and I was born yesterday. Never done a thing wrong in your life, have you?'

'I suppose you want to search.'

'That's why I've come.'

'Do you have a warrant?' Markham asked.

Graham leaned forwards, palms on the desk, until his face was close enough for Markham to smell the decay on his breath.

'Do I need one?' he asked threateningly.

Markham shrugged. 'Be my guest. There's nothing here, I already told you that.'

'We'll see, lad. We'll see.' He stood and looked around, as if he was considering where to start. 'Pull out that filing cabinet,' he told the officers.

Markham kept his face impassive, watching them work, then Graham kneeling, reaching and searching for the envelope.

'Found anything, Sergeant?'

Graham rose slowly. He didn't even try to hide the hatred in his eyes.

'Search everywhere,' he shouted. 'Take the place apart.'

They were thorough, pulling open every file, removing every drawer. Ten minutes later they stood by the door, empty-handed.

'It looks like that little bird of yours isn't too reliable, Sergeant.'

'You'd better watch your mouth,' Graham warned and stormed off, the uniforms trooping behind him.

He waited until the footsteps had receded and let out a long, slow breath. Dodgy money. Counterfeit. That explained a lot. It would have been a few years in jail if they'd found it.

He'd been lucky. He was surviving by the skin of his teeth. But survival wasn't going to be enough.

★★★

When he turned the corner he saw Graham leaning against the car and sighed. He should have guessed. He'd made the man look like a fool; now there'd be a price to pay.

'I thought our business was done, Sergeant.' He had the key tight in his hand.

'You think, lad?' He pushed himself upright, making his large hands into fists. 'I don't know what you did, but that money was there.'

'Was it? Your boys were thorough. They didn't find it.'

'Next time,' he warned. 'Meanwhile, you and me are going to have a little talk.' He nodded at a ginnel that led to the back of a building. 'Down there. Five minutes. That's all I need and you'll be crying for your mummy and telling me everything.'

'Leave it, Ronnie.' Baker's voice was low and even as he emerged from the shadows, hands pushed deep in the pockets of his raincoat. 'You had your chance.'

Graham kept his gaze firmly on Markham.

'This one thinks he's a bright boy. We can't let him get away with that.'

'He's smarter than you. The best thing you can do is let it go.'

Graham was still for a few moments then spat and walked away.

'Good job I was passing by,' Baker said quietly.

'Were you?' Markham asked and saw the man shrug.

'Maybe. I told you, I don't like bent coppers.' He snorted and gave a grim smile. 'I like them even less than enquiry agents. Be grateful for that.'

Markham nodded. 'Thank you.'

'I don't know what's going on but watch yourself. Graham doesn't like to lose. Do you want to talk about it?'

'There's nothing to tell.'

'Have it your own way. Having him after you makes me think you might just have something about you, after all. Just don't be a bloody fool. I don't want to be the person who has to sweep up the pieces. And believe me, Danny boy, you don't want me angry at you.'

Markham unlocked the car door and Baker began to stroll away.

'Remember, though, if you leave the straight and narrow it won't just be Sergeant Graham you need to worry about.'

CHAPTER THIRTEEN

By ten on Thursday morning no one had come out of the Jenkins' house. He poured more tea from the flask and waited.

A pair of women strolled along, pausing for a moment outside the place. One shook her head before they moved on. Odd, he thought.

Markham waited a few more minutes then opened the latch on the gate and walked down the gravel drive to knock on the front door. Nothing. He tried again. No answer.

The grass of the square front garden was neatly trimmed, the rose beds dug and weeded. He peered through the front windows. The curtains were open. Not a stick of furniture inside, just bare floorboards. He darted round to the back of the house. Exactly the same in the living room. Empty.

'They flitted last night.'

The woman leaned against the fence between the drives, puffing on a cigarette and watching him with amusement. She had a pleasant, plump face with smile lines around her mouth and eyes, an apron tied around her waist.

'A flit?' he asked in surprise.

'After dark. It's not quite what one expects around here,' she said with a brief grin. 'A van came and they put in what they had. Not that they had much,' she added with pleasure. 'They'd only been here three days, too.'

'They were here yesterday,' he said. It was a pointless remark, more to himself than to her.

'How do you know?' She jumped on the remark. 'Were you watching the house? What's going on? Are they criminals? I thought he looked a bit shifty. Are you a policeman?'

'No. Mr Jenkins wanted me to keep an eye on things.'

'Who's Mr Jenkins?' she asked. 'The landlord?'

'He's the husband,' Markham said.

She shook her head.

'No. I had her round for a cup of tea. She said they were called Thompson.'

'I see.'

He saw all too well. He'd been conned. A job to keep him out of the office whilst they hid the counterfeit money. And once they were done they'd pulled down the tent and vanished.

'Why were you watching her?' the woman asked. She ground out the cigarette and picked up the butt. 'Did he think she had a fancy man?'

'Something like that.'

'Well,' she said slowly and glanced over her shoulder. 'Would you like to come in and have a cup of tea? I'd love to hear about it.'

★★★

In the office he tried the telephone number on the card. A dead line, of course.

It had taken time and effort to set everything up, to find the couple and make the arrangements. If he dug a little he'd probably discover that Carter owned the house.

If Carter's plan had worked, Markham would be in Armley jail now, on remand and waiting to be tried. *Prima facie* evidence; a five-year sentence. No question about it.

Carter was worried. Now Markham needed to make things bite.

He smoked his way through two cigarettes without finding an answer. It was almost noon. By now Freddie Hart would be in the ground, friends and family getting drunk in his memory.

On the way to the post with his tax return he stopped at the secretarial agency. As he opened the door the staccato clack of typewriter keys hit him like a loud wave. Miss Jacobs sat at her own desk, facing the others like a teacher in front of the class, busy with her own work. He smiled sheepishly as she silently handed over the envelope she'd kept for him. It was still sealed. He thrust it into the pocket of his mac, thanked her and left.

It went through the slot in the post box, two envelopes, one to the Inland Revenue, the other with no name or address. It would sit in the unclaimed room for years before being destroyed. A British bureaucracy was the best place to make anything vanish. He'd learnt that after he was conscripted.

★★★

At five, just as he was taking the raincoat from its hook, the phone rang.

'The bloody bastard came to the funeral!' she shouted down the line.

'Mrs Hart …' he began.

'He was there at the back of the church and in the cemetery.' She sounded drunk, her words slurred and bitter.

'Carter?' he asked. The question was pointless; it couldn't be anyone else.

'Bastard,' she repeated as the fire seemed to drain from her voice.

'Did he say anything?'

'Just his commis–,' her tongue stumbled over the word. 'Commiserations. He said he'd be in touch tomorrow.'

'Then don't worry about it until tomorrow. Where are you now?'

'Mummy and Daddy's.'

'You stay there and sleep it off,' he advised.

'Can't. People still here. Got to go and grieve for them.'

'When will you be back in Leeds?'

'In the morning. I need to start sorting out the house. Bloody thing's mortgaged to the hilt.'

'I'll come by in the afternoon. We can talk more then.'

'What if he rings before that?' A note of panic rose in her voice.

'Then put him off.'

★★★

With her husband in the ground she'd abandoned her widow's black clothes. Joanna Hart answered the door wearing a bright floral dress, catching the last gasp of summer. Her hair was up in a chignon, face heavily made up to hide the lines, all the weariness and the puffiness of her hangover. Another five years and she'd look old.

The dining table was piled high with papers, roughly sorted into piles. She flopped into a chair and reached over to a small table for a glass filled with a clear liquid.

'Did he call?' Markham asked.

'A little after luncheon.' She shook her head. 'Bloody man.' She nodded at the shamble of documents. 'There's no choice. I'm going to have to sell the business very soon. Freddie left me with nothing. This house has to go, too.'

'I'm sorry,' he told her.

'Oh, don't.' She waved his words away. 'I'll get by, I suppose.' She lit a cigarette and blew out a thick trail of smoke.

'Did Carter make you another offer?'

'For what it was worth.' She grimaced. 'I told him I expected better.'

'What about your friend?'

'Will? I asked him after the funeral. I told him what I needed.' Joanna Hart shook her head. 'He said it was a bit rich for his blood.'

'So Carter has the only bid.'

'I need more, though.' She tapped ash off the cigarette. 'Freddie hadn't paid his bloody taxes and they want their pound of flesh. You know what they're like; they're not going to wait. If I don't pay them soon they'll close the business. Then I won't have a damned thing to sell.'

'And you've had no other offers at all?' It seemed strange. This was the age of the motor car, pronounced by the newspapers. They seemed to bring new models out every month. People had money to spend.

'None,' she said. 'Help me. Make him offer more.'

'I can't force him to do anything,' he told her.

'He wants to meet me tomorrow.'

'Where?'

'In town. Jacomelli's at half past twelve. He's booked a private room. I told him you'd be with me.' She looked at him, her eyes pleading. 'You will, won't you?'

'Yes.' He wouldn't miss the chance to see David Carter again.

★★★

Long before that, though, he had a date. Bob Barclay from Studio 20 had rung him during the afternoon, full of enthusiasm.

'You have to come down tonight, Dan. I've got someone special.'

'Who?' he asked.

'A lad called Tubby Hayes. I know, it's a daft name. But he's already been with Kenny Baker and Jack Parnell's bands and he's not even twenty yet. One of the best tenor players you'll ever hear, honest to God. I'm trying to drum up a good crowd.'

'What time will he be on?'

'Midnight or so.'

'I'll be there,' Markham promised.

He'd rung Carla at college, persuading her to come along with him. He'd conceded a meal out. She was the one to suggest going to Donmar again.

'Are you sure you want to?'

'I'll be fine. Guides' honour. No scenes. We'll have a long, lazy supper then listen to this chap you say is so wonderful.'

She'd been as good as her word, enjoying the meal and the wine, a Chianti that tasted like a weak imitation of the one she'd brought back from Italy. They finished the coffee by eleven, a glass of grappa to wash it all down, the last customers in the restaurant.

'There's still time before the music starts,' he said. 'Do you fancy a game of snooker?'

'I suppose we can,' she said guardedly. She'd told him once that she often played with her students in the Union. 'Why?'

'You'll see.'

He led her down the Headrow and into the dark gap between buildings called Bramley's Yard. Next door, the Vine was already closed, the drinkers turfed out into the night. He climbed a set of rusted iron steps bolted to a building at the back of the court. A small bulb illuminated a sign over the door – 'W. Smith and G. Nelson Billiard Hall'. Everyone called it Nelly's. He entered a room where men crouched and concentrated over four billiard tables, lights shining down on the bright green baize. Balls clacked and sped around.

'Good God, I never even knew this place existed,' Carla whispered in wonder. She was the only woman in the place but no one even gave her a glance. Nelly's was where the serious players came. Money changed hands quietly in private games, often large amounts. A small crowd had gathered to watch two men in shirtsleeves and braces playing. Brylcreemed hair shone. A fug of smoke hung in the air. The tension was palpable, the atmosphere was as reverent as a church, no more than small mutters of pleasure and praise as one of the players made a difficult shot to pot one of the balls.

The game ended, the two men shaking hands, and the tension broke.

'This is fantastic.' Carla spoke softly in his ear. 'Are you sure we can play here?'

'If we can get a table.'

In the end midnight had come and gone when they walked into Studio 20. Carla had beaten him in two straight games. Her arm was curled around his. But as he settled and lost himself in the music he forgot about her. Hayes was everything Barclay had promised, exploring his way through a tune and taking off on flights of fancy that spiralled up and up before gliding back to earth. He was still young, full of fire, and played more than an hour before taking the reed from the instrument and acknowledging the applause.

In the orange glow of a streetlight Markham looked at her with a question.

'Can you drop me off at college in the morning?' she asked and he nodded. 'Right,' Carla said, 'let's go home.'

★★★

He'd eaten at Jacomelli's often enough but Markham had no idea it boasted a private room. The waiter escorted him up the stairs and along a thickly carpeted corridor, holding open a polished wooden door of etched and bevelled glass. No one could see in. Private, indeed.

The table was set for three, the window looking down on Boar Lane. Joanna Hart gazed out as she smoked a cigarette, turning as he entered.

'Thank you for coming,' she said with real gratitude. 'I didn't know if you would.'

Yesterday's floral dress had been replaced by a sober grey suit, seamed stockings and a white blouse. Prim and business like, with the hair gathered back off her face. A waiter appeared silently, bringing her a gin and tonic. Markham ordered a lemonade and she chuckled.

'Still teetotal?'

'I've told you. Alcohol and business don't mix.'

'If you say so. I find they go together very well.'

Carter was five minutes late, bustling into the room without an apology.

'Mrs Hart,' he said, shaking her hand quickly before sitting down and nodding at Markham. 'I hope you don't mind, I ordered for us. So much quicker.'

Carter was watching her, appraising each movement, looking like an animal waiting for the moment to pounce. They'd hardly settled before the soup arrived, a spicy Brown Windsor.

'We'll eat first and discuss things later.' Carter gave a quick, tight smile. 'Better that way.'

He was as good as his word, offering nothing more than idle chat about the weather during the sole and the pudding. Finally he poured cream into his coffee and lit a cigar.

'Right,' he said. 'Mrs Hart, you have my bid on the business. I understand everything needs to go through probate yet, but you'll find I'm offering a fair price.'

She sipped at the gin before answering.

'It's anything but fair,' she replied. Markham could hear the faintest tremor in her voice.

'Do you have other bids?'

'That would be telling.'

'It doesn't matter.' The smile showed Carter's teeth, white and even. 'I know you haven't.'

She gave a short nod.

'If you know so much, you'll know what Hart Ford is worth.'

'Oh, I do. To the very last penny. And I know how much you owe the Revenue.' He paused to let his words sink in. 'I think you'll find that an item is only worth what a person is willing to pay for it. I'm sure you'll agree, Mr Markham. After all, you're a man of the world.'

'What if Mrs Hart doesn't want to sell at your price?' Markham asked.

'She does. Even if she doesn't realise it yet. She can't afford not to.'

'You seem to know an awful lot about me,' Joanna Hart said.

'It's business.' There was a brusque edge to his words. 'Knowledge is power, that's what they say. I like to have an advantage.'

'And use it in any way?' Markham asked.

Carter acknowledged it with a nod of his head.

'It's like war or love. Everything's fair.' He smiled. 'I'm sure you understand what I mean.'

'It doesn't mean I agree,' Markham told him.

'You're very presumptuous,' Joanna Hart said. 'You assume I'm going to sell to you.'

Carter shrugged. 'You're desperate for money. Mine's the only offer on the table. You're going to sell to me. If it helps I'll go three hundred higher.'

She pushed the chair back and stood.

'No, Mr Carter, it doesn't help. Thank you for luncheon but it's been wasted. I need the money. That much is true. But I refuse to deal with a bully.'

'It's quite simple, Mrs Hart. You can deal with me now or later.' He kept his voice low and even. 'I'll give you until Monday to decide.'

She stormed out, slamming the door behind her. Silence filled the room in her wake.

'Tell me something,' Carter said eventually. 'Have you always had a charmed life?'

Markham held up the bandaged fingers.

'I'd hardly call these charmed.'

'They'll heal.' He dismissed the injury, then added, 'Of course, if they were broken again you'd probably lose all the use of them.'

'Is that a threat?'

'Mr Markham,' he said with disappointment. 'Why would I need threats when actions can scream so much louder? Don't you remember? I told you I wanted you to persuade Mrs Hart to sell. That's the job I gave you.'

'I don't work for you.'

Carter shook his head.

'You still seem to believe that. You've been harassing the manager of one of my clubs. They've had a raid looking for underage drinkers. And I've had inspectors at my other businesses.'

'That's unfortunate.'

'It's more than that. It's costly.'

'And so you planted counterfeit currency in my office?'

'Did I? Are you accusing me?' Carter asked with interest. 'You might do well to beware of slander.'

Markham took his time gazing around the room.

'As far as I can see, we're the only ones here.'

Carter stared at him for a long time. 'I wonder about you,' he said. 'You don't want to do what you're told and Mrs Hart seems to like you as support. You're an annoyance, like one of those flies that buzzes around the food in the summer. If I removed you from the equation altogether she might be more amenable to selling her husband's business. And my life might be a little simpler.'

It was delivered in a matter-of-fact tone, a passing thought.

'Is that another threat?'

Carter grinned. 'Why would I threaten when I can promise, Mr Markham. After all, who'd miss you? There's no family, only that girlfriend of yours.'

'I could go to the police. They'd look for you if anything happened.' Even as he said it he knew he was wasting his breath. Carter would keep himself well covered.

'Be my guest. But if I were you I'd keep looking over my shoulder from now on.' At the door he turned. 'I believe whatever business you and I ever had is done. Goodbye, Mr Markham.'

★★★

For a while he simply sat and smoked. Murder. Nothing more or less. And casual, as if it was nothing at all.

He felt dazed, as if someone had knocked him out and he was just coming to, trying to find his bearings. He bobbed between the crowds on Briggate like flotsam, pushed this way and that.

Carter was no stranger to murder. It had been part of his job. He'd been forced out of the secret service for it. He'd arranged the death of Freddie Hart. Another body wouldn't mean too much to him. The end would justify the means.

By the time he reached the office he felt bruised and battered, his thoughts still muddled. He sat for a long time, letting the afternoon pass. The sounds of traffic and pedestrians came through the window. Finally he locked up and drove the two short miles to Headingley.

He knew where to find Baker. The man loved his routines and rituals. He always finished his week with a drink in the Skyrack before heading home to his house in Burley.

He was there, leaning against the bar, still wearing his raincoat and hat, talking intently with an older man who had the bearing of an ex-copper. Markham ordered his orange squash and waited for Baker to spot him.

Five minutes later the detective ambled over, a pipe balanced in his mouth, a glass of bitter in his thick hand. There was no friendliness in his eyes.

'If you've come to confess to something I'll be at the station on Monday morning.' He drained the glass. 'Since you're taking up my time you can put another in there.' Baker signalled to the barman and a pint appeared.

'What do you know about David Carter?'

The man took a slow drink and wiped his moustache.

'The one who wants to buy Hart Ford.'

'Yes.'

'Not that much. Why?'

Markham took a deep breath. 'He's said he's going to kill me.'

He didn't want to confide in Baker but he knew he had no choice. The sergeant was the only one who could help him, the only one he could trust. Broken fingers, someone going after his bank account, the possibility of jail: he could deal with those alone. But a death threat … he needed help.

'Can't say as I blame him. I've felt like doing that often enough myself. What did you do, bugger up his marriage?'

'I know he's behind Freddie Hart's murder.'

Suddenly Baker was all attention.

'Go on, lad. You've got something to tell me. But I already looked at him and he's clean.'

He explained some of it, careful to omit his Webley from the tale.

'That's all you've got? Where's your proof?' Baker demanded when he was done.

'He wants Hart Ford. Ask Joanna Hart. He's been pressing her to sell. And his offer is very low.'

'So why's he going to kill you?'

'He wants me to persuade Mrs Hart to sell. I told him I won't.'

'Did he do that?' Baker gazed at the fingers and Markham nodded. 'What does he have on you?'

'Nothing.' It was true, more or less.

The detective stayed silent for a long time, puffing on his pipe and thinking.

'You're not telling me everything, lad. What I want to know is why you're coming to me now. You were eager enough to handle it all yourself before.'

'He hadn't threatened to kill me then. If it happens then you'll know where to look.'

'I don't want any more murders on my patch.'

'Don't you believe me?' Markham asked in exasperation.

'I'm sure it's right enough,' Baker said. 'But I've still not heard any proof. There's nothing he said or did to you when anyone else was around, is there?'

'Not anyone who'll talk. Rob Anderson was there when he broke my fingers.'

'The bruiser,' Baker said with a nod. 'Who's in his pocket besides Ronnie Graham?'

'I don't know. He has connections in London. He was with MI5.'

Baker's eyebrows rose.

'One of those clever buggers, eh?'

'They kicked him out after the Berlin airlift. He went further than he should have.'

Baker gave a faint smile.

'Tell you that himself, did he?'

'I have friends in London, too.'

The policeman was silent for a moment.

'So why did he come up here?'

'I don't know,' Markham answered. 'I haven't managed to find that out. But he's here now and he's dangerous.'

'Maybe I'll take a look at him next week, then.' He finished the beer and placed the glass on the bar. 'And what are you going to do?'

'Bring him down if I can.'

'Very noble.' Baker's mouth turned down. 'But you need to stay alive to do that.'

'That's my plan.'

'Whatever you do, keep it legal,' he advised. 'If not, I'll come down on you. But I'll be keeping an eye on your friend and doing a little digging. That it, lad?'

Markham produced a piece of paper.

'These are the businesses he's taken over.'

'Clubs, garages, shops. A bit of everything in there,' Baker said as he scanned the list. 'No rhyme or reason to it.' He put the pipe away in his pocket. 'You keep breathing 'til Monday and I'll see what I can turn up.'

CHAPTER FOURTEEN

Markham spent the weekend looking over his shoulder. Carla went to visit her parents. For once he was glad; he didn't want her caught in anything. He stuck to busy streets, out only in the daytime then locking and bolting his door at night.

For hours at a time he could forget that Carter wanted him dead, then the thought would come crashing back to leave him paralysed for a few minutes.

He read and listened to music, going through his entire LP collection, everything from Basie to Webster. By Sunday night he'd had his fill of it all. He could skulk around and try to keep himself safe. He could do nothing. He could flinch at every unusual noise and be scared every moment. That wasn't going to help.

Monday morning he drove the Anglia into town and parked outside the office on Albion Place. He took a deep breath as he unlocked the door. The room felt stuffy and airless, but there was no sign that anyone had been there. Markham hung up his overcoat and settled behind the desk, checking the desk drawers before lighting a cigarette. He'd made the decision.

A little after nine he phoned the planning committee. The voice that answered was cool and slightly amused.

'Mrs Kingston?'

'It is.'

'This is David Markham. Ted Smith's friend.'

'Of course. I remember you.' She was suddenly attentive and he wondered what kind of relationship she had with the old man. Smith had been generous with his contacts and his money; there was still plenty left and it was time to spend the rest of it.

'I believe inspectors were out at a few businesses.'

'That's correct. I'm sad to say that they found several violations of use.'

'Did any of the businesses have to close?'

'Under our procedures we issue a notice and give the firm a little time to comply.' The words flowed with professional ease.

'And have they?'

'I don't know. The inspectors haven't had time to return yet.'

'Do you think it might be time they went back?'

'It might.'

'I'd be grateful. So would Mr Smith, I'm sure.'

'I'll arrange it,' Kingston agreed brightly. 'I think we've given those businesses a good chance to do everything we require.'

'Thank you.'

He put another forty pounds of Smith's money in an envelope and addressed it to the woman at the planning committee. No note. She'd know.

One small blow. He smiled.

★★★

Baker rang during the shank of the afternoon. He heard the clunk of coins dropping in the telephone box.

'Meet me in Park Square in a quarter of an hour.' It was a demand, not a request.

'All right,' Markham answered as the policeman replaced the receiver.

He gathered up his coat and left, taking an awkward route through the streets to see if anyone was following him. If they had, he'd shaken them off by the time he reached Park Square.

The houses were old, perfectly laid out around a small, green park. These days they were home to solicitors, dentists and the private practices of doctors. The grass was carefully trimmed, the last of the flowers in the beds hanging on to their blooms. There was just enough of a chill in the air to keep people away from the benches. Only one person was there: Baker, calmly reading his newspaper and puffing on his pipe. Markham sat next to him.

'What is it?'

Baker kept the paper in his lap, eyes searching around for anyone who might be watching.

'You'd better tell me the full story on this friend of yours.'

'Carter?'

The man gave a brief nod, pipe still clenched between his teeth.

'I put in a request for information on him this morning. Came back straight away. The muckety-mucks said no. Orders of the Assistant Chief Constable himself.' Baker turned to face him, eyes blazing. 'I don't like that. We're supposed to work without fear or favour. That means no protection for anyone.'

'I told you that he has friends.'

'He's got more than that. You'd better give me the gen. Everything you know.'

He laid out all he'd learned from Ged Jones. In the end it was very little, more supposition and reading between the lines than fact. Baker listened with close attention, pursing his lips at times and staying quiet until Markham had finished.

'And how did you manage to learn all this?'

'A friend from National Service. They recruited him into the secret service.'

'And he told you just like that?' He sounded grudgingly impressed.

'We were friends. In military intelligence together,' Markham told him.

'Did they teach you all those dirty tricks too, then?'

'Some of them.'

'With that background and the people he has looking out for him, your Carter is quite a slippery customer.'

'A deadly one.'

'Maybe,' Baker agreed. 'But he hasn't killed you yet. Who did you say works for him?'

'John Dodge and Big Chalky White.'

'I know them, right enough. Didn't you have a third name?'

'Rob Anderson.' He felt his fingers throb as he spoke.

'He's the big one with the scar on his cheek, isn't he?'

'Yes.'

'Happen it's time to have a word with them all. I daresay there's something they've done wrong. And if there isn't it'll let Carter know I'm nipping at his heels a bit.'

'Be careful.'

Baker smiled.

'He wouldn't dare hurt a copper, lad. He's not that stupid. Nobody would be mad enough to protect him then.'

'I hope you're right.'

'You just watch out for yourself, lad.' He paused. 'I know there's something you're still not telling me.'

Of course there was. He daren't mention the gun to Baker. Not now. Not ever.

'That's all of it,' he lied.

The detective raised an eyebrow.

'If that's what you want. Just keep your eyes open. Did you do all that fancy spy malarkey to throw off a tail when you were coming here?'

'I did.'

'Next time we meet, don't bother,' he suggested. 'If they know you're seeing a copper it might be good protection for you. At least it could make them think twice.'

He was right; Markham knew that. 'But dangerous for you.'

'Don't you worry about me. It's like I said, Carter wouldn't be daft enough to mess with someone on the force.'

'I meant with your bosses.'

Baker shook his head.

'I'm a detective sergeant, lad. I wasn't going any higher, anyway. Another few years and I'll have my thirty in. There's nowt they can really do to me.'

'All right.'

The policeman pushed himself up off the bench, folding the newspaper and pushing it into the pocket of his mac.

'If you find anything else, let me know right away. And no taking the law into your own hands. You do that and I'll have you in a cell before you can say Jack Robinson.'

★★★

At least he had an ally now, Markham thought as he walked back through town. A van had broken down on Commercial Street, the traffic at a standstill, motorists idling in their cars, a few pushing down on their horns in a sporadic symphony of noise.

He paid little attention as he began to cross the road. He heard the motorcycle's engine growing closer as he stepped off the kerb, then suddenly it was close, a deep-throated roar. Markham turned his head. It was accelerating straight towards him, passing the line of vehicles. Two men, both in leathers, with gauntlets and visors pulled down to cover their faces.

Stupid, he thought and moved back a pace. They couldn't even wait until everything was flowing again. As they passed the passenger raised his gloved hand, formed his fingers into a pistol and aimed it at him as they roared by. It was only a moment. No one else even noticed. It could have been coincidence. But he knew it wasn't. It was Carter's little reminder. Killing him would be so easy. Anywhere, anytime.

He breathed deep, dug out a Craven A and lit it, drawing the smoke deep into his lungs. On the way back to the car he kept glancing back and checking the roads.

***

Markham drove, watching his wing mirrors for anyone behind him. He dodged through the back roads, turning a corner and parking for a minute before moving on again. Every trick from his training until he was satisfied that he was alone.

Only then did he head out to Alwoodley, parking outside Joanna Hart's house. The Humber was in the drive but he still had to knock twice before she answered the door, hair gathered back into a simple ponytail. She had a half-empty glass in her hand and looked up at him with bleary eyes.

'Oh,' was all she said, stepping back down the hall. 'I suppose you'd better come in.'

The room was exactly the way he'd seen it the other day. Papers were scattered across the table and a bottle of gin was on the small table beside the chair. She saw his glance.

'Do you want one?' she offered. 'I've had a couple already, I'm afraid.'

'Not for me. Have you heard anything more from Carter?' She shook her head. 'He'll be ringing you again,' Markham told her.

'Maybe I should sell the damned place to him. Just get the bloody business out of the way.' She flopped elegantly into the chair without spilling a drop from the glass. 'I miss Freddie. He could be fun when he wanted.'

'What about your lover?'

'I'm not seeing him any more. I didn't even have to suggest it. He did.' She snorted. 'Maybe his wife's suspicious or something. I'm glad you're here. I hate being on my own. And I hate being poor.'

Markham looked around the room again. Furniture that would fetch a good price at auction. All the trappings of money.

She crossed her legs and the sound of nylon on nylon filled the room. The skirt rode up enough to show a little thigh and he turned away. He could feel her gaze, intent and trying to be seductive, while all he wanted was to be out of the house before its walls closed in around him. He didn't want to be near her like this.

'Let me know when he does ring,' Markham said, gathering the coat around his body.

'Don't you want to stay a little longer?' There was a tiny, pleading note in her voice.

'I still have to see some people.' He gave her a smile. 'Don't bother getting up. I can see myself out.'

★★★

After the cloying atmosphere of the house the air in the garden felt fresh and sweet. For a moment he wondered what would happen to her. Back to the good time girl she'd been before? Jumping into another marriage that wouldn't make her happy? Or seeing out time in bottles of gin and loneliness? It didn't matter; her redemption wasn't his job.

If she gave in and sold to Carter, that was her decision. He'd done everything he could. If she held on, he'd help her. He needed every lever he could use to bring the man down.

His flat was empty and he relished the peace, the silence that climbed around him. With the lock and the bolt set, he felt safer.

★★★

At eleven, after the pubs had closed and the city had bedded down for the night, Markham drove down to the International Club, the shebeen down towards Sheepscar. Monday night and business was good, a press of drinkers all seeking the thrill of the illegal.

Brian Harding was there, off in a corner with his head down, so still he might have been dead. Markham bought a large whisky and pulled up a chair to sit across from him. He slid the drink across the table and Harding's head rose. His eyes were bloodshot, the tiny veins under his flesh broken and red, and he looked as if he hadn't changed clothes in two or three days.

'Hello, Brian. I thought you could use that.'

'I always can.' He raised the glass and took a sip. 'Better,' he pronounced. 'What can I do for you, Dan? Had *la belle* Hart yet?'

He was surprised that Harding could remember their last conversation; after so many years the man's brain must have been pickled. But he was one of those rare creatures who seemed to function just as well drunk as sober, thoughts and memory still sharp however much he wanted to dull them. God's little joke.

'Not my type,' he replied with a smile.

'Anyone's type if you're desperate enough.' He raised the glass in a toast. 'To poor old Freddie. A long time in the ground now.'

'And now she owns the Ford agency.'

'The first decent offer and she'll sell it. Jo always wanted to be a woman of independent means. It's the main reason she married Freddie. His family has pots of cash. She thought she'd have the high life.'

'And she didn't?' Markham asked with surprise. 'I've been to her house. It's hardly a slum.'

'Well, yes,' Harding agreed slowly. 'But it's hardly *rich* rich, is it? You know what I mean, Dan. Ancestral pile out in the country, walls all around to keep out the peasants. That's what she's been angling for all the years I've known her.'

'What would you say if I told you that she was hardly getting any offers for Hart Ford?'

'Really?' The man frowned. 'I'd say there was something a little odd. Aren't we all supposed to be driving everywhere by 1960 or something? I saw that in the papers. And have little jet cars by the end of the century? You'd have thought they'd be queuing up to take the business off her hands.'

'I was wondering about that.'

'Strange.' He finished the whisky and stared at the glass. Markham bought him another.

'You know the kind of people who'd be likely to buy the Ford place, don't you?'

'One or two, I suppose,' Harding agreed.

'Could you ask around a little and see what's putting them off?'

Harding smiled, showing brown, neglected teeth.

'I can do better than that. Wait here.'

He reappeared a few seconds later, trailing someone behind him.

'Dan, this is George Hatton. He might be able to help you. I'll leave you two to it.'

They shook hands. Hatton could have been anywhere between fifty and seventy, with a paunch that jutted like a prow, a nondescript grey suit and trousers held up by wide blue braces. His hair was grey, combed down hard across his head and thin enough to show the pink of his skull. A pair of shrewd eyes showed behind thick glasses.

'Brian said you wanted to ask about business.' His accent was broad Yorkshire.

'That's right. What do you do, Mr Hatton?'

He tugged at the knees of his trousers and sat down. 'I used to have a boot factory. Started in a back room, ended up with a hundred working for me.'

'Why did you get out?'

'Saw the end of the war coming. It was going to be a different England with peace. Sold at a good price. These days I mostly buy and sell.'

He knew the type. They were all over the West Riding.

'Do you know Hart Ford?'

'I do,' Hatton said. 'Could have been a decent little earner.'

'Could have?' His question was sharp.

'Word is that the young fellow who died owed the taxman and the bank.'

'How did you hear that?'

'Around and about,' Hatton said. Someone turned up the music and he had to raise his voice. 'Keep your ear to the ground and you hear a lot. You can save yourself a few bob, too.'

'Do you know David Carter?'

'I know who he is.' The man was guarded. 'Can't stand the bugger.'

'Why not?' Markham was interested.

'Do you know how he works?'

'Yes.'

'Then you know what I mean. I don't mind paying a fair price for a business if I think I can make money out of it. Don't get me wrong, I'll pay no more than I have to. But I don't press people.'

'Motor cars are a growing business.'

'True enough.' Hatton nodded. 'No disrespect to the dead, but I knew Freddie Hart. I wouldn't have trusted him to make tea, let alone run a business. I daresay what they're saying is true. Is it?'

'Some of it,' Markham admitted.

'There you are, then.' He smiled, his point made.

'But if it's so bad, why does Carter want to make an offer?'

'A low one?'

'Very, I'm told.'

Hatton sat back, rubbing his chin and staring at Markham.

'You seem to know a lot about it, young man,' he said. 'What's your interest in all this?'

'I want to stop Carter.'

'I'd not argue with you on that. But maybe Hart Ford isn't the right ground for your battle.'

'What if Carter is the one spreading rumours that it's in such a bad state?' Markham asked.

'I suppose that's possible,' Hatton allowed after a few seconds' thought. 'Plant the word here and there.'

'It would explain why no one else is making a bid for the place.'

'Happen it might be worth having a look at the books. See how bad it really is.'

'Perhaps it would.'

Hatton gave a brief, thoughtful nod. 'I knew there was a reason I came in here tonight. Besides not having to go home and see the missus.'

***

The phone rang a little after eleven the next morning. Markham answered, once again hearing the metal clunk of coins in the phone box.

'You're buying me my dinner, lad. Lyons at twelve.' Baker replaced the receiver without waiting for an answer.

***

He was already there, sitting at one of the tables, chair pushed back to accommodate his belly, reading the menu as if it was a good book. Markham sat across from him, dark patches on his mac from the rain that had begun as he walked down Briggate. The restaurant smelt of warm, damp wool.

'What's so important, Sergeant?'

'In a minute.' Baker finished the list and waited until the waitress had taken their order. He dragged the pipe from his pocket and lit it, taking his time. 'I pulled in those three who work for Carter,' he said with a smile. 'No shortage of prior offences on them.'

'Still in custody?'

'Had to let Dodge and White go, but Anderson's in the cells. He was carrying a knife when the bobbies searched him. He'll be going down.' He said the words with satisfaction.

The food came and they began to eat.

'It won't stop Carter,' Markham said.

'I know. But it's a start. And out of the three we took in, Anderson's the only one who can think a bit. Carter's going miss that.'

'He'll find someone else.'

'Of course he will,' Baker snapped as if it was obvious. 'But at least the bastard knows he's in my sights now. With any luck I'll be able to get something on Graham, too. Have him bounced off the force and into a cell.'

'Why? Why are you doing all this now?' Markham asked.

'It's not because I've taken a sudden liking to you. Don't worry about that, Danny boy.' He pushed the empty plate away, took a sip of the tea and relit the pipe. 'I've been on the force for a long time. You weren't even thought about when I started out on the beat. I like this city and I'm buggered if I'm going to let someone come in and tear it all down just to make a bob or two. Simple as that.'

'Carter's a dangerous man to have as an enemy.' Markham held up his bandaged fingers.

He snorted. 'You said that before. You should have tried being a bobby here in the thirties if you wanted dangerous. Back before they knocked down all them slums where Quarry Hill flats are now. They only let us go there in pairs back then. He's not going to hurt me.'

'He's killed people.'

'Plenty of us have, lad.' His voice turned harsh. 'What the hell do you think we did in the war? And there's more as never came home, too. It wasn't like your generation, playing bloody games on your National Service.'

Markham didn't try to reply; there was no point. They were unlikely allies, he knew that. But if they brought down Carter it would be worthwhile. After that things could return to the way they'd been.

'What next?'

'What do you have up your sleeve?' Baker asked. 'You're the wonder boy.'

'There might be some other interest coming on Hart Ford.'

'Oh?'

Markham shrugged.

'We'll have to wait and see. But it would make things interesting.'

★★★

Joanna Hart sounded fresh and alert when she rang during the afternoon. She offered no apology for the way she'd been the day before. Most likely she didn't even remember, he thought.

'I wanted to tell you, I've had the very best news.'

'Another offer on the business?'

'How did you know?' There was a trace of suspicion in her voice, then it vanished. 'It's not an offer, exactly. He wants to see the books first. But I'm sure he'll make a bid.'

'You're right, that's wonderful news.'

'If he does, Carter will have to up his price if he wants to buy.' For the first time since he'd met her, she sounded buoyant and hopeful.

'Then let's hope he likes what he sees.'

'His accountant is examining things today. So I could hear something tomorrow.'

'True.'

Hatton hadn't wasted time. But he hadn't seemed the type to miss an opportunity. It was out of Markham's hands now. The figures would speak for themselves. If the potential was there, the man would make his bid.

He stayed in the office until five, pottering at this and that, filling the time in case some new client appeared. They'd been too thin on the ground lately; he could use the business. He'd just buttoned the mac and taken the keys from his pocket when the telephone rang.

'Dan?' It was Carla's voice, close to tears.

'What is it?'

'Can you come up to the college, please? To the studio?'

'Of course. But what—'

'Please.'

CHAPTER FIFTEEN

She was in the corridor, squatting, her back against the wall, head buried in her hands.

'What is it? What's happened?' Markham asked, kneeling in front of her and holding her gently by the shoulders. She looked like a collapsed marionette, tears coursing down her cheeks. 'What is it?'

Carla said nothing, just tilted her head towards the room. Slowly he rose, his heart still thumping in his chest. He'd run all the way from the office. He turned the handle and walked in.

Every canvas had been slashed. Some just three or four cuts, other in ribbons. Brutal light spilled through the windows. The painting she'd started based on Donatello's statue was still on an easel, obliterated by razors. Everything she'd worked on for a year or more had been destroyed.

One picture lay in the middle of the floor. It had been placed there deliberately, a self-portrait, Carla caught in a pensive mood with hair falling across her face. A single cut crossed the neck. He picked up the painting and stacked it with the others. Everything damaged, everything beyond repair. All her work, all come to nothing.

He lifted Carla to her feet and took her in his arms. She clung tightly, pushing her head against his shoulder and letting the tears come again. He reached out and closed the door; no one else needed to see this.

She held him for a long time. He rubbed her back softly, feeling the small shocks of each thought making her quiver. They'd taken away everything she'd created. But the self-portrait had been directed at him.

'Come on,' he said gently when the crying had ended and she was still. He kept his arm around her, gathering up her bag and coat.

In her office she stared at him, her face empty. She lived for her painting. Teaching at the art college just gave her the money and the studio to do it. He took hold of her hand.

'I'm sorry,' he said.

'You know who did it, don't you?'

He nodded.

'Why?' Her voice was bleak and uncomprehending. She pawed at fresh tears, wiping them away with broad strokes. He thought about a simple answer but she deserved the truth.

'It's the man I'm after. He's responsible for this.'

'But *why*?'

'He wants me to stop. He thinks doing this will help.'

She stayed silent for a long time looking into his eyes.

'Dan …'

'I'm sorry. I never thought …' He shook his head. He hadn't imagined Carter would go after her. Carla had no part in their battle.

'I'd been talking to the gallery in London about an exhibition. Maybe next spring.'

And now that was ruined. He let out a long, slow breath, not knowing what to say. In his mind he could see the self-portrait.

'Would the college let you take a little time off?'

'The term's only just started,' she answered automatically, then stopped herself. 'Christ, Dan, what are you saying?'

'That it would be safer if you were out of Leeds for a little while.' He kept his voice steady.

'Safer?' She said the word as if she didn't understand.

'Yes.' He didn't want to have to explain, to make it into bare facts. This was enough, more than enough. He cared about her. But he knew he couldn't protect her.

'Tell me,' she demanded.

'Go and stay with someone for a little while. A week, maybe a fortnight. It'll all be over by then.'

He didn't know if it would, he could only hope.

'And what then? I start everything all over again?'

'I don't know.'

'Would I be in danger if I stayed?'

'I don't know,' he repeated.

Her eyes were hard as she stared at him.

'Be honest, Dan. I'm not a bloody child.'

'You might be.'

She squeezed his hand hard.

'All because of what you're doing?'

'I'm sorry. I didn't expect anything like this.'

Like an invalid, she let him help her into her coat and guide her down to the Victoria Hotel on Great George Street. It was close to college, somewhere they'd gone often enough. But all the old joy and laughter had flown from the place. He bought her a large brandy and watched her drink it. A blush of colour started to return to her cheeks as she smoked a cigarette.

'Did you mean it? What you said about me leaving for a while?'

'Yes.'

'For God's sake, Dan. What have you got yourself into?'

'More than I wanted.'

A vendetta, a war. He owed her the truth and he gave it to her as she sipped the brandy, bringing her up to date on everything. All the twists and turns. When he'd finished she only had one question.

'Do you think you'll win?'

'I hope so.' It was the best he could offer.

She let the silence hang and gazed around the bar.

'I'll talk to my department head tomorrow.' Her voice was quiet and reasonable. 'In the circumstances I'm sure he'll be fine with a fortnight away.' He opened his mouth but she continued. 'Don't worry, I won't tell him the truth. I have a friend I can stay with.' A small, bitter smile crossed her lips. 'Maybe I can do some painting. Try to have enough for that exhibition, if it's any good.'

'You know you have talent.'

Carla shook her head.

'Right now I'm not sure what I have, Dan. I don't even know what I'm feeling.' She buttoned her coat. 'I'm going to stay with Mary tonight and I'll sort everything out in the morning.' She leant across and kissed him on the cheek. 'I'll ring you when I come back.'

He heard the sharp click of her heels on the floor. No goodbye, nothing. But he deserved that for what he'd caused her. Maybe he was saving her life, but would he ever see her again?

CHAPTER SIXTEEN

Friday arrived. Markham hoped Carla would ring before she left town but the telephone was silent all morning. When the bell finally shrilled in the afternoon he grabbed at the receiver. It was only a call from another enquiry agency in Birmingham offering him a little work in Leeds.

It meant money and he accepted gratefully, but he'd have given it up to hear her voice. Still, he understood. He'd brought all this down on her; of course she wouldn't want any contact with him right now.

He'd made notes during the call and began rewriting them, translating his scrawl into legible writing whilst it was fresh in his mind. The door handle rattled then turned and he looked up. Joanna Hart burst in.

She wore a cream dress with black trim under a black coat, her hair was loose and a smile played on her lips.

'Hello,' he said.

'I was coming into town and I wanted to let you know. He's going to make an offer!'

'The mystery interest?'

'Of course,' she said with a touch of exasperation. 'Who else?'

'So you're celebrating?'

'I'm meeting someone for a drink and we might have a bite to eat.'

'Mr Parker?'

'That's none of your business,' she told him. 'But no, if you must know. It's an old chum. A girl.'

'When will the offer come through?'

'Tomorrow. He said he still needed to come up with an exact figure. He was just checking that I hadn't already sold to anyone. So I can forget about our friend.'

He didn't say anything. For some reason Carter had his sights on Hart Ford; he wouldn't be happy at anything that stopped him buying it. And he wasn't a man who liked to lose.

'Have you heard from Carter again?'

'Yes.' She sighed. 'This morning he sent me a big bunch of flowers. The char had to dig out another vase to hold them all. But he won't go a penny higher.'

★★★

In the end, the job for the Birmingham agency only took an hour. He was finished before five and was back in the office, writing out his report and dropping it in the post box on his way back to the motor car.

Sergeant Graham was leaning against the wall. The trilby shaded his eyes and his hands were pushed deep into overcoat pockets.

'Looking for me?' Markham asked.

'I'm not here for my health.' He moved close.

'What do you want?' He knew. Word would have passed about Hatton's interest. Carter would have made a telephone call to send out his pet copper.

'Someone wanted you to do something.'

'I'll tell you what I told him: I don't work for Carter.'

'He's heard that the Hart woman might sell to someone else.'

'If the money's right, I'm sure she will.' He had the car key in his hand, protruding between his index and middle fingers.

Graham shook his head.

'Not good enough. He told you what he was going to do. To make an example of you.'

'Then he hasn't succeeded, has he? I'm still here.'

'If Mrs Hart hasn't signed over the business to him by Monday, you'll be gone. Simple message, even for someone like you.' He brought out one large hand and slapped Markham very lightly on the face. 'He's giving you one last chance. You're a lucky lad.'

'Since you're playing messenger boy you can tell him something.' He saw Graham bristle.

'What's that?'

'To go fuck himself.'

The sergeant smiled.

'You think having Baker on your side will help you? He's on his way out. Coppers like him are the past. The pair of you, you're amateurs.'

'But we're not bent.'

He wasn't prepared for the fist. It sank into his belly and forced all the air from him. Markham sank to the ground and Graham casually brought up his knee to catch him on the jaw and send him sprawling.

By the time he could breathe and start to move, the policeman had gone. People walked around him as he crawled and gathered his keys from the pavement. Very slowly, the paralysis faded from his solar plexus. He spat blood from his mouth where he'd bitten his tongue.

He steadied himself on the car, pushing himself upright and wiping the dirt from his trousers. Finally he lit a cigarette, smoking the whole thing then grinding it out before driving home.

The blows had been Graham's own touch. The hard man giving a taste of what he enjoyed. But the message had been clear. Monday. It was Friday now. A weekend of grace then it would all come to a climax.

★★★

Late in the evening he was back in town, casually dressed in cavalry twill trousers and an old jacket, his shirt collar unbuttoned, the tie in the drawer at home. The end of the week and people were out to enjoy themselves. Crowds spilled out from the pubs, scattering to the late buses. A few revellers remained, a knot here and there on street corners.

He parked and took the stairs down to Studio 20. The music was already roaring, a trumpeter letting his notes soar like Louis Armstrong over a rowdy, bumpy rhythm section. It hit him as he opened the door. Bass, drums, the piano punctuating with jagged chords, a tenor sax taking over the lead on 'A Night in Tunisia' as the crowd applauded.

The group was half West Indian, the trumpeter wiping his face with a handkerchief as he sat down, smiling and nodding his head in time with the beat. The sax spiralled higher, turning the melody inside out before dipping down an octave and starting to climb again on a subtly different route.

Markham nodded to Bob Barclay, in his usual place behind the partition, then sat. His stomach was still sore and a bruise was beginning to form on his chin. His fingers throbbed; he'd taken a couple of pills before coming out. But as the music grew around him, he forgot the pain.

The drummer propelled the group, pushing and nudging, but it was the front men who shone, feeding off each other, swapping phrases, eyes closed to listen then play, their skin wet with sweat. They batted around an idea, smiling as they resolved it into 'A Foggy Day In London Town' to finish their set. It had been ragged at times, but there was electricity in what they played and the audience knew it, clapping wildly.

Markham stood, ready to leave. Whoever else played tonight, they wouldn't top that. Barclay waved him over, watching as two new reedmen set up to play.

'What did you think?' he asked, nodding at the players who'd just finished.

'They're good.'

'Yes,' Barclay agreed with a hint of doubt. 'You know what, though, Dan? Three people in the crowd walked out as soon as they saw those two were coloured.' He shook his head. 'People, eh? Who do they think made jazz in the first place?'

'So who are this pair?'

'They came over three months ago. Tony and Terry. Working as street cleaners for the council. They play for fun.'

'Maybe they'll make money from it sometime.'

Barclay shook his head.

'Money and jazz, Dan. Don't go well together. Never have.'

Out on Briggate he looked around as he walked to the car. Monday, Carter had said, but he wasn't going to put his trust in a word. No one was waiting. No one had broken into the flat.

***

By eleven on Saturday he was parking in Ilkley. He'd dressed for the occasion in dark trousers and a tweed jacket, with a checked shirt and pale tie. Respectable but casual. He knocked on Ted Smith's door and heard footsteps shuffling along the hall.

'Hello, Dan.' The man beamed. Maybe so few people visited him that anyone was welcome. 'Come on in, I'll put the kettle on.'

They settled in the kitchen, teapot and a pint bottle of milk between them, a fresh packet of digestive biscuits tipped on to a plate.

'Right,' Smith said. 'I know you're not here to pass an hour. Is everything over? Do you need more money?' His voice was eager, his eyes shining and curious.

'No more money,' Markham told him. 'I still have some of what you gave me before.' He began to reach for his wallet but Smith reached out a hand to stop him.

'You keep it, you might need it. Have you won?'

'Not yet.' He detailed everything that had happened, the pushes forwards, the steps back and the threats. Smith listened closely. When Markham finished, he asked,

'What's so special about this Ford place?'

'I don't know.' He'd wondered about that himself, unable to find an answer. It was just a business. If Carter really wanted a motor car agency he was able to open one of his own. Everything perfectly legal.

'Seems an odd thing to me. But how can I help you, Dan?'

'I just wanted you aware of everything. In case something happens to me.'

'You really think it will?'

'I think he's a man who does what he says. And he's well-protected. He has friends in Whitehall.'

'Is it worth it?'

'Yes.' Markham didn't even have to think. 'It is.'

'Right. The Chief Constable's a friend of mine. Owt happens, I'll have a word with him. I can do it now, if you prefer?'

Markham shook his head.

'No. But thank you.'

'It's your choice.' Smith gave him a curious look. 'But you look after yourself. I respect a man who'll stand up for what he believes, but I don't want to read about you in the *Evening Post*. I'm not sure anything's worth that.'

'I'm not sure it is, either,' he answered with a wry smile. 'But here I am.'

'Make sure it's not the last time.' He poured another cup of tea, draining the pot, and taking one more biscuit. 'You said that girl you like has gone away for a little while.'

'I think so. She promised she would.'

'I saw your face. You're sweet on her, aren't you?'

'A bit.' He didn't want to say anything more. For all he knew, everything was over with Carla. If it was, he could hardly blame her. If she hadn't been involved with him then her paint-ings, everything she'd created, would still be whole. Her art was who Carla was. It was everything that mattered to her. She might care about him, but he'd always play second fiddle to her work. He couldn't afford to dwell on it now.

'Think about what matters. You get to my age, the only regrets are the things you didn't do.'

'I will.'

***

The hard metal ringing of the alarm clock woke him at half past one. Outside the window the night was silent. No cars on the road, no stragglers on the pavement making their late way home.

He dressed in a dark suit and tie, topping if off with the overcoat and trilby. The effect was exactly what he'd hoped, an anonymous young businessman who might be a guest at an expensive hotel. In town he parked on Basinghall Street, away from the lights.

On the way home from Ilkley he'd stopped on King Street and walked through the ground floor of the Metropole Hotel. It was as grand as its name, an old Victorian building that kept the old standards of luxury and service.

There was no doorman in the small hours, but nothing to stop him walking in, either. He smiled at the desk clerk and passed quickly, walking with the assurance of a guest. The thick carpet muffled his footsteps. Down the corridor he waited ten minutes, long enough for his face to vanish from the man's mind.

Then he reached up and pulled the fire alarm before slipping through a door and out of sight to hide among piles of towels and sheets. A cacophony of bells began to sound. Within a few seconds Markham could hear voices and footsteps on the stairs as people tumbled from their rooms and staff shouted ques-tions and instructions.

He waited eight minutes. Time enough for everyone to be up and outside and the fire engine to arrive. At the second floor he listened carefully then put on a pair of leather gloves. At room 203 he brought a thin piece of plastic from his pocket and pushed on the door, enough to force a gap between wood and frame. Markham worked the perspex between them to force open the Yale lock, exactly the way the army had taught him. A quick turn of the handle and he was in.

The light was still on, the bedclothes were thrown back; there was still a dent in the pillow. Like a good guest, Carter had abandoned his room when the alarm sounded. Papers sat on the table. He took them without looking, then emptied the contents of each drawer into a pile onto the floor.

With a Stanley knife he slashed the mattress and pillows, then the twelve suits in the wardrobe, cutting a sleeve off each one. Finally he attacked the shirts and looked around at his handiwork.

Back in the corridor he closed the door gently, checking that the lock held. His footsteps echoed lightly on the concrete of the service stairs. Down on the ground floor he found a rear door that was unlocked and slipped out into the night. He walked to the car, forcing himself to stroll and not run, sucking the smoke of a cigarette deep into his lungs.

In the flat he undressed and glanced through the papers he'd taken. More letters relating to the businesses Carter owned. Several were from the council, violations and fines and threatening closure. Good, he thought with a smile. A couple of notes from friends awaiting replies.

The man would know who was responsible. He'd want his revenge. Markham was banking on that.

Part Three

ROUND ABOUT MIDNIGHT

CHAPTER SEVENTEEN

The car was waiting on Town Street, pulling into traffic directly behind the Anglia. The driver didn't even try to disguise his actions, staying close on the drive into town. Markham turned off, cutting through back streets and bouncing over the cobbles, the car sticking close as he headed away from Leeds.

He knew the spot he wanted. Out in Shadwell, just beyond the suburbs. A lazy little stream where he'd gone fishing with his father, riding bicycles into the country. He'd been back several times since, when he wanted solitude close to home.

There was only one man in the vehicle behind him. Markham pressed down on the accelerator just after a corner and pulled ahead, keeping up the speed as the road snaked. Around a second bend, out of sight for a few seconds, he stamped on the brake and yanked on the wheel to turn onto a small track.

The other car dashed past, then stopped, reversing slowly. It gave him the time he wanted, to leave the Anglia and run down a path. He picked up a branch, weighing it in his hands. It hurt to grip with his injured fingers, but was worth the pain. The trees were thick; plenty of places to hide.

He heard the man, the crack of twigs on the ground. Markham tightened his grip on the wood, scarcely daring to breathe. The man was blundering along, confident and contemptuous. As he passed, Markham brought the branch down hard on his head.

He fell with a small sigh and lay still. Quickly, Markham felt for a pulse then emptied the man's pockets – wallet, grubby handkerchief, change, keys. He took the thirty shillings in notes, the keys and most of the coins, leaving tuppence for a telephone call; there was a box a mile down the road.

He stripped the man naked, throwing clothes and possessions into the stream. It ran deep here; everything would sink. There was no need for more. With a final glance he walked back to the cars and put on his gloves.

The boot of the man's car was empty but he found a gun wedged under the front seat, a Colt automatic with a full magazine, the safety catch on. He put it in his overcoat, locked the door and tossed the keys into a hedge before driving away.

Whoever he was, the man would wake in a while. Sooner or later he'd be able to raise some help, if he wasn't arrested for exposure first. Either way, Markham had sent another message to Carter. Now it was time for one more.

★★★

Eleven on a Sunday morning and Joanna Hart was up and dressed. She showed him through to the living room, the sun through the window catching dust motes in the air.

She glanced at the grandfather clock.

'I'm meeting some people in a little while,' she announced.

'Have you had that offer yet?' he asked.

She shook her head. 'Tomorrow, he said.'

'I want you to ring Carter and arrange to meet him in the morning.'

'Why? I don't have the offer yet.'

'Tell him someone else is putting in a bid for the business and you're giving him a chance to increase his offer.'

She looked at him with curiosity.

'Is there any point?'

'Make it early,' he continued. 'Nine o'clock. And tell him I'll be with you.' With the shops shut on Sunday Carter would have had no chance to buy new clothes.

'I'll ask again, Mr Markham,' she said impatiently. 'Why?'

'He'll try and put you off until later in the day. Insist on it being early.'

She sighed and lit a cigarette.

'All right,' she agreed finally. 'Where?'

He thought quickly.

'The Kardomah, up in the restaurant.'

'What sort of game are you playing, Mr Markham?'

'One that puts Carter at a disadvantage.' He stood, feeling the weight of the gun pulling down his pocket. 'I'll see you in the morning.'

'I trust this won't end up being a wasted trip.'

He smiled.

'Believe me, it won't.'

★★★

Markham spent the rest of the day on edge, playing Ellington and Basie records, big bands to distract him. He tried to read but couldn't settle long enough as he anticipated the meeting the following morning.

Wearing his best suit, he was in the office a little after eight. No one else had been there but why would they? Carter wanted his revenge on the man, not the place.

He smoked four cigarettes, grinding one out in the ashtray then immediately lighting another. Every few seconds his eyes flicked to the clock. The telephone rang and he jumped to it.

'He said ten o'clock,' Joanna Hart said. 'He wouldn't budge from that.'

Markham smiled. Carter needed time for new clothes to be delivered. Good. He'd be awkward and angry, wrong-footed. That was when men made mistakes.

'Still at the Kardomah?'

'Yes.'

'Why don't you come to the office? We'll go down together.'

'If you like,' she agreed with reluctance. 'Will you tell me what this is all about?'

'Yes.'

'I'll be there in an hour.'

★★★

He dialled Millgarth police station and asked for Detective Sergeant Baker.

'Carter will be at Kardomah Tea Room at ten.'

'So you kept yourself alive over the weekend. Why do I want to be there?'

'Our man will have a new wardrobe.'

'Oh?' Markham heard the rustling of papers. 'That wouldn't have anything to do with a fire alarm going off at the Metropole on Saturday night, would it?'

'I've no idea what you're talking about.'

'Or there's this one. We received a complaint yesterday about a naked man out past Shadwell. They sent out a car to pick him up.' Baker chuckled. 'Turns out he works for Carter. Said someone had assaulted him and taken everything.'

'I wish I'd seen that.'

'So do I, lad.'

'Did he say who did it? Or why?'

'Never saw him, he claims. Record as long as your arm. He was out on probation. Banged him back inside. Can't have people exposing themselves in public like that.' He paused. 'Looks like I might have underestimated you,' he said with grudging admiration.

'If I'd done anything.'

'Aye, of course. So is something going to happen this morning?'

'You never can tell.'

'Maybe I'll wander over for a cup of tea, then. Ten, you said?'

★★★

Joanna Hart was as good as her word, appearing on time and wearing a Chanel suit that cost more than Markham had made in his very best month. She wore it as casually as anything from a department store.

'You didn't ask about the other offer,' she said as she settled on a chair and crossed her legs.

'Has he rung?'

'Just before I left. It's less than I'd wanted but a lot more than Carter has bid.'

'That's good, isn't it?'

'I suggested a higher figure. We're haggling.' She eyed him with curiosity. 'You've never asked me who it is. You know, don't you?'

His answer was a fleeting smile.

'So why do you want me to meet Carter again, Mr Markham? You obviously have a reason.'

'See if he's willing to top the bid.'

'Why would he?' She narrowed her eyes. 'I don't know what you're planning, but unless you tell me I'm going home right now.'

'Because he needs to squirm a little. His clothes were ruined on Saturday night and yesterday one of his men was humiliated.'

'You did all that?' she asked, impressed.

'Yes.'

'Why?' She eyed him curiously. 'This can't all be to do with me.'

It was safe enough to tell her now; she knew he was on her side.

'Carter wanted me to persuade you to sell.'

She glanced up sharply, surprised.

'But you haven't even tried.'

'I know. I told him from the start that I wouldn't.'

'You never said anything.'

'If I had, would you have trusted me?'

'I … I don't know. Maybe not,' she accepted and looked at his fingers. 'Did he do that?'

'He wielded the hammer himself.'

She winced. 'God.'

'He's also threatened to kill me.'

'Kill you?'

'Don't worry. He'll find it's a difficult job.'

★★★

By five to ten they were sitting upstairs at the Kardomah, a table in the window that looked down on Briggate. People thronged by, some moving quickly, others ambling and window shopping.

'That man over there, he's the detective who kept asking me if I'd killed Freddie.' Her hiss was full of outrage.

'He's here to keep an eye on things. Don't worry, he's as honest as they come.'

She looked doubtful and opened her mouth to speak just as Carter appeared at the top of the stairs. His shirt was a brilliant white, the tie dark blue silk. But the suit was an ill fit; he'd had no time to have it altered. The trouser legs were a little too long, light flashing briefly on the pins that hemmed them, and the cut of the jacket emphasised the bulge of his belly.

He crossed the floor quickly, fury on his face as he saw Markham.

'Mrs Hart,' he said. 'A pleasure to see you again.' He waved Joyce the waitress away. She rolled her eyes at Markham. 'You said you wanted to discuss my offer for the business.'

Joanna Hart gave a charming smile.

'I wanted to give you a final chance to increase your offer. It's only courtesy.'

'You have my terms.' His voice was grave. 'I see no reason to change that.'

'You should know that someone else has put in a bid. A serious one,' she added. 'And it's rather higher than yours, I'm afraid.'

'I see.'

Markham kept his eyes on Carter's face. His eyes flickered between doubt and possibility.

'Might I ask who's been so generous?' Carter asked eventually.

'I couldn't say,' she told him. 'I'm sure you understand.'

'You're hoping I'll increase mine?'

'I'm giving you the chance. After all, you were so eager. You approached Freddie, and you've been after me from the moment he died.' The sweetness never left her voice but acid flowed beneath the surface.

'How much is he offering?'

'Mr Carter, you can't expect me to reveal that. I've put the ball in your court. Whether you play it or leave is completely up to you now.' She took a sip of her tea and raised an eyebrow. 'Well?'

'I'd like until tomorrow.'

'Fine,' she agreed. 'But not a moment longer. If I haven't heard from you by ten o'clock tomorrow morning with a figure that beats his, that'll be the end of our business.' She paused for a heartbeat. 'I must say, you're looking very smart today. A new suit?'

Carter coloured but said nothing as he rose.

'I'll be in touch,' he promised.

'How was that?' she asked as the man disappeared.

'Perfect,' he told her. She'd played her part convincingly. The next twenty-four hours would be interesting.

★★★

They parted on Briggate and he watched her walk away, hips swinging under her coat. He was still standing there when Baker drifted out.

'Looks like Carter called in at Burton's on the way.'

'Austin Reed. I saw the label in the jacket.'

The policeman shrugged. 'Either way, they didn't do him any favours with those clothes. What happened?'

Markham recounted it all.

'A day, eh?' Baker said thoughtfully. 'Plenty can happen in that time.'

'I'm hoping it does.' He had the gun in his pocket, careful to wear gloves when he touched it. Today was the deadline Carter had given him. Deliver Hart Ford or die. Plenty would definitely happen before tomorrow arrived.

'Watch out for yourself. I can't keep an eye on you all the time.'

'I am, believe me.'

★★★

He spent the rest of the morning in the office, alert for footsteps on the stairs. Nothing. Only the pigeons on the rooftops and the staccato click of typewriters from the secretarial agency downstairs.

Carter wouldn't let a deadline pass. He'd want revenge. He needed to keep his reputation. At half past twelve Markham put on overcoat and gloves and went down to Albion Place.

The man set to follow him turned away whenever Markham looked back and halted when Markham paused to glance at shop windows as he walked up Briggate. Across from the Grand Theatre, he slipped into the Riviera Café and sat at a table by the kitchen.

It was a tiny place, just six tables, the air heavy with the smells of grease and cooking. He ate slowly, finishing with a cup of lukewarm tea and a cigarette. As he paid the bill he asked casually,

'Is there a back door?'

'Course there is,' the harried woman replied. 'Don't be daft.'

'Do you mind if I use it? There's someone outside I don't want to see.' That piqued her interest. Her hand was in the till, reaching for his change. 'Angry husband,' he said with a smile and a wink.

'Been a bad lad, have you?' Her voice was stern but her face softened. 'Aye, go on, then. Straight through there.'

He came out into a ginnel, following it around until he was back on the street. Watching the watcher. The man waited five more minutes, constantly glancing at the time, before he darted into the cafe, then left again in a panic, looking around help-lessly. A black Riley pulled up to the kerb and he got in.

The car turned and headed back down Briggate. With heavy traffic and the Monday throng crowding the street, Markham could trot and stay close enough not to lose the vehicle.

It crossed the bridge then turned the corner on to Dock Street, and he knew exactly where it was going.

In the daytime this was an area of small factories and work-shops. There was the constant noise of machinery and voices. The spark of a welding torch and the clang of a hammer. The heat of a forge and water thrown out across the cobbles.

The car was parked where he expected, on the small side street by the blank wooden entrance to a building. The door stood open. Markham crept close enough to listen.

'You fucking lost him?'

'He must have gone out the back way from the cafe.'

'What about you?' the first voice asked. 'You were driving the car. Did you see him?'

'No.'

He waited through a few moments of silence.

'He must have spotted you,' the first voice said with disgust. 'Go back to his office. He'll be back there sometime.'

Markham stepped into the doorway. The three men turned as he blocked the light. His broken fingers throbbed. The place was exactly as he remembered, empty, the bare bulb, two chairs and a table. The only difference was the large carving knife sit-ting on the wood.

'Looks like you don't have to bother, lads,' the first man said with amusement. 'He's come to us.'

Markham knew him now. He was the one who'd held a blade when he'd been driven here before. A bulky man with a pale complexion and dark, wavy hair, eyes full of confidence. Big Chalky White. Back then the man hadn't spoken. Now he didn't seem to want to shut up.

'You might as well come in.' He grinned 'Even if you run we're not going to let you go far.'

His hand snaked out towards the table.

'Don't,' Markham said quietly and drew the pistol. The man froze.

'And what were you going to do with me?' He moved the barrel between the men, waiting for an answer.

'Mr Carter wants you dead,' the second man said nervously.

'Really? Another dead body would bring down the law.'

'Only if they find it.' White didn't seemed frightened. 'You won't be seen. Not for ten or twenty years, any road. Who'd care by then?'

It was hard to bring a murder case when you didn't have a body.

'Kick the knife across the floor,' he ordered. 'And the keys to the car and the door.'

'Or what?' White said.

'I shoot.' He raised the gun and aimed at the man's chest.

'You wouldn't bloody dare.' White was smirking. 'Not when everyone could hear.'

'Plenty of noise out there. Banging, booms. Do you think anyone would really notice?' He paused. 'Do you really want to bet your life on that?' He raised the pistol and waited.

Finally, turning his head to spit, White dropped the blade to the floor and kicked it across to Markham.

'Keys, too.'

With a gesture of disgust, the man brought a keyring from his pocket and tossed it at Markham's feet.

He picked them up, backed out and slammed the door behind him. It was solid wood, the lock old and heavy.

Footsteps rushed across the concrete floor inside as he turned the key. They wouldn't be out of there until someone came to free them, he thought.

Markham sat in the Riley, the gun back in his pocket, knife half-hidden under the seat. The engine started on the first attempt. He bumped it back over the cobbles, then through the city centre and parked in front of the Metropole. The old car stood out among the polished Wolseleys and Jags. The commissionaire came across, a dark frown under his shiny top hat.

'You can't leave that here,' he insisted.

'Mr Carter asked for it,' Markham said. He handed over the keys. 'You know what he's like. You'd better tell him his car's arrived.'

'He's not even here,' the man blustered. 'He left not five minutes ago.'

'Don't ask me.' Markham shrugged. 'I was told to bring it here, that's all.' He walked away with a smile.

CHAPTER EIGHTEEN

So far he'd infuriated Carter. What he'd done had been nig-
gling and annoying, but not dangerous. He needed something
bigger. Something audacious. Something final.

He wanted this to be over. He wanted Carla back in Leeds,
to see if anything was still possible between them. He looked at
his watch: a little after three. He couldn't face the climb to the
third floor and the empty office. Instead, he started the Anglia
and went home.

He filled the flat with piano music. From Bach and Schuman
to Shearing. Sounds to sit at the back of his brain as he thought.

What could he do that would really hit Carter hard? What
could he do to topple the man? By midnight he'd found nothing. Plans skimmed through his mind, none of them workable.
With the door double-locked and bolted, he went to sleep.
Maybe the answer would arrive in his dreams.

★★★

The morning was dreary, grey skies and sharp, squally show-
ers that sent people running under shop awnings for cover.
The windows on the buses were steamed with condensation.
He parked on Albion Place, dashing between the car and building, the rushing to unlock the office door before the telephone
stopped ringing.

'Where have you been?' There was fear in her voice. 'I tried ringing you all yesterday afternoon.'

'I was out,' he answered. 'What's happened, Mrs Hart?'

'He came here.'

'Carter? When?'

'About three o'clock yesterday. He had someone with him. A big man.'

'What did he want?'

He heard her take a deep breath.

'He said he'd indulged my little games, but it was time to stop and sign the papers. He wasn't going to offer a penny more than he already had and I was going to take it.'

'Did you sign?'

'No. But he's coming back this morning.' She hesitated. 'There's a strange car parked outside the house.'

'Is there anyone in it?'

'I don't know. I can't see.'

'Call the police,' he advised. 'Tell them about the vehicle and Carter. They'll send someone out.'

'There's one more thing,' she said quietly.

'What?'

'He hinted that you were out of the picture.'

'I'll bet he did. I'm here. Look, I'll drive up there. It'll only take a few minutes.'

'Thank you.' She sounded as if she was starting to cry. 'When I couldn't get hold of you, I thought …'

'He's going to have to work a lot harder to get rid of me.'

★★★

Before he left, he needed to make one more call.

'Jones,' the man answered, his voice somewhere between boredom and exasperation. The secret service, or whatever name it had, wasn't keeping him busy enough.

'Ged, it's Dan.'

'Again, boyo?' He chuckled. 'What's it this time? What's been happening up there?'

He gave a very brief outline, hearing the soft scrape of a pencil taking notes.

'You're sure about all this, Danny? It's not your imagination or anything like that?'

'I'm positive. Christ, Ged, the man smashed my fingers with a hammer. His men were going to kill me and bury me somewhere I'd never be found. You think I'm making this up?'

'Calm down,' Jones said quietly. 'You need to think straight.'

'Right now he's threatening my client. He wants her business and her won't take no for an answer.'

'Wherever she is, get her out and somewhere safe.'

'I'm just about to.' It was the procedure, one the army had taught him.

'Let me talk to some people here and I'll see what I can do. We both know he's well connected but I think they'll draw the line at a murder spree.'

'I bloody well hope so.'

'I'll keep trying until I reach you,' Jones promised. 'Make sure you stay safe, Dan.'

***

There was no black car on the street when he parked. A police car sat there instead, one constable inside, the other banging on the door of the Hart house.

The officer turned as Markham marched down the drive.

'We received a message about a car here, sir. Do you know the owner of the house?'

'I do,' he answered with concern. 'She's not answering? I'm the one who told her to ring you. It was only a few minutes ago.'

The bobby shook his head.

'I've been knocking. There was nothing here when we arrived.'
Markham could feel his heart beating faster. His mouth was dry.
'Have you tried the door or looked in the windows?'

'Sir?' the constable asked.

'She should be here,' he insisted. 'I told her I was coming over.'

'She might have gone out, sir.' He shrugged. 'Women, you know.'

Markham thought for a moment then dashed to the garage
and pulled the door open. The Humber sat inside.

'If she'd gone out, she'd have driven.' He moved into the back
garden, peering through the windows of the house, seeing no one
inside. He tried the back door, then the front door. Both locked.
'Can you pass a message to Detective Sergeant Baker at Millgarth?'

'Because she's not here, sir?'

'Yes.' His voice was sharp.

'Sir, she's over twenty-one,' the policeman said. 'She can
come and go as she pleases.'

'She's part of a bloody investigation.' He almost shouted the
words then took a breath. 'Baker will want to know.'

'Yes, sir.' He sounded doubtful but went to the car. A minute
later he returned with his notebook open. 'They'll pass it on.
I just need some details from you.'

Name, address, relationship to the woman of the house.
The constable raised his eyebrows at enquiry agent but said
nothing. The patrol car pulled away in a shower of gravel.
Markham looked around. The house stood by itself, surrounded
by a tall privet hedge. Plenty of privacy but no help for him.
In an area like this people didn't look to their neighbours. Not
openly, anyway.

He caught his reflection in the window and straightened
his tie. The creases in his trousers were sharp, shoes shined.
He smoothed down his hair. Presentable enough to go around
and ask questions here.

Markham started with the house across the street. The woman
who answered his knock was in her late fifties, grey hair in a

severe perm, the scent of lavender water around her. She'd seen the parked car, she claimed, but it had been empty.

'Did you see anyone else arrive?' he persisted.

'There was a motor car,' she answered. 'It was only there for a minute.'

'Did Mrs Hart leave in it?'

'I wouldn't know.' She sniffed. He waited. 'I went to make a pot of tea. By the time I came back, it had gone and so had the other car.'

That was all she knew. By the time Baker pulled up in a plain black Ford, Markham had been to four other houses. There was no answer at two of them; the others had seen and heard nothing unusual.

He pushed the brim of the hat back. 'You'd better tell me what's going on.'

Markham condensed it into a few sentences, watching the man frown as he glanced at the house.

'Are you sure Mrs Hart isn't inside?'

'I haven't been in.'

'Good. That's copper's work. Come with me.'

At the door Baker took a set of lock picks from his pocket. A few deft flicks of his wrist and the lock clicked. He turned the handle and they were inside. The smell of beeswax filled the air.

'You look downstairs,' the policeman ordered. 'I'll go up.'

The rooms were empty. In the kitchen a half-drunk cup of tea stood by the cooker. The liquid was still warm. Hart's handbag, the purse still inside but no keys, was on the floor next to her chair.

'There's nothing upstairs,' Baker said as he returned. 'She's a messy cow, though. Clothes and towels all over.'

'Her keys have gone. Everything else is here.'

'Carter, you think?'

'I'm sure of it.'

'Where would he take her?'

'There's the place off Dock Street where they took me.'

Baker shook his head.

'I'll have someone look but it's too obvious. Where else?'

'I don't know.'

'You get searching,' Baker told him. 'I'll go back to the station and organise things. I'll tell you what, though, if she's just nipped out for a pint of milk I'm not going to be happy with you.'

'She's gone, Sergeant. You know it as well as I do.'

'Aye,' the man agreed grimly.

★★★

Where, Markham wondered as he drove back into town. Where would he have taken her? And what had happened to Carter? Why was he so obsessed with owning Hart Ford? What was there that he needed? What the hell did he hope to do by taking Joanna Hart? It was guaranteed to set the police after him.

He needed to find her, and find her quickly. In the office he pawed through the papers taken from Carter's room. He noted down every single address. She might not be at any of them, but it was somewhere to start. It made him feel he was doing something.

After half an hour he had a long list. It was time to begin looking. He ignored the businesses that Carter owned; there'd be too many people around and too many awkward questions.

On a hunch he drove out to Carr Manor Parade, to the house where he'd been duped by Jenkins, the man who never really existed. He didn't try the door but went next door. The woman had been helpful before.

'Come back to see me?' she asked with a smile as she answered his knock.

'Just a quick question. Have you seen anyone next door today?'

'Today?' she asked in surprise. 'There hasn't been anyone there in a week or more. Why?'

'I just wondered.'

'There's something going on, isn't there?' Her eyes were full of curiosity.

'Can I use your telephone?' He'd seen the wires running to the house. She looked uncertain. 'I'll pay for it.'

'Of course. It's in the hall.'

As he talked to Baker at Millgarth station he sensed the woman hovering at the kitchen door.

'I've made a list of places she might be,' he told the detective.

'And how did you do that?'

'Some of Carter's papers.'

'I'll not ask how you got them.'

'There are too many for me to check myself.'

'I'll have the bobbies go to them.'

Markham rattled off eight addresses.

'Right. If you find anything, let me know. I kept someone at her house in case she comes home.'

He hung up and folded the list before returning it to his pocket.

'It sounds urgent,' she said, holding out a mug of tea. 'You look like you could use that.'

He drank gratefully.

'Someone missing.' It was all he was willing to say.

'Very hush-hush?'

'For now.'

'Will I hear about it on the radio?'

'I don't know.' He finished the tea in a long gulp and took out a business card. 'If you see anything next door, ring me, please. Or call the police.'

'All right.'

He trailed to houses and businesses all over Leeds, pushing and darting through traffic, from a street of back-to-backs in Armley to a cleaning business based in Roundhay. Nothing. No sign of Joanna Hart or Carter in any of them.

Markham's head was throbbing as he drove back into town and parked at the office. As he reached for the telephone it began to ring.

'Markham,' he said, surprised at how jumpy he sounded.

'It's Ged.'

'Things have changed. Carter's snatched my client.'

'They've changed here, too. The brass decided to send someone up to take care of him.'

'Take care of?' he asked.

'You know what I mean, boy. The powers-that-be have decided that he needs to be stopped.'

'I see.'

'If he's caught, then his past is going to come out. A matter of national security.'

'Of course.' He gave a small, cynical snort.

'I'm the one who's coming up,' Jones told him.

'You? You've done this before?'

'Once or twice.' He kept his voice bland. 'I'll be there at seven. Can you meet me at the station?'

'Of course.'

'One thing, Danny. Are you armed?'

He felt the weight of the pistol in his coat.

'Yes,' he answered, reluctantly.

'If you're somewhere quiet and can get off a clean shot, take him out. There won't be any comeback. Our people will clean up.'

'And if I can't?'

'Then I will,' Jones promised.

★★★

He rang Millgarth again.

'Anything?' he asked Baker.

'Not a dickie bird. I sent the uniforms out but no luck.'

'What about Sergeant Graham? He might know.'

'He rang in sick this morning. He's not at home. His missus doesn't know where he's gone. Someone rang him and he told her he had to go out. Any more ideas?'

'MI5 or someone is sending a man up.'

'How the hell do you know that?'

'It's a friend of mine. Their plan is to kill Carter.'

'Not in my bloody city, they don't,' Baker exploded.

'I think it's out of our hands now,' Markham told him.

'No, it's not,' he said, but the truth was apparent in his voice. MI5 trumped the local police.

'We'll have to find him first.'

'Just tell me where.'

That was the problem. He didn't know. He'd run out of places to look.

'I have no idea,' Markham said with a sigh.

'There's a bulletin out about Joanna Hart and Carter. That's all I can do for now. If you come up with anything else, ring me.'

'I will.' He glanced at the clock. Half past two. He locked the office door and started walking briskly through the city centre.

★★★

It took a while before anyone answered the door at the Kit Kat Club. Will Dawson was in his shirtsleeves, holding a mop, his collar undone and tie pulled down, a pair of braces holding up his trousers.

'It's you,' he said without any welcome in his voice. 'I thought you were the bloody cleaner. She hasn't shown up again.'

'I just need a word, Mr Dawson.'

'I suppose you'd better come in.' He led the way into the club and sat at a table facing the small bandstand. 'What is it?'

'Have you seen your boss today? Or Mrs Hart? Have you heard from them?'

'I only got in half an hour ago. Why? What's wrong with Jo?'

'It looks as if Carter's snatched Mrs Hart to make her sign over the Ford business to him.'

'Christ.' He sat back, shook his head and lit a cigarette. 'Are you sure?'

'It looks that way.'

'David? Why would he do that?'

'She'd had a better offer from someone else.'

'But …' he began, then words failed him.

'I need to know where he could have taken her.'

Dawson thought for a while, drawing hard on the cigarette.

'Have you tried his other businesses?'

'The police have. And I've been to other places he owns.'

'Then I don't know. He's never told me much about what he does. Bloody hell. Jo.'

'She's in danger, Mr Dawson. I need to find her before anything bad happens.'

'I'm sorry.' He ran a hand through his Brylcreemed hair. 'I don't know where they could be.'

Markham stood.

'The last time we talked I suggested you find another line of work. It's time. This place won't be around much longer.'

'Yes,' Dawson agreed bleakly. 'Maybe you're right.'

★★★

He went through Carter's papers one more time, desperately searching for any addresses he'd missed before. Baker rang at five. Not a sniff of Joanna Hart and Carter. They'd simply vanished. But Leeds was a big city; there were too many places to hide, especially for someone with connections.

'When's this secret agent of yours arriving?'

'Seven,' Markham answered.

'Bring him down to the station in the morning at nine and we'll have a confab.'

'If they're not found first.'

'Aye.' He didn't sound hopeful.

★★★

The station stank of dirt and smoke. The glass ceiling was covered in grime. Newspapers and sweet wrappers littered the floor. Markham waited by the barrier at the end of the platform, smoking a cigarette. The last time he'd been here was when Carla returned from Italy. And where was she now? Off somewhere, safe from Leeds, safe from him and all he'd brought down on her. He hoped so, anyway.

Exactly on time, the train pulled up to the platform, brakes squealing. Carriage doors opened and porters swarmed around. Jones strode through the crowd, carrying one small suitcase, raising a hand in greeting as he saw Markham.

'You're not looking too well, boy.'

'Good to see you too, Ged.' The man had filled out a little but he needed that; he'd been a skinny runt on National Service. His face was brown, as if he'd been abroad recently.

'Nothing new?'

Markham shook his head.

'Let's find a hotel and you can fill me in over dinner.'

'Carter has a room at the Metropole.'

'Expensive?'

'Very.'

'I'll need somewhere cheaper. HMG won't spring for the best. Not at my level, anyway. But they'll buy us something to eat.'

★★★

They'd finished their food, plates pushed aside. Markham drank his coffee while Jones toyed with a Scotch and soda.

'Right, tell me what you know.' Ged lit a cigarette and listened intently as Markham ran through it all. 'You've no idea where they could be?'

'None. I've checked some places and the police have been to the others.'

'This copper you're working with. Do you trust him?'

'Sergeant Baker? Yes. But there's another one named Graham. He's in Carter's pocket.'

'We should start with him, then.'

'Evidently he received a phone call then called in sick. Hasn't been seen since.'

Jones frowned.

'Has anyone talked to his snouts? Where does he like to go?'

'I don't know.'

'Right. We'll look at that in the morning. You said you're armed?'

'A Colt 1911.'

'Smuggled it back from Germany?'

'Not quite.' He recounted what had happened at the stream near Shadwell.

'You left him stark bollock naked?'

'The police arrested him for exposure.'

Jones roared.

'You should be back in the service, Danny. They'd bloody love that.'

'Right now I'll be happy to find Jo Hart and Carter.'

'We will,' Jones said with certainty.

'Do you have any ideas?'

'One or two. I'll tell you in the morning. Do you have a phone at home if I need to get hold of you?'

'No.'

Jones brought out a notebook and scribbled something.

'Right, we'll take care of that tomorrow.'

'Just like that?' He couldn't believe it. The waiting list for a telephone was eighteen months.

Ged smiled.

'We tell the GPO to jump and they ask how high.' He glanced at his watch. 'Right, I need to ring a few people. So it's the police station at nine?'

★★★

197

There were cups of tea and a plate of biscuits on the table.

'I hear you've come to kill Carter,' Baker said with disgust.

Jones opened a briefcase and took out a thick folder with a red stripe.

'That tells you all about him, Sergeant. Read through it. By the count in there he's killed twelve people himself. And only six of those were during the war. That doesn't include Mr Hart.'

'We all killed during the war. But you were too young for that.'

Jones shrugged as if he was used to the criticism.

'Doesn't matter.'

'I don't want any murder on my patch. You kill him, I'll arrest you.'

'You won't.' He spoke quietly but there was command in his voice. 'And that's from the highest levels.' He wrote a telephone number on a piece of paper and pushed it across the table. 'If you don't believe me, ring them.'

Baker snorted but put the paper in his pocket. He lit his pipe.

'Right, smart boys, where do we go from here, because I'm buggered if I know.'

'Go back and look at yesterday's places again,' Markham said. It was what he'd been taught. 'Just because he wasn't there then doesn't mean he isn't now.'

'The bobbies are already going round,' the detective said sourly. 'What do you think we do? Sit on our arses all day?'

Jones produced a piece of paper from the folder.

'I had them put this together before I left yesterday. These are all the properties Carter owns.'

'We already know them,' the sergeant snorted.

'Not all of them, you don't,' Jones told him, his voice cold. 'You don't have our resources. There's a man on the house Carter has in London in case he goes there.'

Baker and Markham scanned the list. There were two they didn't know, one in Holbeck, the other close to Harewood.

'There,' Markham said. The sergeant nodded his agreement.

'Nice and quiet. Wait a minute.' He returned with an Ordnance Survey map of the area and pointed with a stubby finger. 'That's it. A farm sitting off by itself.'

'What about the other place?' Jones asked.

'I know the street,' Baker told him. 'It's all garages and lock ups.'

'Why don't you take the place in the country,' Jones suggested, giving Markham a look. 'We'll go to this one.'

'If you want. I'll need to clear it, it's outside Leeds.'

'Don't worry about that. You have my authority.'

'Cocky little bastard, aren't you?'

Jones stared at him. 'I'm in charge of this, Sergeant. Please don't forget that.'

'What do I do when I find Carter?'

'You hand him over to me. Then forget you ever met him.'

'Simple as that?'

'Simple as that.' He stood, motioning to Markham. 'Remember, Sergeant, Carter's dangerous.' He patted the folder before returning it to his briefcase.

CHAPTER NINETEEN

'Why do you want the place in Holbeck?' Markham asked as they walked back from the police station. Jones smiled.

'Because I read Carter's file properly on the way up here.' He glanced around. 'Not a bad looking city, Leeds.'

'As long as you like everything to look as if Victoria's still on the throne.'

'Back when Britain was great, boy,' Jones said with a grin. 'Carter likes towns and cities. He'd rather have someone down a back street than out in the country.'

'As long as we find them I don't care.'

'We will.' There was confidence in the voice that Markham didn't feel.

***

It was a short trip through cobbled streets, past factories that spewed smoke into the sky. Leeds might as well still be a Victorian city, Markham thought. So little had changed. All the stone was still black from decades of dirt in the air, the houses back-to-backs and terraces. He parked beside a tall brick wall.

'Down there,' he said, pointing to the corner.

'Right.' Jones tossed the briefcase into the back seat. 'You have your gun?'

'Yes.'

'Keep it close.'

'For Christ's sake, Ged, this is Leeds. It's not the bloody OK Corral.'

'Have your hand in your pocket, then.' He closed the car door. As they turned into the street of small buildings, half of them empty, he said, 'It's that one. Hardisty and Sons.'

A welding shop, from the name on the fading sign. It was a street awaiting demolition, silent and empty. Broken cobbles on the road and glass from smashed street lights.

The place had a door large enough for a lorry, the blue paint flaking away in fistfuls. A smaller door, big enough for a man, fitted within it.

'How do you want to play it?'

'I'll go in first,' Jones told him. 'I'm trained for this, Danny. You come in behind me. If you see Carter, shoot the bastard.'

He glanced at the lock and brought something from his pocket. Three quick movements and the door swung open. He heard Jones take a breath as he took the gun from its shoulder holster. Then he was inside.

Inside it was black. The only light was a small rectangle from the open door. Markham stood, letting his eyes adjust, the Colt heavy in his hand. Metal filings glittered on the floor. In a few seconds he could make out another door in the back wall. With a nod, Jones motioned him to the side as he turned the handle and dashed in.

She was there, tied and gagged on a dirty old mattress in the corner. The dress was bunched around her thighs. Her eyes were wide with fear. Markham knelt next to her.

'It's fine,' he said, keeping his voice soft as he pulled the gag from her mouth. 'We're here, we've found you. You're safe now.' He talked while his fingers worked on the knots that kept her wrists bound behind her back, trying to sound soothing even as he saw the terror in his eyes. 'Come on,' he told her, lifting her up gently, and keeping his arm around her. 'Hold on to me. Everything's going to be fine now.'

'No sign of him,' Jones said. The only other furniture in the room was a straight chair covered in cobwebs and a cheap old desk.

Out in the light she kept blinking, leaning heavily against him as she hobbled. Silent tears ran down her cheeks through a dried trail of mascara. She began to shake, quietly at first, but by the time she reached the car, her body was wracked. Markham took off his raincoat and wrapped it around her like a blanket. He gave her a cigarette. Her hand trembled and she drew the smoke in deep.

'We have a safe house where we can keep her,' Jones said. He turned to Joanna Hart. 'Do you know where Carter is?'

'Leave it, Ged.' He looked at her. 'You're safe now,' he repeated, waiting until she gave a small, fearful nod.

Jones was rummaging through his briefcase, finally drawing out a paper.

'We can take her here,' he said. It was an address in Leeds 8, off Street Lane.

'In a little while.' She needed time.

'Bloody well think!' Jones' eyes blazed. 'We're out in the open here.' His hand was in his coat, clamped around his gun.

He was right. There were no other cars around, just the dull sounds of machines from the factories in the distance. Easy targets for anyone who wanted to take a shot.

'We're going to take you where no one can hurt you,' Markham told her. She huddled in the corner of the back seat, clutching the coat, still saying nothing.

'You still remember how to throw off a tail?' Ged asked.

'Yes.' His hands were so tight on the steering wheel that the knuckles were white.

'Then do it. Just in case.' He adjusted the wing mirror so he could keep watch.

Markham was cautious, taking half an hour to reach the house. It was an Edwardian villa, well kept, all red brick and fresh paint, identical to its neighbours. He pulled the Anglia into the drive.

'Round the back,' Jones ordered. 'So no one can see the car from the road.' He knocked on the kitchen door of the house, rapping his knuckles in a shave-and-a-haircut code. The woman who answered was as anonymous as the house, somewhere between forty and sixty, hair set in a wave, a floral pinafore over a skirt and twin set.

Markham escorted Joanna Hart into the building, her arm through his. The kitchen was warm, a pot simmering on the stove. A large table sat in the middle of the room, on a floor of Yorkshire flagstone. He sat her on one of the chairs as the woman bustled around, heaping sugar into a steaming cup of tea.

'She's in shock, poor love. You drink this, pet, it'll help. My name's Maggie. Maggie Cornwall. I look after the house here.'

Joanna Hart clasped her hands around the mug to take in the heat. Markham sat close, smoking, motioning for the others to leave the room. They were strangers; she knew him. She trusted him; he hoped she did. He needed to talk to her, to discover what she knew. Where Carter might be.

'He won't find you here.'

'He said he'd be able to find me anywhere.' Her voice was husky and broken.

'Not here,' he assured her. She pushed her lips together, staring straight ahead. Without thinking, she took a drink.

'Do you have another cigarette?'

He lit one for her, waiting. She'd say more in her own time, when she was able. She smoked greedily, finally stubbing out the butt in a clean glass ashtray.

'He said he'd kill me if I didn't sign over the business,' she said eventually, then turned to him. 'I didn't do it.'

'Good.' He squeezed her hand.

'He had a man with him. He had his hands all over me.' She took several deep breaths.

'Did either of them hurt you?'

'No.' She pushed the answer out too quickly.

'Did he …?'

She shook her head.

'He said he'd let him but he didn't.' A shudder of memory ran through her. 'He told me no one would ever see me again.'

'We're going to find him.'

She pushed her hands against her eyes, keeping out the light, trying to block out all the images of the last twenty-four hours.

'What will you do then?'

'Kill him.'

'I hope you do,' she told him after a long silence.

'Did he take you anywhere else?'

She shook her head.

'Did he mention any other places?'

'No.'

She'd spoken all the words that would come for now, he decided. She was drained. Sometime later, when all this was past, all the rest would come out in small floods.

'I need you to stay here for a while. Until we catch him.' The fear returned to her eyes. 'You're safe now. Honestly. No one can find you here. I promise.'

She didn't move as he left the room. Mrs Cornwall stood in the hall.

'Do you have a doctor you use?' Markham asked.

'Yes, of course,' she replied.

'Give him a call. She'll probably need something to sleep.'

'I've already done it,' she told him with a smile. 'He'll be along in a little while. I'll look after her, don't worry.'

'Thank you.'

'Mr Jones said you're an enquiry agent.'

'That's right.' Right at the moment that job seemed far, far away. 'Where is he?'

She pointed to the closed door of the front room.

'He said for you to just go in when you were done. I'll go and sit with Mrs Hart until the doctor comes.'

★★★

204

Ged was talking to someone on the telephone, waving Markham to a seat. After a moment he replaced the receiver.

'Baker didn't find him out at that cottage.'

'And we don't have him.' He sighed.

'How is she?'

'How do you think?'

'Did he rape her?'

'She said not.' A moment later he asked. 'Why? Does he have a record of it?'

'In the war and after.' There was sweat above Jones' lip. 'Not just women suspected of working for the enemy, either. We had to pay out and put pressure on the West German police a few times to keep it quiet.'

'What the hell were they doing letting him carry on? Christ, Ged.'

'He was good.' Jones shrugged. 'That's why. Results are what count in this game. You remember that.'

'But he became too wild?'

'We're pretty sure he was responsible for killing someone important on the other side. Someone we wanted alive. That was too much. But there were still a number of people who believed he should have stayed.'

'His friends.'

'The ones who helped him up there in the first place. But they've been overruled. Carter's on his own now.'

'We still have to find him,' Markham said. 'He might have left Leeds.'

'The department has people checking. Wherever he is, we'll find him. If you ask me, though, he's still here.'

'Why?'

'He's tied himself to the place. All these businesses he owns. I can't see him leaving all that. He's invested too much.'

'Why Leeds?' Markham asked. 'What's here for him?'

'I don't know, Danny. There's nothing in his file. It's like he stuck a pin in a map and decided on it.'

'Something's snapped in him.'

'Maybe it has. Who bloody knows, boy?' He shrugged. 'You'd need the trick cyclist for that. All I'm here to do is stop him.'

'To kill him.'

'Yes. Those are my orders.'

'Obeying orders. We heard that a lot from the Jerries after the war, Ged. Remember?'

'Different things, Danny. Completely different.'

'So where is he?' Markham asked. 'You have any other secrets in that folder of yours?'

'I wish I did, boy. What about the people who work for him?'

'Two of them have been arrested.'

'Then we'd better go and have a word with your tame copper.' He pulled down the knot of his tie and loosened the top button of his shirt. 'I'm not kidding, Danny. The people in London want him out of the way sharpish before anything can reach the papers. They don't like issuing D-notices for something like this.'

'Is she really going to be safe here?' Markham asked as he started the Anglia.

'Even if Carter finds out where she is, he doesn't stand a cat in hell's chance of getting in.' He passed across a piece of paper. 'By the way, you have a telephone in your flat now. That's the number. I want to be able to get hold of you.'

He didn't ask how it had happened.

At Millgarth they were shown through to an office. Baker was waiting, his jacket draped over the back of a chair, braces a tired blue against his white shirt.

'How is she?'

'He didn't hurt her,' Markham said guardedly.

'But?'

'She's in shock. Terrified. Not in good shape.'

The detective nodded.

'And we still don't have the bugger. Didn't look like anyone had been at that place out in the country for a week or more.' He glanced at the other two. 'Any ideas?'

'What about Graham?'

Baker shook his head.

'Still no sign. I talked to his wife. She didn't have any idea what he was up to. I think she's glad the bugger's gone, to be honest.'

'Then we're back where we started,' Jones pointed out. He paced up and down the room.

'Not quite,' Markham told him quietly. 'We have Joanna Hart. That's the important thing.'

'He's right,' Baker agreed. 'We'll catch Carter sooner or later. The lass is safe.'

'My job is Carter,' Jones said. His voice was hard. 'The ones who work for him. You need to talk to them again.'

'Don't be so forward, laddie,' the sergeant said. 'Someone's already doing it.'

★★★

They sat in Lyons, drinking tea and smoking. Jones' actions were quick and jerky. He kept glancing around the restaurant, eyes restless.

'Looking for something?'

'Habit.' He shrugged.

'This isn't your first operation, is it?'

'No.' He didn't elaborate.

'You've been abroad.'

'A few times.' He smiled. 'Free suntan.'

'And how many have you killed, Ged? All this rubbish about being an office boy, it's a lie, isn't it?'

'Don't ask, Danny. You know I can't tell you.'

'It works well for you, though, doesn't it? This act of the young Welsh lad amongst the toffs.'

'You believed it.'

'I'm just a poor provincial.'

'If you say so.' He kept his tone even. 'How are the fingers?'

Markham shrugged. He'd felt twinges of pain all through the

morning. The dressing needed to be changed again. But he felt that they were healing. 'Don't look around, but I think there's someone on the other side of the road keeping an eye on us.'

'What do you want to do?'

'Split up when we leave here. Make him choose who he follows. How much of your training do you remember?'

'Enough,' Markham said.

'You were good. Better than me.'

'Rubbish. I lacked the dedication.'

'Do you think you can still take someone down?' Jones asked him.

'I don't know,' he answered honestly. 'What does he look like?'

'Brown suit, red tie. Moustache. Short ginger hair. Trilby.'

'Right. I'll see you at my office.'

The man would follow him. Markham was certain of that. He was the one Carter wanted to kill. He crossed Briggate close enough to note the man's features, then along Kirkgate before turning up Fish Street. It was quiet, the cafe on the corner empty. He slipped into a deep doorway and put a hand into his pocket of his overcoat, gripping the gun.

The man followed a few seconds later and stopped, trying to see where Markham had gone. He stepped out into the street.

'Looking for someone?'

'What?' He tried to hide his surprise but the man simply wasn't that good.

'You're following me.'

'Don't talk rubbish!' It was all bluster, colour rising on the man's face.

Markham drew out the gun, just far enough for the man to see.

'We're going to take a walk,' he ordered.

It was like something from a detective picture, he thought. Something that happened in Hollywood, not in the centre of Leeds. It was ridiculous. Unreal. People passed, not even giving them a glance. The man was biting his lip, a thin sheen of sweat on his face.

Jones was waiting at the top of the stairs, casually leaning against the wall.

'Good to see you haven't forgotten it all,' he said.

'Like riding a bike?'

'Something like that. Who's this, then?'

Markham unlocked the door and pushed the man inside. Jones followed and turned.

'Take a walk for half an hour, Danny.' His face softened a little. 'Please.'

'Why?'

'You won't want to see what happens here.' When Markham didn't move, he continued. 'It's for the best, boy. Just keep your eyes peeled. Carter might have others out there.'

He closed the door quietly.

★★★

Markham strode through town, to City Square, up to the Town Hall then along the Headrow, thoughts shifting to the rhythm of shoe leather on pavement. Anger simmered under the surface. He didn't like being kicked out of his own office, to have a friend become something more, to see the professional take over.

He sat on a bench, smoking. It had all been so ordinary in the beginning, nothing more than finding out about a husband's affair for a vengeful wife.

Even when Carter entered the picture, even with Freddie Hart dead, Markham had thought he could handle it all. He ground out the cigarette butt and kicked out at a pigeon that came to investigate.

It had all spiralled out of control. At the end of this someone else was going to die. All he could hope was that it was Carter and not him. He flicked up his sleeve and checked the time.

★★★

Ged was behind the desk, arms splayed out at his sides, his eyes focused on something far beyond this world. There was a neat, small bullet hole in the middle of his forehead, the air heavy with the bitter smell of cordite.

For a minute all Markham could do was stand, to try and take it all in. He thought of Ged in Germany, laughing, drunk as often as not. Now he was nothing more than a bag of bones and skin. Then he took out a handkerchief, picked up the telephone receiver and dialled.

'I need to speak to Detective Sergeant Baker.'

CHAPTER TWENTY

He arrived in ten minutes. No shrill bells, no police cars, no mass of footsteps on the stairs. Just one man, his face grey and weary. Baker examined the body quickly and said,

'Christ, what have you got me into?'

'He's dead,' Markham answered bleakly.

'I can bloody see that.' Baker rounded on him. 'I've had to ring a number in London and tell them. Do you know what they said?' Markham shook his head. 'To let them handle it. They want you and me out of the way.'

'You know who did it.'

'Aye, of course I do.' His face was mottled red with fury. 'But they're telling me not to look into a murder on my own patch.' He shook his head.

'He was one of theirs.' Even as he said the words, he knew how they sounded. Ged had been much more than that. He'd been a friend, right from the day they began their National Service together.

'If he's up here, he's one of mine,' Baker said. 'What's downstairs?'

'A secretarial agency.'

'Do you know them?'

'Yes.'

'Go down and see if they heard anything. I'll bet my hat they didn't. I'm going to have a nose around here. Sod what they want in London.'

★★★

He asked Miss Jacobs for a quiet word outside while the typists kept up their clatter of keys, raising their eyes in a mix of flirtation and curiosity. She closed the door carefully behind her and looked him in the eye.

'I do hope it's important, Mr Markham. We're rather busy.'

'I was just wondering …' How could he put it? 'Did you hear any unusual noises from my office in the last hour?'

'Unusual?' She peered at him. 'What do you mean? And weren't you there yourself?'

'I had to go out for a while. Was there anything? Shouting? Maybe something sharp?'

'Not that I noticed. Simply people going up and down the stairs, but that's quite normal. If there'd been anything very strange I'd have telephoned the police. Was that it?'

'Yes. Thank you.'

She returned to work with a pitying look in her eye.

★★★

'Nothing,' he said as he walked back into the office.

'Then Carter used a suppressor on his gun. If it was Carter himself who killed your mate.'

'Does it matter who pulled the trigger?'

Baker had been kneeling on the floor. He stood slowly, pushing himself up with his hands, until his face was no more than two inches from Markham's.

'Of course it matters. This is murder. Deliberate, cold-blooded murder. Get that into your head.'

'You're not leaving it?'

'Of course I'm not,' Baker answered angrily. 'Are you telling me he doesn't deserve something? I thought you liked him.'

'I did.'

'All they'll do is sweep it under the carpet. Send his parents a medal and a "died in the course of duty" letter.' He paused and looked hard into Markham's eyes. 'The poor bastard was killed here. That makes it my business, whether they like it or not. If you're too scared to keep on, you'd best tell me now.'

'I'm in.' He kept glancing at the corpse, hearing the lilt and laughter of Ged's voice. He couldn't let it lie.

'Right.' Baker stepped back and began pointing. 'There's no casing on the floor. I can't see any powder burns on the wound. Whoever shot him must have been standing near the door. Tell me about the man you brought here.'

Markham gave a quick description. 'He was no one special.'

'And your friend told you to leave for half an hour?'

'Yes. He said I'd be better off not seeing what happened.'

'Well, he was right enough there. If you want my guess, the man following you was a set-up. Someone else trailed you back here. They wanted you two somewhere private so you could be killed. You were lucky.'

Markham stood, frowning and thinking. Maybe he was right. Maybe luck had saved him again. But Ged had paid the price.

'I still don't understand why Carter's doing all this.'

Baker sighed. 'I don't think reasons matter any more. We just need to find him before it happens again. Or it'll be you I'm sending to the mortuary next.' He looked at his watch. 'Right, we need to be out of here before their clean-up crew arrive. I meant it, lad. Keep your eyes peeled.'

★★★

It was a stark drive home. Ged was dead. In his office. In his chair. And tomorrow morning it would all be gone, as if nothing had happened. Pictures came into his mind. The pair of them in basic training. The military intelligence classes. In the NAAFI, chatting up the nurses. Walking around the Talstrasse black market in Hamburg, where survivors sold anything and everything to last for another day or week. Ged, flushed with excitement after his first small mission. The way they'd promised to keep in touch when Markham finished his National Service.

The gun was in his hand as he climbed the stairs to his flat but the place was empty. The new telephone, black shiny Bakelite, sat on the table next to his chair. A final gift. He picked up the receiver and listened to the tone. But the only person he wanted to ring was Carla, and she was gone.

The door was locked and bolted, the pistol sitting on the table, ready. He ate and raised a glass of wine in silent toast to Ged while Monk played a lurching melody, pauses and discords ringing through the flat.

★★★

In the morning he drove into town, constantly checking the mirror. But no one was following him. He unlocked the office door and held his breath, scared to go in. But when he turned the handle, everything was pristine and normal inside. Blotter square in the centre of the desk, chair neatly pushed in. There was no smell of death in the air, not even a bloodstain as a memory of what had happened. Nothing. He might have dreamed it all.

He sat down and looked around. The phone started to ring, jarring him back to reality.

'Just checking you're alive,' Baker said.

'I'm here,' he said slowly. 'I'm thinking of those who aren't.'

'That happens after every battle. Any more ideas?'

'Not yet. Has Graham surfaced?'

'Not a dickie bird,' Baker said. His voice was grim. 'People have been looking into things he's done. There's a warrant out for him now. About bloody time, too. Meet me at the cafe in the market. Ten minutes.'

★★★

The shouts of the traders rose from the market, 'Ten for a shilling', 'You won't do any better than this', as they stirred tea and sat at a chipped wooden table in the cafe at the top of the stairs.

'How do we find him?' Markham asked.

Baker puffed on his pipe for a long time before answering.

'Well, we haven't a clue where he might be. There's a way, but I don't like it.'

'What?'

'Offer up some bait. Something he wants.'

'Me.' He gave a wan smile as the policeman nodded. 'I'd thought about that, too.'

'It's dangerous, lad.'

'We don't have much choice, do we?'

'Not at the moment,' Baker admitted.

'Then we'd better try it.'

'What about Joanna Hart. How is she?'

He didn't know. Ged's death had pushed everything else from his mind.

'I haven't been by there. I'll find out later,' Markham told him.

'She's our best witness against Carter.'

'You want him in court?'

'I want him to hang for what he's done.'

'They'll never let it go public.'

'We'll see, lad. Depends who finds him first.'

It wouldn't make any difference. He knew that, so did Baker. If they arrested Carter he'd soon be spirited away and that would be the last anyone heard of him. But Markham knew that the copper had his pride. He wanted to be the one to find him, to do his duty.

'I'll go and see Jo.' He cocked an eyebrow. 'Tell me, if I'm the bait, who's looking out for me?'

'I'll have a couple of people watching.'

'What do the brass say?'

'Catch the bastard. Those were the exact words.'

'Then we'd better make sure we do it.'

***

He was careful, taking a roundabout route to throw off anyone following. Driving along the street to the safe house he glanced into every parked car. No one.

Markham gave the coded knock on the door, waiting as Maggie Cornwall undid the locks. The glass in the windows was thick, curtains closed.

'I had a telephone call about Mr Jones,' she said.

'Yes.' It was all he could manage. If he said anything more, it would all gush out. 'How's Mrs Hart?'

'She's still asleep. Best medicine. The doctor gave her some pills. I looked in on her a few minutes ago.'

'You haven't told her about Ged?'

The woman shook her head.

'Don't you go doing it, either,' she warned. 'It'll only terrify her.'

'I won't,' he promised. He watched her fill the kettle and wash the leaves from the teapot, making a fresh brew.

'She'll be safe here. Don't you worry.'

'How long can you keep her?'

'As long as she needs. Or wants. Just so you know that I don't have the authority to stop her leaving.'

'She's upstairs?'

'Second door on the right.'

He could hear her breathing, soft and even. For a moment he considered waking her, taking a pace into the room, then decided to leave her be. Let her sleep and recover. The world would crowd back around soon enough.

***

216

A startled pigeon outside the window flew off as he entered the office. The folder Ged had brought with him was gone; the clean-up crew at work, of course. All Markham still had were the papers from Carter's hotel room. He pored over them again, looking for something, anything he might have missed before. Any clue to where the man might be.

Twice through and finally something caught his eyes. It was just a scrawl on the margin of a letter – 'ask about progress on old Reginald building.' He'd seen that name before. Where the hell was it?

Baker was out, the desk sergeant at Millgarth station told him when Markham rang. Following up on an assault on New York Street.

He couldn't settle. Every few minutes he stood, glancing around the office in disbelief and staring out of the window at the rooftops. Finally he left, starting the car and driving out past Quarry Hill flats and along Regent Street.

Hart Ford was open, shiny new vehicles on display, temptation behind plate glass. The motor car agency took up half the block. Beyond it was the old building, some of the stonework crumbling, doors and windows boarded up.

A name had been carved in the lintel. The painted letters, once smart, impressive gold, had faded to almost nothing. He pulled to the side, craned his neck to make out the word. It took a few moments, but then everything made sense. Reginald.

Owning Hart Ford and the Reginald Building would give Carter real property. An entire block where businesses were eager to be, on a main road into town. The money that could bring in would make the rest of his businesses seem like small change.

It took ten minutes to reach the Town Hall, then another ten to find a clerk in the office he needed. The woman was little more than twenty but she knew her job well, vanishing into a back room and emerging with a heavy, leather-bound register.

With quick movements she leafed through the pages, moving a bright red fingernail down the lines. Everything was in ink, the writing a neat, archaic copperplate. Markham waited, nibbling at his lip as she worked.

'Found it,' she said finally. 'Three months ago, a company called DC Limited bought the building.' She followed the line across the page. 'Very reasonable price, from the look of it.' She glanced up. 'Does that help you?'

DC Limited. David Carter Limited. Jones' people probably knew about it. But Ged was dead. There could be more property under the name, places where Carter could be hiding.

'Is there any way you can find what else the company owns?'

'I'm sorry, love. Not here.' She leaned forward, glancing around. 'Between you and me,' she whispered, 'if that company leads to another company, you can hide half of England. It's all for taxes, stops them paying it all to the Revenue.'

'Thank you,' he told her before he left.

'Anytime, love.' She gave him a wink.

★★★

Baker was back the station. They sat in an interview room with its tired green paint, grey light filtering through dirty, barred windows.

'It makes sense,' the sergeant admitted when Markham told him. 'Keep everything legal but shady. I daresay we can dig deep enough and find it all through official channels, but it'll take weeks.' He ran a hand through his thin hair. 'Have you taken a look in the building?'

'Not yet.'

'Happen we should.'

★★★

It only took two minutes to drive there. Markham parked out of sight, the engine ticking slowly as they walked away. Baker had his trilby pushed back at a jaunty, cocky angle, the mackintosh flapping around his knees.

'You have a gun in your pocket?' he asked casually.

Markham's hand was wrapped around the butt.

'Yes.'

'Keep it there. I don't want all the paperwork if you shoot the bastard.' He nodded towards a door at the back of the building. 'We'll go in that way. It's out of sight of the road.' He smiled. 'Don't want anyone calling the coppers.'

There were no cars around or indication anyone might be around. The only sounds drifted over from Regent Street. Baker tried the door handle, pulling and pushing then finally ramming with his shoulder until the wood splintered around the lock.

'Rotten,' he said, shaking his head and fishing out a torch. 'If there's anyone inside they'll know we're here now.' He played the beam around a large room. 'How many floors?'

'Two,' Markham said.

'Doesn't look like there's much down here. Stairs are over there.'

He marched across the floor, stepping over old newspapers and pieces of wood and metal, then testing each step as they climbed. Markham followed. The wood of the rail felt spongy under his fingers. He looked up. Nothing but darkness. The only light leaked around the boarded windows. The building was filled with the thin chill of neglect, every footstep echoing around.

There was an office in the corner, partitioned off from everything else. Baker strode over to it, waving the torch into the far corners and catching a reflection of rats' eyes. But before he'd gone five steps, two shots rang out.

Markham dropped to the floor, fumbling to free the pistol. Baker was three paces away, crumpled on the ground. The torch had fallen, pointing uselessly at a wall. There was nowhere to hide, no cover.

He breathed slowly, extending the weapon, alert for the slightest sign of movement, a sound, a flash, anything. Nothing. Inch by inch he began to crawl over to the policeman, keeping his eyes forward, hand tight and ready against the trigger.

Closing the distance seemed to take an age. Sweat ran down his forehead and into his eyes. Finally he was close enough to extend a wary hand, but Baker didn't move when Markham touched him. He risked a glance, eyes accustomed the gloom now, and saw a dark pool under the policeman's body.

There was a faint pulse at the wrist.

He didn't have a choice. Baker would die without help. Markham needed to run, to take the risk. He tensed, then rose into a crouch and sprinted for the stairs, expecting a shot and the burn of pain. But there was nothing as he crashed along, sprinting to the square of light in the distance. Outside, he paused for a second to push the pistol out of sight in his pocket and dashed on.

Heads turned as he burst into Hart Ford. He heard someone draw in breath sharply. A woman covered her mouth. He knew what he looked like, his face grubby, his clothes covered in dirt. A secretary stared at him.

'Ring nine nine nine,' he ordered. 'Police and ambulance. There's a policeman shot next door.'

Without even thinking, she did as she was told. Customers twinkled away. The staff vanished until he was alone in the show-room. He turned, hands deep in his pockets, and walked back to the back door of the Reginald Building, lighting a cigarette.

Within three minutes he heard the bells of the ambulance and police cars roaring along. A dark Humber sprayed gravel into overgrown bushes as it slewed to a stop and a man in plain clothes, with a sandy moustache and accusing eyes, climbed out.

'Who's in there?'

'Sergeant Baker.'

He frowned. 'And who the hell are you?'

'Dan Markham. The building belongs to David Carter.' The man's eyes flashed. Good. He knew the name. 'We were upstairs and someone shot twice. One hit Baker.'

'You stay here. I don't want you in there again.'

He waited until the police were all inside the building and casually walked to his car. The ambulance men were waiting with the canvas stretcher, all of them looking worried. Markham opened the door of the Anglia and hid the Colt under the seat before lighting another Craven A.

So close. The first time anyone had taken a shot at him. He could still hear the hiss of the bullet as it passed. Before he had time to think about it he heard shouts and made his way back. They were carrying Baker out. A blanket was pulled up to his chin, his face so pale it looked lifeless. He watched them put him in the vehicle, strapping an oxygen mask over the man's face. The doors closed and the vehicle raced away, bells clanging loud. He watched until it disappeared round the corner.

'Right.' He turned at the voice. The copper from the car. 'Millgarth.' It wasn't a statement; it was an order. Markham began to move towards the Anglia but the man shook his head. 'With me. Your car will still be here later.'

He sat in the back of the Humber, the cracked seats smelling of old leather and fear. In the car park, the man opened the door and escorted him into the building. Bobbies in uniform gave half-glances as they passed. The news about Baker was already out.

The interview room felt cold. Markham sat and lit another cigarette. The man took off his mac and folded it neatly over the back of his chair, then placed his trilby on the table.

'I'm Detective Inspector Crowther.' He leaned forward, hands on the desk, his face just a few inches from Markham's. 'So we understand each other, I'm not going to piss around. I want to know everything and you're going to tell me. Right?'

'Yes.' His voice was nothing more than a croak. 'How is he?'

'They'll ring us as soon as they know.'

He went through it all. Crowther flinched as Markham described the way Ged's body had been taken by the service as if the shooting had never happened. Then the Reginald building, hearing the gun again and closing his eyes as he finished.

'Whoever it was, he'd gone by the time we arrived,' Crowther said.

'Carter,' Markham told him. 'It has to be.'

The man nodded slowly.

'So where is he?'

'I don't know.

'He shot a police officer.' Crowther's voice was hard. 'He might have killed him. That means we don't stop until we find him.' He stared at Markham. 'It also means that you're out of it.'

'Yes.' It was going to be a manhunt now. Everyone on the force would be looking for Carter. 'What about Sergeant Graham?'

'Nothing.' Crowther snorted. 'Can't find hide nor hair. His wife doesn't know. We've talked to her twice. He's cleaned out their bank account.'

'Long gone.'

'We'll catch up with him sooner or later.' It was a grim promise.

Markham stood.

'When you hear …'

Crowther nodded.

'I'll let you know.'

★★★

He walked back along Regent Street. The wind had kicked up, swirling empty cigarette packets and chocolate wrappers around the pavement. He tried not to think about Baker, but the sound of the shots filled his mind, so loud they drowned out everything else.

He liked the man. Respected him. If he believed in God he'd offer a prayer for the man's recovery. He'd survived a war and years as a beat bobby during the Depression. He deserved better than a bullet from a madman.

And Carter had to be mad. It couldn't be anything else. Something had turned in his mind.

Markham unlocked the Anglia and sat wearily. He reached under the seat and slipped the Colt into the pocket of his overcoat. There was one thing he knew about luck. It always ran out sometime.

CHAPTER TWENTY-ONE

Three police cars were still parked at the rear of the Reginald Building. The back door hung open. As he turned the Anglia he could see torch lights playing inside. It was their problem now. He was out of it, ordered away.

But this wasn't the end of it; he knew that. Carter might be a hunted man now, but he was still a hunter. He checked the mirror as he drove, turning into side streets and taking a careful, twisted route to the safe house.

He parked and knocked on the door. Mrs Cornwall let him in with a serious face.

'Is it true what they're saying on the radio?' she asked.

'What's that?' Markham said, as if he didn't know.

'About that poor wounded policeman.'

'I'm afraid it is.'

She took in his appearance, the dirt on his face, the marks on his clothes, and raised an eyebrow.

'Were you there?'

He nodded. She bustled around the kitchen, filling the kettle and emptying the teapot.

'Have yourself a good wash; get rid of all that muck. You'll feel better.'

He went through the motions, lathering the soap, rubbing it on his cheeks and hands, then rinsing it off. Dark water ran down the drain but he didn't feel any cleaner.

'Is she upstairs?' he asked.

'In the bath. I had the immersion on for over an hour to heat it for her.'

He knocked on the bathroom door, hearing a slosh of water before her voice came with a muffle 'Yes?'

'It's Dan Markham.'

'I'll be ten minutes.'

He drifted away again, looking around the house. On the surface, everything seemed so ordinary, all the furniture and decorations perfectly normal. But the glass on the window was thick enough to stop a bullet, and the outside doors were far heavier than they looked, three strong locks on each one.

Nets were hung inside the windows to stop people looking in, and the curtains were all lined so every room could be in complete darkness. He tried a desk drawer in the front room. Locked. Every drawer was locked. That was interesting.

There was only one room he couldn't enter: Mrs Cornwall's quarters, he assumed. Finally he heard a door open and the creak of footsteps on the stairs. Joanna Hart stood in a thick dressing gown, a towel wrapped like a turban around her hair.

'Do you have a cigarette?' she asked.

The living room was warm, autumn sun pouring through the windows. She curled up in a chair, smiling her thanks when Mrs Cornwall brought tea and left quietly.

'How are you?' Markham asked.

She blew out smoke.

'All right, I suppose. Have you found him yet?' She gave a small shudder. He noticed that she didn't say the name.

'No. That policeman …'

'The fat one, you mean?'

'He's been shot.'

'God!' She put a hand over her mouth. 'Is he …?'

'I don't know yet,' Markham said softly. 'It happened next door to your Ford agency.'

'Where? In the Reg?'

'Yes. It turns out that Carter owns the building.'

She frowned, suddenly more attentive.

'He does? When did he buy it? Before he went after Freddie?'

He nodded. 'A few months ago.'

'That explains a lot, doesn't it?' Her voice was low and thoughtful.

'I want you to stay here until Carter's in jail. For your own safety.'

'You think he'd come after me again?'

'I don't know. There doesn't seem to be any rhyme or reason to what he's doing.' Or maybe there was a method that only Carter saw.

'Can you get some decent gin?' Joanna Hart nodded towards the door. 'She doesn't approve of drinking.'

'Next time,' he promised.

★★★

'Do you mind if I use your telephone?' he asked. Joanna had gone upstairs to dress. Mrs Cornwall was in the kitchen, rolling out pastry.

'In the hall.' She smiled. 'Help yourself, love.'

The desk sergeant at Millgarth answered on the first ring.

'Detective Inspector Crowther, please.'

'He's out.'

'My name's Markham—'

'I know who you are.' The tone was abrasive.

'Is there any word on Sergeant Baker?'

'He's still in surgery. That's the last we've heard.'

'Thank you.'

'Pity the bugger didn't hit you instead,' the sergeant said before slamming down the receiver.

★★★

Climbing the stairs to the flat Markham kept his right hand wrapped around the gun. He locked and bolted the door behind him and turned on the two-bar electric fire to heat up the room.

He wanted music, anything to swallow up the silence. The sweet, formal tinkle of Scarlatti sonatas came from the speaker. He changed into clean clothes, wiping dried blood from the sleeve of his suit, made tea and stood by the window to look down on the road.

After a long time, he picked up the phone and dialled the Infirmary.

The patient was out of surgery and in a stable condition, a dispassionate voice told him. Markham gave a slow sigh of relief. Baker would survive. He lit a Craven A, watching smoke curl up to the ceiling. Now they just had to find Carter.

At six o'clock it was the first item on the Home Service news. He listened, trying to relate the words to what he'd experienced. The sharp ring of two shots, the echo round the big room. Baker's stillness. The faint hint of the pulse in the man's wrist.

Maybe it had been like that in the war.

★★★

By eleven, he knew that he wouldn't sleep. Everything was churning in his mind. He grabbed his overcoat and drove into town, parking outside Studio 20. The streets were empty, just a few souls wandering lost and lonely.

The musicians were already building the heat. The pianist usually worked at City Varieties, but he had jazz leaping in his soul. Head down in fierce concentration, he was creating magic around 'I Got Rhythm'. All the bass and drums could do was follow, and the alto player was sitting out, listening and nodding his head to the beat, smiling as the lines took another flight of fancy. It lasted a full ten minutes before the melody returned and the man glanced up, nodding an ending to the others, back to the theme and wrap it up.

It was one of those times that made Markham understand why he loved jazz so much. It existed in the moment. Any performance could be explosive if the mood was right. There was no score to follow, no conductor in charge, nothing exact. Each time it was as good as the imagination of the people playing it.

A trombone joined the line-up, a man from the pit orchestra at the Grand, and they felt their way through a couple of Basie and Ellington tunes. Competent enough, but the real spark had already passed. He closed his eyes, not sleeping but not quite there, roused when someone tapped his shoulder. Bob Barclay was holding out an envelope.

'Someone pushed this through the letter box for you the other day,' he whispered. 'You haven't been in since.'

Markham nodded his thanks and left the room. On the stairs he ripped open the envelope. Inside, there was a single piece of paper with two words written on them in black ink: DEAD MAN.

What was it supposed to do, he wondered. Terrify him? That morning he'd been shot at and seen the man next to him almost die from a bullet. He'd seen the terror on the face of a woman who'd been kidnapped. He'd discovered an old friend, dead. Words didn't have any power after those things. He crumpled the note and dropped it on the floor.

He'd seen the best of the music for the night. The truth was that he couldn't settle. His mind wouldn't slow down. The music followed him out on to the street until the door swung shut.

★★★

The International Club was quiet. A few men sat talking. He scanned the room, looking for a particular face. Finally he spotted Brian Harding in a quiet corner, staring at the empty glass in front of him.

Markham ordered a whisky and carried it over, placing it on the table. Harding looked up with a start, his eyes glazed.

'Hello, Brian.'

'Dan Markham. You're a sight for sore eyes.' His voice was steady as his hand snaked out for the drink.

'How are you, Brian?'

'So-so. You know.' He shrugged. 'You were asking about Jo Hart a while ago, weren't you?' He frowned as he tried to remember. 'It was you, wasn't it?'

'Yes. Why?'

'They're all saying she's disappeared. Did you know?'

'Who's saying it?'

'People. You know.' He thought. 'You know,' he repeated.

'She's gone away for a few days. Mourning,' he lied.

'Ah.' Harding downed the whisky then looked wistfully at the glass.

'Want another?'

'I wouldn't say no, old man.'

Markham brought a double and Harding smiled.

'I'm looking for someone else who's vanished.'

'Oh? Who's that?'

'David Carter.'

Harding shook his head.

'I don't know him. Should I?'

'Probably not. He's dangerous.'

'Can't be more dangerous than some I met in the war.' He opened his mouth to say more then closed it again.

'If you hear anything about him I'd like to know.'

'Of course, old man.' He sipped the whisky and smiled. 'David, you said?'

'Yes.'

'If the name comes up I'll be on the blower.'

Markham knew it was a lie. Another five minutes and Brian would probably have forgotten the conversation. Tomorrow morning, none of this would ever have happened in his mind. But it was impossible not to like him.

'Thank you.'

He stood. Outside, he paused on the small porch, eyes moving around for movement or silhouettes. Nothing, but he kept his hand on the gun, out of sight in his pocket as he walked to the car.

★★★

It was sheer habit that took Markham to the office the next morning. Maybe someone would come in needing a divorce, pictures of a spouse caught with someone else. He could use the money.

He'd been sitting there for fifteen minutes, reading the *Yorkshire Post*, when the telephone rang. As he answered he heard the rattle of coins in the slot of a phone box.

'Dan?' Carla's voice sounded half a world away.

'Hello.' He sat upright and she flooded back into him. Her scent, the feel of her, the texture of her hair as he stroked it. 'How are you?' he asked cautiously.

'Fine,' she answered. 'I've been wanting to call for days …' He understood. She'd been hurt to her core, everything she'd created destroyed because of him. She was hiding.

'I've missed you.'

'Have they caught him yet?' It was the question she needed to ask.

'No. Not yet.' She didn't need the details, only the answer. 'Where are you?'

'I came to stay with a friend in Whitby.'

'Have you been painting?'

There was a pause as she pushed in more coins.

'Yes.' He waited. 'I want to come back to Leeds, Dan.'

'I know.' Her life was here. But she wouldn't return until Carter was caught. That was understood. 'Soon,' he promised. Soon, he hoped.

She stayed quiet. This was how it had to be for now, a conversation full of silences and hesitations. Things half-said, where the spaces spoke louder than the words.

'How are you?' she asked finally.

'Fair to middling.' He tried to smile.

'Safe?'

He thought about the gun in his coat pocket. 'Yes.'

'I don't have any more change. I'll ring soon, all right?'

'I have a telephone at home now,' he began, but the pips had sounded and she was gone. He sat holding the receiver for a while then dialled Millgarth station.

'Crowther,' the man answered eventually. Markham didn't expect the inspector to tell him much.

'It's Dan Markham.'

'Mr Markham.' There was no friendliness in his voice.

'I wondered if you'd heard more about Sergeant Baker.'

'He's going to be fine,' Crowther said grudgingly. 'It'll be a while before he's back to work, though.'

'But he will be back?'

'In time.'

'Thank God for that.'

'The doctor said he'd have died if he'd lost much more blood.'

'What about Carter?'

'I can't tell you, Mr Markham. You know that. It's a police investigation.'

'And I told you that he's after me.'

Crowther gave a long, patient sigh. 'I've got a copper who was shot and a dead body, sir. Do you really believe I'm going to allow anything else to happen?' He didn't mention Ged's death, Markham noted dully, as if that belonged to another place.

'I don't think you can stop him.'

'We'll catch him.' The man slammed down the phone.

Markham knew what it meant; they had no idea where Carter was. They'd keep searching. They'd look everywhere and quiz all their snouts because he'd shot one of their own. But Carter was smarter than them. He knew all the tricks, all the places to keep out of sight.

The morning passed with desperate slowness. He smoked too much, filling the ashtray by eleven, a pall of smoke hanging below the ceiling. Finally, as the walls seemed to close in on him, he put on the overcoat and walked out into Albion Place. There was no one standing suspiciously still, not a soul who moved off to follow him.

It was still early, well before people crowded the Kardomah with their luncheon vouchers. Markham took a table by the window, exchanging pleasantries with Joyce the waitress as he ordered. He gazed down on Briggate as he ate, trying not to think, to stop his mind whirring. He'd barely managed three hours' sleep the night before, waking and moving in the bed until the sheet and blankets were twisted all around him.

After the phone call with Carla he'd replayed every word of it in his head. She was still scared. But at least she missed him enough to ring.

By the time he finished his tea he still couldn't find meaning in any of it. He paid, walked to the car and drove out to see Joanna Hart.

Mrs Cornwall let him in quickly, careful fingers on the locks behind him.

'I'm so glad you came, Mr Markham. I tried ringing you a little while ago.'

'What's wrong?'

'Mrs Hart keeps saying she wants to leave. It just started about eleven; she'd been fine until then. I asked her to wait until I'd talked to you.'

He sighed and glanced at his watch. One o'clock.

'Where is she?'

'In the front room. She's got a right mood on her.'

Joanna Hart was sitting in an armchair, handbag clutch tight on her lap. A cup of cold coffee, still full, was on the table next to her.

'I hear you want to leave.'

'That's right,' she snapped. 'I've had enough of it here. Did you bring that gin you'd promised?'

Markham looked at her. He'd forgotten. But her life was in danger and that was all she could think about? He shook his head.

'Do you remember what happened to you? What Carter did to you?'

'Of course I do.' There was ice in her voice, but he could see the memory made her blanch.

'He's still out there. He shot that policeman.' She didn't say anything. 'Sergeant Baker will live, but you're safer here where Carter can't get you. Do you understand?'

'And how long will I be here?' she asked.

'Just until he's arrested.'

'And what if you don't find him? What am I supposed to do, stay here forever?'

'The police are looking. They'll find him.' The same words Crowther had used, and they didn't sound any more believable when he repeated them.

'No.' She shook her head. 'For God's sake, look at me. I've been wearing the same clothes for days.'

'I'll go and fetch you more,' he offered.

She stood, shaking her head and looking determined.

'Take me home,' she said, and he caught a glimpse of the wilful girl she'd been a few years before. 'Now. Please.'

He couldn't keep her in the house if she didn't want to be there. She could walk out whenever she demanded. At least if he was with her, there might be some small safety.

'All right,' he agreed after a while.

'I'm sorry,' he told Mrs Cornwall as she unlocked the door. 'And thank you.'

Joanna Hart didn't look back or even say goodbye.

CHAPTER TWENTY-TWO

As soon as they entered the Hart house she marched into the living room and poured herself a large gin and tonic.

'Switch on the immersion, would you?'

In the kitchen, plates sat on the draining board, old, dried food stuck to them. Dirty pans littered the stove. He filled the kettle and heard her footsteps on the stairs. The garden looked unkempt, the grass starting to grow wild. A thought struck him.

'Don't you have someone who comes in and cleans?' he shouted up to her.

'Once a week.'

'Does she wash the pots?'

'Of course.' Mrs Hart sounded bored. 'Why?'

'When was she here last?'

'It should have been two days ago,' she answered after thinking. 'Why?'

Hurriedly, he began to search. The bed in the spare room had been slept in, covers roughly thrown back. An empty glass sitting in the kitchen. He sniffed it. Whisky. Carter was clever, he had to give the man that. He knew they'd taken Joanna Hart somewhere safe, so her house would be empty. It was perfect, the last place anyone would think to look.

'What is it?' She came and found him in the kitchen, turning off the gas under the whistling kettle. 'What?'

'Carter's been here. He slept here.'

He saw her fingers tighten on the glass and she took a quick drink.

'Christ.' He saw the panic rise in her face. 'Is he going to come back?'

Would he? The sensible thing was to keep moving. That was what they taught, he remembered that; a moving target was always harder to hit.

'I don't know. He might try.'

'I have a gun.' He looked at her sharply. 'Freddie brought it back from the war. And Daddy taught me to use a shotgun.'

'Where is it?' When she didn't answer immediately, he asked again. 'Where is it?'

'He used to keep it at the back of the top shelf in the larder.'

Markham pushed the tins and packets aside, his hand scrambling along the wood. Finally his fingers closed around the cold metal and he sighed with relief. He pulled out the weapon. A Webley, just like the one he'd owned.

'Do you know how to use this?'

'Yes,' she replied. 'Freddie showed me. We'd go out in the country and shoot at things. I was better than him.'

'I want to take you back to the safe house.'

'Not until I have a bath and pack some more clothes,' she told him, finishing the drink and pouring another. 'I'm not spending another bloody day wearing these.' She vanished up the stairs.

He paced, checking every door and window to be certain they were all locked. His hand remained on the gun in his pocket. The Webley sat on a ledge at the top of the stairs. She took her time, half an hour passing, then an hour, before he heard her emerge.

Markham couldn't settle, couldn't relax. The spare bedroom gave a view of the empty street whilst a box room looked out over the garden. There was nothing, but that didn't stop the growing sense of fear. Fear was good, he told himself. It kept you alert. It kept you alive.

He heard a car engine and dashed to the window, but it was just a husband returning from work, parking down the street and vanishing into a house. The start of the suburban evening ritual.

Finally Joanna Hart came downstairs. He hadn't seen the dress before. It was black and blood red, the skirt flaring below her hips. She'd caught her hair up somehow to show off a long neck. Her makeup was so subtle that it looked completely natural, and there was the faint drift of perfume as she passed him and poured more from the bottle of gin before adding a small dose of tonic.

'I feel better for that.'

'Have you packed?'

'Not yet,' she said casually. 'Do you have a cigarette?'

He gave her a Craven A and lit it.

'We need to get you back to the safe house.'

'I'll go,' she agreed. 'But we're all right for a little while yet, aren't we?' She took a long sip of the drink. Her eyes were starting to shine. 'It's so boring there. Nothing to do except listen to the bloody wireless or read. That woman's always off doing something and she doesn't have anything to say when she's around. I want to do something before I go back to that jail.'

'What did you have in mind?' She was tipsy, her skin glowing a little.

'Oh, I don't know. A meal out. Something like that.' She turned to look at him. 'What do you do, Mr Markham? You must do something for fun.'

'I go and listen to jazz.'

'Jazz?' She stretched the word out as if it was a foreign idea. 'Isn't that all noise?'

'Sometimes it's beautiful.'

'Is there a place in town that has it?'

'Yes.'

'Right. We'll go to the Red Lion to eat. I adore it there. Then you can take me to this jazz place. *Then* I'll go back to that house.' She kept her gaze on him. 'God knows I need to have some fun first.'

He had to be careful. If he insisted, she'd baulk. What he needed was to make her believe that returning to the house was her idea.

'He's out there.'

'I know. But how's he going to find us?' she asked defiantly. 'How many people live in Leeds, Mr Markham? Do you know?' Hundreds of thousands? He had no idea. She smiled when he didn't respond. 'We'll be lost among all of them if we go into town.'

He wasn't going to dissuade her. She might be terrified inside, but she wasn't going to budge. The little girl inside her was petulant enough to demand fun and even fear wasn't going to deny her. With luck, there'd be nothing good at Studio 20 and she'd want to leave quickly.

The long evening was gliding by as he drove into town, watching in the mirror for any cars that seemed to be following them. They knew her at the restaurant, offering their sympathies on her husband's death, and guiding her to a good table. He simply followed in her wake, watching faces.

She was effusive with the waiter, too loud and bright, ordering a gin and tonic and making a face when Markham asked for orange squash.

'How can you drink that stuff?'

'It's fine.' He didn't want to explain himself.

She ate hungrily, relishing each mouthful. Soup, a steak with chips then pudding, finishing with coffee and another gin. He had little appetite, picking at a chop and leaving most of it. His gaze flickered constantly around the room. Joanna Hart was eager to make small talk but all he managed were brief, inconsequential replies.

Finally she was done, crushing out her cigarette in the ashtray.

'Shall we go and listen to this jazz of yours, then?' She glanced in the handbag. 'Can you be a love and pay? I don't seem to have any money on me.'

He looked at the bill and drew out his wallet. After paying he had a pound left, along with the change in his pocket. Hardly a fortune. The woman was costing him far more than she'd ever given him. Outside, in the dark, she tucked her arm through his.

'Are we going to walk?'

'No.' He guided her back to the car and drove up to New Briggate, taking his time before opening her door and escorting her down the stairs into the club. The music had barely begun as they sat at a table.

It was an ordinary room, linoleum floor, cheap wallpaper, a collection of signatures in one corner from the stars who played there, and Bob Barclay on his chair behind the plywood partition.

They sat through the first number: a short, ragged version of 'A Night in Tunisia' that only brought polite applause. She leant towards him.

'Can we get a drink?'

'There's no licence,' he told her quietly and she pouted. With luck, that would be enough for her to leave. 'They have squash. Or there's tea or coffee.'

Her mouth moved into a determined line.

'I'll have a coffee, then.' It came in a cracked white mug, a slur of milk at the top. She spooned in sugar, took a drink and frowned. 'God, that's awful.'

'People don't come here for the drinks.'

She nodded at the musicians. 'For that?'

'When it's good.'

'Are these good?'

Markham shook his head.

'Bloody awful,' he whispered. 'Do you want to leave?'

Her eyes blazed for a moment.

'No.' She was firm. 'I told you, I came out for fun and I'm going to have it.' She grabbed his hand. 'Come on, let's dance.'

It sounded like a dance band tune, and they could at least keep the rhythm. She pulled him close and began to shuffle around the dance floor. He tried to move with her but he'd always been a listener, not a dancer. He felt embarrassed to be on show this way.

'You could try to look like you're enjoying yourself!' she hissed in his ear.

'I'm not.'

'Then you're bloody well going to.'

She was light on her feet, happy to lead until the music ended, when he returned to his chair. A few of the musicians changed, adding a couple of horns, the guitarist and cornet player packing up their instruments.

Markham glanced at his watch. Quarter past eleven. He wanted to leave before midnight, to have her safe again. Joanna Hart opened her handbag, searching for cigarettes. The light caught her silver hip flask.

'You brought that?' he asked.

'Of course. I filled it before we left. I told you that bloody woman at the house wouldn't get in any gin and you didn't bring any.' She pulled out the flask and took a nip. 'Want one?'

'No.'

'You're a bit of a prig, aren't you, Mr Markham? I should call you Dan, shouldn't I?'

'I told you, I want to be alert. And call me Dan if you like.'

She took another nip from the flask. Christ. That was all he needed, to have her drunk and in a strop. The music started again, a piece by Gershwin, and once more she wanted to dance, pressing herself close against him. Her hair tickled against his cheek and her perfume filled his senses. He tried to relax into the music, to simply feel it and move, but he couldn't do it. Barclay smirked at him from beyond the partition. They were the only couple on the floor. The other people stared ahead, watching the musicians and nodding their heads in time.

By quarter to twelve he'd danced three more times. She'd taken a few more quick drinks. Her eyes shone brightly.

He made a comment; she threw back her head and gave a full-throated laugh that made people turn to look at her.

'Have you had enough yet?'

'Of what?' she asked sharply.

'Everything.' If Markham had come here alone, he'd have left long before: there was much better music on his gramophone. He just wanted to deliver her, to have the day over, to push Carter from his mind for a few hours. He glanced at his bandaged fingers. All he wanted was for this to be over, for the man to be caught. For Carla to come home and life to return to the way it had been before.

'Another few minutes.' She pouted. 'Please?'

He nodded. They'd leave at midnight. He'd insist on it. Whisk her out like Cinderella before the clock struck twelve. He was grateful when the musicians changed again to tenor and alto saxes, bass, drums and piano. The kicked up an Ellington piece and Joanna Hart glanced at him for one last dance.

At least it was short, no more than three minutes until he was back in his seat. He checked his watch again.

'Now,' he told her.

'I want to stay.'

'It's late. I'm tired. And I need to get you back to the house.'

'All right,' she agreed with a reluctant sigh. She lit a cigarette, puffing quickly and moving a spoon in the cup of scummy coffee. He waited patiently as she snapped the handbag shut and gathered her coat before crushing the butt in an ashtray.

Markham shrugged into the overcoat, giving a small wave to Barclay as they left. He closed the door, muting the music. She began to climb the stairs but he put his hand on her arm.

'I'll go first,' he said. 'Just in case.'

The wind had turned cold, whipping rubbish along the street. Somewhere in the distance a drunk was trying to remember the lines of a song. The lamps glowed yellow. Not a soul to be seen on New Briggate. He kept his hand on the Colt in his pocket.

'It's fine,' he told her. 'Come on.'

He held the car door, closing it once she was seated, then settling in the driver's seat. He placed the key in the ignition. Before he could start the engine he heard a click from the back seat. In the mirror he saw a shape rise from the back seat and the black shape of a gun barrel.

'Well, well, both of you together,' David Carter said. 'It's my lucky night, isn't it?'

CHAPTER TWENTY-THREE

'Drive, Mr Markham,' he ordered, waiting until the engine caught. 'Go north, out past Alwoodley. I trust you're well, Mrs Hart. Recovered from your ordeal?'

She kept her lips pushed together, turning her head to look out of the window. The only sound was the motor and the tyres on the road.

'Keep it under the speed limit,' Carter said. 'I don't want to attract any attention.' After a moment he added, 'Reach into your pocket and take out the gun, Markham. I know it's in there. Pass it back to me.'

'While I'm driving?'

'It'll make you think. And please, put any ideas out of your mind. Not unless you want to drive with Mrs Hart's brains on the inside of the windscreen.'

Markham saw her shiver and try to move down in her seat. Carter laughed.

'You're going to kill us anyway,' he said. He tried to sound offhand but inside he wanted to yell. Sweat trickled down his back. 'That's the point of all this, isn't it?'

'Of course,' Carter acknowledged. 'But in the right place at the right time. The gun, please.'

He eased it out of his pocket and placed it on his lap then picked it up with his other hand before passing it over.

'A Colt. Lovely weapon,' Carter said with admiration. 'And how are the fingers? Healing well?'

A few minutes later they were out in the country. Just darkness to surround them. The headlamps picked out the few yards of road ahead of them. No other traffic, only emptiness.

He needed to concentrate. At the corner he geared down, the lights picking out the eyes of a rabbit on the verge. Then he pressed the accelerator and moved back into third as the car climbed the hill. Carter was silent for a while. Markham glanced over at Joanna Hart and squeezed her knee lightly. She didn't turn to look at him.

'About another mile and you'll see a road that goes off to the left,' Carter instructed. 'Just past a sharp corner. Turn there.'

As he braked for the corner he considered simply driving on. But then the man would do exactly what he'd threatened. She'd be dead. If he did what he was told there was a faint chance they'd survive. Right now that seemed better than nothing.

'Here,' Carter ordered. He was down in first, poking his way along gravel between two overgrown hedges. 'A quarter of a mile along there's a track to the right. Follow that.'

Markham felt the barrel push against the back of his neck. He swallowed and took a deep breath before making the turn.

It wasn't a road, only hard-packed dirt and gravel, rutted with potholes. He parked next to the faint outline of a building.

'Here?' he asked.

'That's it. Welcome to my country house. It's nothing much, but ...' He let the sentence trail away. 'Hand me the keys.' Markham took them out and passed them to a gloved hand. 'Now, out you get. The pair of you. Chop chop.'

It was colder out here. That was the first thing he noticed. The wind was blowing. The leaves rattled, although he couldn't see the trees. The only light came from the headlamps, shining on a small piece of ground. Around them, the darkness was complete.

He heard Carter's footsteps behind him on the gravel.

'What now?' he asked, hearing the fear in his own voice.

'Into the cottage.' A set of keys landed at his feet. 'You go first, open the door. It's the large key. So you know, I have hold of Mrs Hart.'

He did exactly what Carter wanted. His hand was shaking; it took three attempts to work the key into the lock. He took two tentative steps inside, sensing the others behind him.

'There's a candle on the table right in front of you. Be a good chap and light it.' After a second the flame caught on the wick. Light and shadows flickered in the room. 'On the sofa. Both of you.'

They sat side by side, facing Carter. Markham squeezed Joanna's hand. Her eyes were firmly on the man in front of them, the handbag on her lap.

'The police know about this place,' Markham said.

'I heard about it. That policeman friend of yours searched it, didn't he?'

'Yes.'

'And all they saw was that I hadn't been here for a little while. Is he going to survive, by the way? I saw them cart him off to hospital.' Markham didn't respond. 'Well, it was a bad shot. I was aiming for you.'

Carter stood, nonchalant. He wore a new suit, beautifully cut, the creases sharp on his trousers, brogues shining, a pleasant, easy smile on his face.

'Still,' he continued, 'since they know it exists, it means they'll come out here again. So they'll find you in the next day or so.'

'And you?'

'I'll be on the Continent. New name, of course.' He shrugged. 'I have enough of them. Take your car, ferry from Hull and I'll have vanished. Plenty of opportunities for an enterprising man over there. Germany's starting to boom and I speak the lingo. Austria. Too late for you two, of course.'

Markham stared. His hands were shaking but he felt a curious, odd calm inside. He was going to die. This was it. There was nothing he could do about it.

'Why?' he asked.

'Why?' Carter rolled the word around in his mouth. 'Because Freddie Hart decided he wanted to keep his business. He should have been doing well but he wasn't.' He nodded at Joanna. 'I'm sure you've learnt that by now, my dear. I could have sold that block and made a great deal of money. But he refused my offer.'

'So you killed him.'

'I gave him his chances to sell. He turned them all down. What else could I do? People really need to learn not to say no.' A memory came and the man's eyes clouded. 'Lie down on the floor, Markham.' He pointed the gun. 'Now, if you please. Arms out in front of you.' He obeyed. He didn't have a choice. He stretched out on the stone floor. The cold penetrated his shirt and sucked the breath from his chest. This was how it was going to be. Shot through the back of the head. 'I'm sure you recall the night you ruined my clothes,' Carter continued. 'Very clever, I'll grant you that. But I'm sure you realise, everything comes with a price. Close your eyes.'

He squeezed them shut, ready for the end. At least it would be quick. The moment stretched out. The pounding of blood was the only sound in his head. He waited, ready. Then pain jolted through him. He yelled, a raw cry, and tried to draw back his left hand. His broken fingers were on fire, crushed under Carter's heel, the full weight of the man's body grinding down.

He shouted until his voice was hoarse, until he could barely breathe. Carter stepped away. Markham pulled the hand back. The bandages were soaked with blood, bright, terrible red. A trail of it ran down his palm. Tears poured down his cheeks, unbidden and blurring his vision.

'Hurts like hell, doesn't it?' The voice was faint. It seemed miles away. 'Jerry did it to me once. If you were going to live you'd never use them properly again.'

Markham shifted on to his side. Each small movement was agony, a shock that made him gasp. All he could feel was pain.

Slowly, he blinked until he could see. Carter stood, the gun steady in his hand, staring down at him.

'You'll remember me as you die, Markham.' He turned to look at Joanna Hart. 'He's hardly your knight in shining armour now, is he? Not going to save you, is he?'

She didn't respond.

Gradually, an inch at a time, Markham shuffled until he was sitting. It hurt to breathe. He cradled his hand. Blood dripped on his suit but it didn't matter anymore. He wasn't going to leave this place. He'd given up; he couldn't beat Carter. The fingers sent waves of agony through his body. Another minute, once the first sense of shock passed, he'd begin to shiver.

'Be a man, Markham. Stand up. Take a seat next to your client.'

He didn't move. He couldn't. The effort of standing seemed impossible. Carter was doing it to humiliate him. The thought roared through his brain. He bit his lip and forced himself up, feeling as heavy as the world.

Standing, he was dizzy. Each breath was quick and shallow as he tried to steady himself. He stared at Carter. There was satisfaction on the man's face. Pleasure. He waved the gun lazily.

'Very good. Now sit down properly.'

He felt Joanna's hand against his back, guiding and supporting him. He glanced at the floor, spots of blood dark against the stone. The muscles in his legs ached. Time seemed to slow, every heartbeat lasting a year until he was next to her.

He gazed at the hand. Useless, broken.

'You've won,' he said. The words scraped out, a croak.

'No,' Carter said slowly, shaking his head. 'Not this time. A pity, really. I could have enjoyed Leeds. But life doesn't always do what one wishes. The Continent has its appeal, though.'

'I'd like a drink and a cigarette,' Joanna Hart interrupted.

'There's nothing here, I'm afraid, my dear. The cupboard is rather bare.'

'I have a flask in my bag.'

'Always prepared? Very good.' Carter smiled. 'Help yourself. It looks as if your friend could use one, too.'

Light reflected off the silver hip flask. She unscrewed it and drank, then held it to Markham's lips. The gin burned in his throat but it helped. Then she took out her cigarette case, flicked the lighter and the smell of tobacco filled the air.

Carter watched her for a moment then turned his gaze back to Markham.

'Which of you should go first, do you think? The gentleman or the lady?'

'Does it matter?'

The man pursed his lips for a moment.

'In the end I suppose it doesn't. Two quick shots, perhaps? Luck of the draw.' He raised the gun, finger tight around the trigger.

Before he could fire, a roaring sound filled the room. Joanna Hart was holding the Webley, her mouth wide in a silent O. Smoke curled up from the barrel. Carter clutched his belly. A flower of blood was blooming on his shirt.

He pulled the trigger and there was a second explosion as he fell. She jerked back, one eye gone, a small clatter of noise as she dropped the gun.

Carter tried to raise his pistol again as he slumped but he had no strength. His mouth turned into a tight, twisted grin as he crumpled on the floor.

Markham turned slowly. He tried to form words to say to her but she was already dead. He spoke but he couldn't hear his own voice. What remained of her face was empty. Brains and blood were spattered over the cushion. All her beauty had turned to nothing in a moment. He forced himself back to his feet, pushing himself up with his good hand, and kicked the weapon away from Carter. There was still the faint glint of life in the man's eyes, fading quickly as he took his keys from the man's suit.

The candle guttered and died as he forced the door open, the cold air a shock against his face. Stars were up there, a sliver of moon, the sky as dark as the Bible. He stumbled to the car, keeping hold of his left wrist.

The motor caught and he switched on the lights, then yelled in pain as he touched the gearstick and set off down the track. He winced with each bump and bit his lip until his mouth was filled with blood.

He'd left the Webley on the landing in her house. Trying to get her out of there, he'd forgotten it. She must have picked it up and put it in her handbag.

He was sweating although the night was bitter. The smell of cordite was heavy on his clothes. The old bandage around his fingers was sodden. The car rattled through potholes. Christ, how far from the main road had they been?

Finally he reached it, signalling by habit, then turned, speeding up and seeing no traffic until he reached Harewood and the single, welcome light of the telephone box. He forced his finger into the hole in the dial and dragged it round three times. Nine, nine, nine.

CHAPTER TWENTY-FOUR

A soft metallic tinkle brought him awake. Markham opened his eyes, blinking away the sleep. A face was staring down at him, a pretty young woman with guileless green eyes.

'Good,' she said brightly. 'You're awake. About time, too.' Light glinted on the watch that hung upside down on the apron of her nurse's uniform. He turned his head left and right, not sure where he was or how he'd ended up here. In a bed, wearing a pair of old pyjamas that didn't belong to him. All around him he could hear the coughs and wheezes of a hospital ward.

'What time is it?' His voice was thick. He tried to push himself up and pain shot through his body. The fingers. He raised his left hand. A fresh, clean bandage, virgin white.

'A little after nine,' she told him. 'You were in quite a state when they brought you in. And you have someone watching over you.' She nodded towards a uniformed policeman who sat by the nurse's station, reading a newspaper. 'Here you go.' She moved the pillows then eased him to a sitting position with practised strength.

'Thank you. Could I have some water?'

He drank, draining the whole glass before he set it down.

'I can probably find a cup of tea if you'd like,' she offered. 'There might be some breakfast.' She leaned closer and lowered her voice. 'Between you and me, you're better off without.'

'Where am I? What hospital?'

'Harrogate. You're a bit of a mystery man, aren't you, brought in by the police. Did you do something very bad?'

'No,' he answered. 'I just saw something awful.'

★★★

Inspector Crowther sat awkwardly by the bed, mackintosh open, hat sitting on the blanket. He'd made notes of everything Markham told him and leafed through the pages.

'So Mrs Hart shot him then he fired at her?'

'Yes.' He could see it all clearly. He could hear everything, every single word. He'd never be able to forget them. 'His finger was already on the trigger. I think he did it automatically. Just a reaction.' The film of it played over and over in his head.

'They were both dead when we arrived. Took ages to find the place in the dark.'

'She died immediately.' His voice was bleak.

'The gun was in her handbag?'

'Yes.' He'd explained it once. He didn't want to go through it again.

'Carter ruined your hand.'

Markham didn't reply. The consultant had done his rounds earlier. There was a chance he'd be able to use the fingers again, but it wasn't a good one. There'd been so much damage to the nerves. With time and good help … the man's words had tailed away and he'd shrugged. In the lap of the Gods. But there was no other damage. As soon as Crowther had finished, he could leave.

So many bodies. So much death. And for what? One man's greed. He sighed. Joanna Hart. Freddie. Ged Jones. Carter himself. Baker wounded. He glanced down at his useless fingers. He was the one who'd got off lightest of all.

'Where's my motor car?' he asked

'In the car park,' Crowther replied and fished the keys from his pocket. 'We brought it down.' He stood. 'You've been in the middle of quite a sensation, Mr Markham.'

A sensation? He thought about the word. It felt more like a horror story. There was no happy ending. There was nothing, only a void. Carter had been clever, but in the end he'd underestimated Joanna Hart.

She'd saved him. He knew that. Another few seconds and it would have all been very different. He couldn't dislodge that from his head.

Crowther put away the notebook and stood slowly.

'There won't be any charges against you,' he announced gravely.

'What?' Markham asked in surprise.

'No charges for you,' he repeated. 'The case will be closed.'

'What about Ged Jones?'

'Out of my hands,' the inspector said, his voice flat.

'Sergeant Baker?'

'He should be back at work by the New Year.' He held the hat in front of him. 'That's the end of it.' It was more than a statement. It was an order.

***

Half an hour later he sat in the car. The sun came and went as clouds scudded across the sky. He was dressed, discharged with a bottle full of painkillers.

He hadn't been able to knot his tie and ended up stuffing it in his pocket. His suit stank, stains of blood and more across the material. It was only good for the bin but he'd worn it anyway. As soon as he was home he'd throw it away. He didn't want it. He didn't want to carry any of the memories but those wouldn't be discarded so easily.

On the road back to Leeds he tried to pick out the lane leading to Carter's house. But it had been dark; the man had been directing him. He kept slowing, ignoring the vehicles blaring their horns behind him, but he couldn't spot it. Finally, he speeded up again. Maybe it was better never to be certain.

***

He made a cup of tea and looked down from the window. By the time he reached the flat his fingers had started to throb and he'd taken two of the pills. Now he felt as if the world was on the other side of a curtain. The physical pain had gone. But there was nothing that would stop everything spinning over and over in his mind.

He'd locked the door and pushed home the bolts, then put Monk on the gramophone before taking off the record. It mirrored his thoughts too much, disjointed and awkward. Instead he chose Billie Holiday, the sorrow pouring out of her voice. He knew nothing about her, just another American jazz singer, but for today at least, she understood him.

***

Carla had pulled her hair back at each side with a barrette. It hung down on to her shoulders. She looked healthy, skin glowing in the light from the candle on the table. The plates in front of them were empty. She'd sipped at her coffee and a small glass of grappa. Markham still had the remains of his wine, turning the glass in his good hand.

She'd rung from Whitby two days before, the cry of seagulls faint in the background. She'd heard the news on the radio and wanted to hear his voice, to know he was safe. And now she was here. They'd met outside Donmar and lingered over dinner. He told her everything that had happened from the moment she'd gone. It was all there, fresh at the front of his memory. It wouldn't leave.

'I'm sorry, Dan.' She reached out and put her hand over his, her skin warm and soft.

'It's done.' He paused. 'What about you? You look well. Did you do any painting while you were there?'

'A bit. Plenty of walking and thinking.' She seemed hesitant, as if they were acquaintances rather than lovers.

'But you're back now.'

'Yes. Look …'

'What?' he asked quickly. A sick feeling crept up from his stomach. He lit another cigarette to try and keep it down.

'I've been offered something.'

'Something?'

'A friend of mine knows someone in the art department at Durham University.' She spoke slowly, keeping her gaze on the table. 'They have an opening.'

'Doing what?'

'Sort of what I'm doing here.' He heard the rustle of nylon as she crossed her legs. 'More of it and the money's better. The head of the department has seen my work in London. He offered me the job.'

It felt as if he stayed silent for a long time.

'When do you start? After Christmas?' At least they'd have some more time together first. After that he could drive up on the weekends. She could take the train to Leeds.

'Right away. They're short on people. Someone's been doubling up. I've already given in my resignation at the college. It's just … after what happened, I need a fresh start. I'd always be worried here. Scared.'

'I'd look after you,' he said.

She tried to smile.

'I'm sorry, Dan. I really am. I know it's a bloody awful time for it to happen. But it's too good a chance to turn down.'

'When do you go?'

'The day after tomorrow. I still have to do all my packing. Everything from the flat and see if there's anything I can salvage from the studio at college.'

'How are you getting up there?'

'I talked to Daddy. He said he'd come up and drive me. He has that big Wolseley.'

He took a deep breath.

'After you're settled …?'

She looked into his eyes.

'Dan?'

'What?'

'I want it to be a fresh start. A clean break from everything that happened here. You don't understand what that did to me, do you? He took two years of my life. Two bloody years I'd worked on those paintings he ruined.'

'But–' he began and stopped. Words wouldn't make any difference. She was right. He could never understand. Not really. He could admire what she did but he couldn't feel himself inside it. 'I hope Durham is good to you.'

'Thank you.' Her eyes shone, on the edge of tears. 'Look, I … I'd better go. There's still so much to do.'

'Of course.' She reached into her handbag. 'Don't,' he said. 'It's on me. A bon voyage present or something.'

She leant across the table and kissed him lightly on the lips.

'I'll ring you once I have somewhere.'

He watched her walk away, stopping at the door to give a small wave and blow a kiss, then he asked for the bill. By the time he reached the street, she'd gone. A bus passed, the lights inside bright.

He could go over to Studio 20. There was always music.

ABOUT
THE AUTHOR

CHRIS NICKSON is the author of the Richard Nottingham series (Severn House). A well-known music journalist, he has written many celebrity biographies as well as being a frequent contributor to numerous music magazines. He lives in Leeds.

For a track listing of the music featured in *Dark Briggate Blues* visit: www.thehistorypress.co.uk/dark-briggate-blues

PRAISE FOR
THE CROOKED SPIRE
BY CHRIS NICKSON

'The author powerfully evokes a sense of time and place with all the detailed and meticulous research he has carried out for this very suspenseful and well plotted story of corruption and murder.'

Eurocrime

'[A] convincing depiction of late-medieval England makes this a satisfying comfort read.'

Publishers Weekly

'[Nickson] makes us feels as though we are living what seems like a fourteenth-century version of dystopia, giving this remarkable novel a powerful immediacy.'

Booklist (starred review)

Also from The History Press

We are proud to present our historical crime fiction imprint, The Mystery Press, featuring a dynamic and growing list of titles written by diverse and respected authors, united by the distinctiveness and excellence of their writing. From a collection of thrilling tales by the CWA Short Story Dagger award-winning Murder Squad, to a Victorian lady detective determined to solve some sinister cases of murder in London, these books will appeal to serious crime fiction enthusiasts as well as those who simply fancy a rousing read.

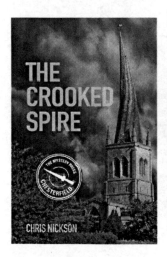

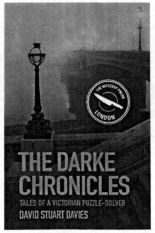

Find these titles and more at
www.thehistorypress.co.uk

Lightning Source UK Ltd.
Milton Keynes UK
UKOW02f0842181114

241782UK00002B/5/P